THE VILLAIN'S FATAL PLOT

GRAVESYDE VILLAGE MYSTERIES
BOOK ONE

PATRICIA RICE

PLEASE JOIN MY READER LIST

Please consider joining my newsletter for exclusive content and news of upcoming releases. Be the first to know about special sales, freebies, stories from my writer life, and other fun information. You'll even receive a thank-you gift. Join me on my writing adventures!

To Join, Please Visit —
https://www.subscribepage.com/ricewebsite

AUTHOR'S NOTE

In the Gravesyde Priory Mystery series I introduce readers to the heirs of Wycliffe Manor, who turn a derelict manor into a home. Each of the couples have their own romance and mystery to solve and some of those couples will continue to appear in this spin-off. There's a list of which couples star in which book at the end.

In this new series, I'm writing about the people who bring Gravesyde Village back to life. The history of the village is wrapped around the manor, the ancestral home of the Earls of Wycliffe, built on a former priory. In the way of medieval fiefdoms, the earls resisted district boundary changes, so the estate, in 1815, is an exclave of Shropshire, although south of Birmingham and surrounded by Worcestershire, creating legal havoc when it comes to crime. As appointed executor of the trust operating the manor, Captain Huntley has been chosen as the local magistrate.

Due to various circumstances, the manor has been empty, or nearly so, for decades. The village has been left to die. With the return of the manor's inhabitants and the war's end, spurred by the industrial revolution, the locals are gradually returning to their ancestral homes.

As the series continues, we can watch the village and its inhabitants grow and find romance—and solve a few crimes along the way.

As a side note, I occasionally reference the town of "Stratford" where the bankers and solicitors reside. Although there is a Stratford in London and the famous Stratford-on-Avon nearby, this Stratford exists only in my mind. Birmingham, however, is completely real, an industrial and technology center akin to today's Silicon Valley at the time.

CHARACTERS

VILLAGE:

Faith Palmer/Verity Porter— orphaned and homeless; *Mrs. Milton Palmer*—deceased mother
Sgt. Rufus Russell (Rafe)— retired army and former innkeeper
Sgt Major Fletcher Ferguson (Fletch)— retired army, Rafe's friend
Miss Ann Edgerton— Verity's former governess
Paul Upton— curate
Wilhemina Underhill— Verity's companion
Clement— apple picker
Rose Holly— Miss Edgerton's next-door neighbor
Amos Culliver— Miss Edgerton's solicitor
Mr. Sullivan— hardware merchant
Nate and George Blackwell— father and son construction workers
Mr. Oswald—mercantile proprietor and postmaster
Charley Jones— church deacon
Mrs. Milton Palmer—Verity's deceased mother
Warren Palmer— Verity's uncle
Luther— Warren Palmer's footman

MANOR:

Captain Alistair (Hunt) Huntley— US Army engineer
Clarissa (Clare) Huntley— wife of Hunt and secret novelist
Arnaud Lavigne— Hunt's artist cousin, former French comte
Henri Lavigne— Arnaud's younger brother, tavern owner, peddler
Lady Elsa Villiers de Sackville— manor cook
Honorable Jack de Sackville— stable owner; Elsa's husband
**Benedict Bosworth Jr. **— banker
Lavender Marlowe— seamstress
Dorothea (Thea) Reid Talbot—interior decorator
Sofia Lavigne— cousin of Arnaud and Henri; perfumer
Daniel Walker— Hunt's friend, steward; Meera's husband
Meera Abrams Walker— physician/apothecary; Clare's best friend
Henrietta (Nettie) Upton— curate's stepmother; housekeeper
Patience Upton— Nettie's daughter and curate's stepsister; gardener
Minerva Peniston— librarian; curate's fiancée
Mr. and Mrs. Dorian Prescott—antique collectors; Thea's guests
Garret Browning III—one of manor's estate solicitors

ONE

London, September 1815

"You've most likely fractured a bone or two, Miss Palmer. You don't keep off that foot, you could be crippled up for life." The apothecary wiped his hands after tying off the bandage. "Best to rest and keep it raised."

The bruising and swelling had made it almost impossible to remove her once-overlarge boot. Putting it back on. . . Faith winced as she attempted to ease on her footwear, leaving the laces untied. "Then I shall have to sit by the fire and knit, shan't I?"

Complaining got her nowhere, so she refrained from saying she was crippled for life already, in more ways than were visible. Mr. Thomas looked at her with too much pity as it was. She refused to be pathetic.

"If you have a cane you'll sell me, I'll stay off it all the way home," she vowed. She hated spending one of her few coins, but stalwart as she had learned to be, even she knew she'd never make it home elsewise.

She would have to buy a larger shoe to accommodate the

bandage, which seemed a dreadful waste, but a lovely excuse for a stronger boot.

Or maybe she could steal one of the boots her uncle used for his clubfoot, she thought meanly. Pain apparently brought out her bad side.

"Aye, a stick will help." The old apothecary brightened momentarily, then shook his head. "Don't know how you'll manage your satchel. That looks heavy. Where's your footman? Don't know what your uncle is about, sending you out at all hours on these streets with those papers."

The satchel didn't contain just papers, which made her lazy footman's defection all the more irritating. When she'd explained she needed to stop at the chemist, Luther had decided he'd worked enough for a day and taken himself off to his pub. He knew she wasn't that far from home. People looked after her here, so she didn't fear the dark streets, even this close to the wharf. But the satchel was heavy and her foot *hurt*.

The apothecary rummaged through a stand of walking sticks, settling on a smaller one. "See if this don't fit."

Not answering his question about her footman, she tested the stick, and smiled in gratitude. "This works well, thank you, sir. I shall look very elegant swinging a walking stick."

She removed the necessary coins from her meager purse, knowing she'd replace them with ones from her uncle's satchel later. She'd paid for her mother's physicians that way for years. She'd felt guilty at first, but Uncle Warren never lowered himself to touching filthy lucre. If his bookkeepers noticed a shortage, he blamed it on his incompetent clerks or the bank. He had wealth enough not to miss a few shillings—or even sovereigns. And he owed her far more than spare change.

She had come to consider theft a form of spreading the wealth to those who needed it. Just call her Robin Hood.

Mr. Thomas looked dubious at her claim of elegance but he'd known her family long enough not to comment.

Faith was perfectly aware that she was anything but elegant.

Stout, possibly. Dowdy, certainly, and as plain of face as her mother had been. But as *the Mrs. Milton Palmer*, her mother had been wealthy and money could buy elegance. Faith couldn't. And what would she do with it anyway? Having no wardrobe to store them in, her mother's silk gowns hung uselessly over a line strung across a storage room. Faith loved trying them on, but they were too ostentatious for these back alleys her mother had never set foot in.

In the early September evening, fog had already closed in. She pulled her cloak hood over her recently refurbished bonnet. Having lived in sight of the wharves for her entire twenty-five years, she navigated the treacherous shoals of dark alleys without fear, even though her father had died on these streets where he'd built his home. He had loved watching his ships come in.

Only tonight, she was much later than usual. Hobbling, with the stick slipping and sliding on the cobblestones, she knew the counting house had closed. Her father had taught her how to open the vault. She didn't need anyone's supervision, but her uncle loved seeing his money as much as his brother had his ships.

After the house closed, though, her peevish uncle worked himself into a drunken state that easily erupted in rage. She hoped he had gone home. Her foot ached like the very devil, had ever since the carriage horse stamped on it earlier. She'd still made it to the bank before it closed. That wouldn't appease Uncle Warren.

She'd love to blame his nasty carriage driver for her lateness, but Uncle Warren would simply say she was clumsy. She supposed she was. Only, she wasn't the one who'd deliberately driven the horse over her foot because she hadn't moved fast enough.

Ah, the alley—a shorter distance and unpaved. Balancing the strap of the heavy satchel over one shoulder and leaning on the stick was wearisome—especially for clumsy her, she added with wry amusement. Elegance wasn't for Faith Palmer.

3

A piteous mew in the shadows offered her excuse to rest for a minute. "Kitty?" More mewling followed.

She'd tried to keep cats for years, but someone always let them out, and life on the wharves seldom came to a good end. But a hungry kitten. . .

Eyes adjusting to the darker shadows, she sorted a ragged bundle of ginger from the debris behind the ash cans. Remembering a bit of cheese in her pocket, she set down the satchel and rummaged in her cloak.

She inched closer, awkwardly holding cheese and stick. The kitten watched warily, sniffing with suspicion. Marmalade, most likely, under all that filth.

"I bet you'd make a good mouser," she murmured as the tiny bundle of fur lay flat to study her.

Perhaps she could train this one not to leave the kitchen? She'd love a little company to fill the lonely hours. Uncle Warren never entered the cellar. He wouldn't know.

The moment the kitten snatched the cheese, Faith caught the handful of fur and cuddled it inside her cloak. "There's more where that came from, Marmie. And there's a fire where you can dry off."

As if accepting the offer, the kitten snuggled into her warmth, tiny, frightened heart beating against hers—someone to love. It had been so long. . . A light lit her dreary evening.

Only now she had a dilemma. Stick, satchel, and cat. And she was later than late. She was a ninny for taking on any more responsibility, but the kitten made her unreasonably happy.

She slipped her new pet into the satchel and appropriated a few coins while she had it open. Now that her mother was gone, she took the extra coins for her trouble. It wasn't as if her uncle paid her for running his errands. He assumed allowing her to live in her own home was sufficient recompense.

"He's a mean cheat, Marmie," she whispered, retrieving her stick to limp down the mews leading home. "Why hasn't anyone taken a cudgel to his head? Run his black heart through with a sword. . ."

Before she could imagine any more bloodthirsty fates for her father's brother, an earth-jarring explosion rattled windows and doors, and she stumbled. Shouts of alarm broke out in the distance.

Steadying herself on the stable wall, clinging to the shadows, Faith peered from the mews and watched in shock as the windows of the four-story mansion her father had built glowed from within. Had that been a trick of candles, it would have been a gorgeous sight.

Except the glass exploded, and flames roared from those lit windows. A moment later, fire licked at the roof, and the foggy night sky reflected orange.

Stunned, she froze against the brick, watching the inferno in horror. Shouts, people running. . . She crumpled into the shadows, fingers digging into the rough brick of the stable.

Her home, everything she'd once owned, all her memories of a happier life, everything she'd hoped someday to claim again. . . *gone*? Horror engulfed her as she watched her future and past burn to fiery cinders. Her soul shriveled like the once lovely damask draperies, her mother's silks, and her father's books. Tears coated her cheeks. And then, a stray idea caught her. . .

Like a snail without its shell, *Faith Palmer died with her home.*

She blinked, not certain from what depth of hell that thought arose. Her insides churned. She swiped at the tears streaming down her face. . . Without her home or family, dull, clumsy Faith Palmer was quite effectively *dead.*

Oddly, that notion left her. . . *free?*

"If heaven means dropping the chains that bind us to earth, is this what it feels like to be an angel, Marmie?" Watching her home blaze into a bonfire, she stroked the kitten's head—the kitten that had saved her life. Had she not been late, had she not stopped to rescue a kitten. . .

She would have been in her cellar kitchen, fixing her tea as she had for nearly a decade. Flaming timbers would now be falling on her head, taking with them the last of all she was, the memories of her mother's laugh, her father's beloved books, the wardrobe of beautiful hats and silks. . .

Everyone would believe her *dead*. How very odd to think no one really knew her except as an inhabitant of that house. She didn't really know herself. She'd had a few dreams, impossible to execute, but now. . . Absorbing the disaster and grasping her new freedom, she squeezed the knob of her walking stick and tried to find a different footing.

In the stable were the dreams she'd lived on these last ten years: the books and coins she'd squirreled away, bits and pieces she'd hidden, cautiously planning for that day she might have sufficient funds to either reclaim her home or escape it. She had letters offering hopes she couldn't redeem. . .

Until now—well before she was prepared.

The kitten yowled a protest from the satchel—a satchel filled with bank notes and coins. Out of the ashes. . . hope flared.

Faith Palmer might be dead, but whatever tiny spark of life remained inside the woman standing there, struggling to stay upright, was not. "I can be anyone, kitty. . ."

Dread and excitement tightened her throat.

SATURDAY

TWO: RAFE

"I hate showing up at Jack's door as a beggar." Sgt. Rufus Russell rode through this aging hamlet some miles off the main highway south of Birmingham, searching for anything resembling a wealthy estate.

Not the world's friendliest man, Sgt. Major Fletcher Ferguson, Rafe's former commanding officer, continued through the village to the far end—still with no sign of so much as a manor house.

The village was even further from civilization than Rafe's former home in Norfolk. He'd spent these last years at war because of a highway that had bypassed his home, leaving his family penniless. Since the war's end, he'd traipsed for months looking for another place he might fit in. This rural nowhere did not appear promising.

He curbed his gelding in the non-existent grass of the village green and rubbed Wolfie's wiry gray head. Nearly as tall as a small pony, the wolfhound had followed him home from the wars. They'd both like to try peace for a while—but the repose of a graveyard had little appeal. A chilly wind blew as he studied the

rotting thatch and timber of the village with the ominous sobri-
quet of Gravesyde Priory. "Did Shakespeare misplace one of his
stage settings?"

. Seeing a tavern sign creaking in the breeze, Rafe called a halt
and swung down. He and the hound could both use food. He tied
the reins to a fence post with no fence.

"We are officers and gentlemen," Fletch contended grumpily,
looking around for water for the horses. "Besides, Jack passed the
word he needed help. That doesn't make us beggars."

"Non-commissioned officers are not gentlemen." Rafe found a
pump, but the handle fell off in his grip while he argued his case.
"The right-honorable Jack de Sackville we knew intelligently
resigned his commission and made his fortune in India, while
ungentrified louts like us all but begged our way though mud and
snow on the Continent."

Fletch shrugged. "If Jack can't find enough men to guard his
stable or train his horses, then his fortune did not buy him any
fancy estate. We have come to offer our services, so we're not
beggars."

"He's married an earl's daughter and is no doubt wealthier
than Midas," Rafe maintained. "We're *beggars*."

"Beggars are those poor lads they sent home without legs or
arms or a ha'penny to their names. We have blunt. We just don't
have enough." Fletch studied the sprawling half-timbered structure beyond the non-fence that most likely had once been an inn
before the roof fell in.

"A few coins in our pockets and a banknote or two barely
count as blunt." Rafe had convinced his equally penniless friend
that they needed to set up their own business. Yon fire trap wasn't
what he had in mind.

With the expertise of an innkeeper's son, Rafe examined the
decrepit inn's yard, the crumbling stable, the. . . lack of potential
patronage. Gravesyde seemed to consist of a dozen cottages and
an invisible manor. Maybe the people were invisible too.

To disabuse his thinking, an auburn-haired gent wearing a

clerical collar and a shabby frockcoat opened a gate in a nearby hedge. Rafe judged the clergyman to be younger than himself and no doubt even poorer. At least his uniform had been tailored to properly fit his barrel shape. Maybe beggars could survive here.

"Good afternoon, gentlemen. May I help you? Gravesyde receives so few visitors that we like to greet each one. I'm Paul Upton, the local curate." He swept off his workman's cap and bowed.

Rafe had already collapsed his frayed bicorne under his arm. He bowed and introduced himself and the major. "We're on our way to Wycliffe Manor and thought to seek accommodations and refreshment first." He'd traveled on an empty belly far more often than he cared to remember. Here, in the midst of a bounteous English harvest, on a late September day, he shouldn't have to starve.

Parson Upton looked chagrinned, glancing at the empty inn. "I fear Gravesyde has no accommodation other than the manor. If you're familiar with the owners, I'm sure they'll put you up. Their drive is only a little further down the road, past the chapel."

"What about the tavern?" Fletch asked, nodding at the swinging sign of The Monk. It appeared freshly painted, at least. "We could use a quaff to clear the road dust."

The curate brightened. "You're in luck. Henri is here today, restocking. I was just heading over to see if my sister brought down victuals for a noon meal."

Rafe half listened as the young curate explained his sister had only recently married the tavern owner and lived in the manor. Perhaps Jack and his wife had turned a manor into an inn. Tavern owners did not generally reside in mansions.

Henri Lavigne appeared to be a French émigré about Rafe's age. He would resent a Frenchman living off the fat of England while he starved trying to save the man's home, but he was amiable by nature. He felt even more generous toward the gent when the tavern owner claimed the first round was free and offered to share his bountiful repast.

"There's enough here to feed half a village," Fletch exclaimed as Henri emptied the basket of food and the curate helped himself to a healthy loaf loaded with what appeared to be ham, cheese, and relish.

Since Upton's mouth was full, Henri responded for him. "Our curate's mother is the manor's housekeeper. She fears he'll waste away if he must live on his own cooking. And my wife sneaks in extra for me. I'm thinking we could open the place as a pub with the leftovers."

Rafe bit into the fresh bread with a groan of delight. He hadn't half-finished chewing when he had to say, "All you need is a good variety of brown ale and stout, and your pub would exceed the finest of London."

An eager discussion of breweries ensued, much to Rafe's contentment. He'd spent a great deal of time learning brewing processes. Fletch lacked knowledge and merely admired the mural of a blond goddess on the wall.

They were in the midst of an argument over hops when Wolfie barked a warning, just before a raspy voice behind Rafe said, "Look at the ginger with the long ears! Both rabbit and carrot!"

His mood soured from genial to hostile in the time it took to swing around on an older, unshaven gent with a bulbous, red-veined nose. "Your proboscis protrudes too much, old man. Let me flatten it—"

The curate grabbed Rafe's arm before he could swing. For a man half Rafe's size, Upton was surprisingly strong.

"Clement, The Monk isn't properly open yet. Henri is entertaining a few friends." Releasing Rafe, Upton caught the dolt's arm and steered him toward the door. "Is the apple picking done for the day? I thought my sister planned to work until dark—"

The door shut behind the pair.

"Heard that a time or two, have you?" Henri refilled Rafe's mug.

Not since he'd grown broad enough to fill a doorway, but there always had to be one genius in the crowd.

"The good curate likes to keep our rougher customers in control so my wife can continue singing here of an evening." Henri polished a mug.

Rafe processed the relationships—Henri's wife—the curate's sister?—sang at the tavern and picked apples? And lived at the manor.

"You invite a *woman* into the tavern?" Fletch asked, his attention still on the mural.

"Her singing raises funds for the church, while increasing my sales with her mournful voice. Cuts down on fights and broken glass, as well." The Frenchman seemed satisfied with the situation. "The locals are normally a good lot, but the manor has been bringing in apple pickers for the season. A few are a bit rough."

A woman, in a tavern. Rafe began to suspect this isolated area was a trifle more than eccentric. He drained his mug. "Apple picking? Harvest time already?"

Where did harvest workers sleep? A roof over his head would be a pleasant change.

"Such as it is. I was hoping to make good cider, but the orchard has been too neglected to produce much. Patience is trying to restore it. Local farmers and their families used to help, but they're long gone. The manor has been hiring anyone with enough limbs to pick. Clement. . ." The tavern owner lifted his wide shoulders. "Won't last long if he's shirking already."

If they wanted a place to sleep tonight, they should apply for an apple picking position? And beat Clement into tree fertilizer.

At the door, Wolfie yipped, and Rafe caught the jingle of reins and clop of hooves. His canine companion had a fear of wheels. Rafe had impulsively rescued him after an artillery cart had run over his paw—not considering how he'd feed an animal this size

"Huh. The village doesn't get many carriages." Henri set down a mug.

The tiny tavern had only one small window, and that was in the rear. Fletch ambled over to peer out the door. "Some portly gent and a widow. Nice rig."

13

Holding the last of his most excellent ale, Rafe watched over his friend's shoulder. The curricle halted in front of a mercantile. Before the driver could descend to help his passenger, the widow climbed down on her own with the aid of an elegant ebony walking stick bearing a handle that gleamed silver in the sunlight.

Rafe admired her sturdy curves, but the black veil falling from the wide brim of her preposterously elaborate hat prevented seeing more. He couldn't tell her age, but a lonely widow in town. . . might be reason to linger. Women seemed to like him, but available ones were hard to come by in rural England.

"That's the manor's banker, Bosworth." Henri came from behind his counter to look out. "No notion of why he'd drop a lady off here instead of at the manor."

Rafe wasn't in any position to look at *ladies* of any age. And he'd had more than his fill of greedy, cheating money men. If he was to hold onto his hard-earned blunt, he needed to invest in something substantial instead of castles in the sky for a change. .

He slapped his mug down on the bar. "Let's get this over with, Sarge. We can put a tent up for the night, if naught else."

And scavenge apples for dinner. The bread and cheese Henri had offered, no matter how enjoyable, hadn't begun to fill his empty belly.

THREE: VERITY

Faith—now *Verity Porter*—thanked the kind banker, Mr. Bosworth, for transporting her. She all but leapt out of the curricle into what she prayed would be her new home, one completely different from her old one. If her former governess was happy in this tiny village. . . so could she be.

The past ten days had not fully knitted the bones in Verity's foot, but her new walking stick suited the identity she was trying on. She might not know exactly who she was any more, but she had acquired a new name and was about to find a new home. Limping clumsily, she climbed the stairs to the mercantile. The kitten in her cloak pocket stuck its small head out, and she soothed it—and her nervousness—before entering the shop.

These past days had been a nerve-wracking, terrifying trial by fire, quite literally, but safety was almost at hand. A week of astounding accomplishments had given her a semblance of confidence. But she was still raw and a little fragile, and now her plotting had delivered her far outside familiar environs. She needed the reassurance of an old friend.

Miss Edgerton had promised to give her guidance should she ever escape London. It had taken time for cautious Faith to gather

her wits and create a bold new persona, one with the courage to buy a coach ticket and leave behind all she knew, but having little choice, she'd done it. She wasn't witless. Once she'd verified that her uncle was still alive, she knew she couldn't tolerate being his lackey any longer.

She watched Mr. Bosworth turn his carriage around at a sad, dead patch of weeds in the middle of the rutted street. He'd pointed out the drive to Wycliffe Manor as they passed, as if she might know the owners, but she knew no one except her former governess.

The mail coach from London had been a horrible journey, but she had remembered Miss Edgerton did her business in Stratford, so Verity had stopped there. After she'd brought the contents of her satchel to his bank for deposit, the banker had been very helpful and informative. Wealth had many uses. He'd promised to tend hers carefully.

She let her eyes adjust to the dim interior of the store until she located the gray-haired, diminutive shopkeeper behind the counter. He watched her with suspicion, rightfully so, she supposed.

"Good afternoon, sir. I am Mrs. Porter. My former governess, Miss Edgerton, has asked me to call. Could you direct me to her home?"

He appeared reluctant to do so. She'd never lived anywhere except the city, but she recognized the clannish protectiveness of a small community. The wharf area wasn't that different from a small town.

"And would you have any flowers or sweets I might take to her as a gift? I've traveled a considerable distance and was unable to bring much with me." She'd left her new piece of baggage by the door—a lovely tapestry to hold the remains of her childhood and new acquisitions for her future.

"Aye, she likes these here." He poured a paper of licorice candies. "You'd have to ask Mrs. Lavigne for flowers, but she's up to the orchard today. Besides, Annie has a yard full of flowers."

Annie? The lovely, softspoken, well-educated governess she remembered had been reduced to Annie? Come to think of it, she had never known Miss Edgerton's first name, only that it began with A, since that was how she signed her letters. Faith/Verity had been fifteen when her father's death had ended her schooling.

Since then, their correspondence had been limited to those times when Faith could steal stationery from her uncle's office. Unwilling to cost her governess too much in postage, she'd kept her letters to a single sheet, and Miss Edgerton had returned the favor. Although, since the post mostly belonged to her uncle, Faith had paid for it with his coins.

"Then the candies will do, unless you know of anything else she might like?" The tiny spark of the personality she'd crushed for ten years lurked behind her veil. *Faith* would have smiled ingratiatingly because she had little to spend. *Verity*—was trying on her mother, who had impressed with wealth and generosity.

"I've some of the manor's first apple crop here." He pointed at a basket on the counter. "Reckon she'd like a taste of those."

"And so would I, excellent. I'll take two. If you will just direct me, I'll be on my way." She left coins on the counter in excess of her purchases.

"Picket fence with the roses, just past the green and across the road. Tell her I expect her elixir to arrive in Monday's delivery." He bowed, all smiles now.

"You are a gentleman, sir, I thank you." She'd ascertain his name another time. These past days, she'd lived in dread of being arrested for theft and had traveled apprehensively with strangers to an uncertain future. It was lonely being dead to all she knew. She had exhausted her bravery.

Miss Edgerton had been offering a safe haven for years. At least she knew one person in this wicked world who accepted whoever she was. Verity hoped her wise governess understood her circumstances once she explained.

She tucked the gifts into her cloak pocket and rubbed Marmie's now-clean head. Without the sack of coins, her satchel was much lighter. She limped down the dirt street in the direction of the weedy patch of dirt implausibly called the town green, studying her surroundings with interest. This might be her new home. Curtains twitched as she passed but she encountered no one on the rutted street. Accustomed to the crowded noise of the city, she didn't know how to take the emptiness of the village.

Terrified of her uncle coming after his money, she'd nervously watched over her shoulder the whole time she'd spent gathering the beginnings of her new life. Not until the newssheets reporting the fire came out had she been able to unclench and breathe a little. Faith Palmer had been officially declared dead, even though they'd found no bodies. She was relieved that no one had lost their life.

Rather than mourn his niece's loss, her uncle had condemned the new fire company for not putting out the flames, for what little good that would have done. He no doubt planned to sue the city and the fire company and anyone else his attorneys recommended, if only to recover lost funds.

So she knew the drunken miser was alive and kicking. Here in the village, she'd see him coming from half a mile away. She really didn't expect him to care where she was. And even if he did, he wouldn't know about Miss Edgerton. She simply couldn't shake years of walking on eggshells.

The rural air was fresher than the city. Autumn smelled different, of old leaves, pine, and wood smoke, with none of the stench of sewers and rotting fish. Although there was a faint fragrance of manure. . .

She found Miss Edgerton's garden gate and admired the cottage yard of autumn blooms. She couldn't identify most, but the wealth of colors and peaty scent was welcoming. The gate opened without creaking. Moss grew between the flagstones. More greenery danced along the border. She recognized some of it as herbs she'd seen in the market. She usually bought her dinner from carts and knew little of cooking beyond eggs and rashers.

Living in the country, she'd have to learn how to cook. She

feared she lacked qualifications, but she hoped Miss Edgerton might show her a place where she might become a teacher. At home, she'd been helping a few of the locals learn to read. A school of young students, where she could go to her own small house at the end of the day, sounded like heaven. No more living in cellars at the beck and call of others. She might not know Latin or science, but Miss Edgerton had taught her well, and her father's books had taught her more. She wasn't ignorant.

The half-timber and wattle cottage appeared freshly painted, the mullion windows recently cleaned. Accustomed to the tall brick edifices of the city, Verity thought the cottage quaint and charming, but she did wonder about the thatched roof. Surely that wasn't safe?

The door had been painted a sparkling red to contrast with the black timbers and white wattle. She used the brass knocker tentatively, at first, then a little harder when she heard no response.

She was wondering if she ought to go around back and was examining a narrow stone path through the tall flowers when she thought she heard a cry. Marmie must have heard it, too, because she stuck her head out of her pocket.

Swallowing hard, she tried the door latch and found it unlocked. Pushing the door open, she called, "Miss Edgerton? It's me, Faith Palmer. Are you here?"

She hadn't dare write for fear her uncle would learn she was alive.

Another cry that sounded distinctly like *help* followed. Panicking, Verity dropped her satchel at the door and rushed into the low-ceilinged cottage, watching for the usual threats of men or fire, finding no more than a pleasant parlor with two sofas and a rocking chair. The mullioned bay window lit the interior.

Another cry, one that almost sounded like relief and *Faith* had her crossing the rush carpet, heart in throat.

On the sofa, the one with its back to the door, lay Miss Edgerton, an arm dangling over the edge, her head bent awkwardly as she appeared to struggle to push up with the arm under her.

19

"Tea," she whispered. "Papers. Under. . . bor. . .sssss." She collapsed and quit moving.

Verity screamed. Falling to her knees to help her former governess, finding her completely limp, she screamed again, while tears rolled down her cheeks, unchecked.

FOUR: PAUL

AFTER ESCORTING DRUNKEN CLEMENT BACK TO THE ORCHARD footpath, Paul Upton didn't return to the tavern. He sat on a bench in front of the parsonage, contentedly finishing his lunch and admiring the lovely day. And studying the firewood needing cutting and the garden he'd promised Patience that he'd weed.

He had seen Bosworth's carriage drop off a passenger, but he'd been too far away to greet the visitor. She'd been gone by the time he reached the street again.

Odd to have three new visitors. Perhaps they knew each other.

The two male arrivals in the village wore the uniforms of soldiers, and the unshaven beards of travelers. He'd gathered they were friends of Jack, so he thought no more of them. Jack had a stable where he raised and sold carriage horses to city folk. Paul's duties were firmly rooted in helping the village survive.

His stepsister and stepmother were part of the manor folk, but he was the orphaned grandson of Irish immigrants. Even though Oxford educated, he'd known since childhood that he'd follow his adopted father into the ministry. The world held so much suffering, someone had to lend a hand.

He was dusting off bread crumbs when he heard a woman's scream. Or thought he did. It was a fair distance.

He pushed through the chapel gate to the road and saw men and the pony-sized hound running from the tavern toward the other end of the village. Gravesyde wasn't large. Mr. Oswald from the mercantile stepped onto his porch, and a few women peered around their front doors. He wasn't the only one hearing screams.

Paul picked up his pace and was on Henri's heels by the time the men halted at the end of town, glancing about in puzzlement. The screams had stopped.

"Miss Edgerton's," Paul said tersely, pushing the half-open gate into the flower garden. "Her door is open."

He'd only arrived in Gravesyde in the spring. He'd spent a great deal of the time since then helping at the manor, while learning his congregation as he could. The smiling former governess had attended services regularly and aided his other church ladies in restoring the neglected chapel to order. He couldn't say he knew much of her beyond that. He pushed the door wider.

Inside, a veiled stranger knelt on the carpet, clinging to a pale hand and weeping silently. At the arrival of four bulky men, she merely wept harder, shoulders shaking. Mercifully, the hound remained outside.

Biting back an epithet, Paul slipped into full parson command. "Henri, Minerva is with Betsy's mother. Send her over, if you will, then fetch Meera." Slighter than the two bulky soldiers, Paul pushed past to kneel beside the woman.

Clever-witted Henri understood immediately. He ran out, muttering French imprecations under his breath.

"I've sent for a physician," Paul murmured, for the benefit of the widow as well as the looming soldiers. He took Miss Edgerton's limp hand in his own and knew at once that a physician couldn't save her. "Sgt. Russell, Major Ferguson, if you would, guard the doors. We don't need curiosity seekers. Whoever takes the kitchen might make a fresh pot of tea."

Well-versed in death and taking orders, the soldiers did as

told. The major took the front and the sergeant retreated to the kitchen.

Paul didn't explain that Gravesyde and Wycliffe Manor had more than their fair share of inexplicable deaths, and he was taking no chances that this might be one.

The governess wasn't exactly elderly, possibly in her fifties, as best as he could ascertain. Blond hair fading to silver, she'd worn spectacles, which had fallen on the floor. Two teacups sat on the table between the sofas, along with the teapot. He touched the pot. It wasn't quite cold.

Paul pried the weeping widow off the floor and led her to the other sofa, offering his handkerchief since her lacy one was sodden. Having been brought up as a cleric's son, he had a natural facility for speaking on all occasions, but he was at a loss here.

"I'm Paul Upton, the local curate, Mrs. . . ?"

She shook her head and pushed her veil aside to wipe her cheeks. She wasn't a beauty, but she was much younger than he'd expected. Silky, light brown hair framed a clear, rosy complexion and big dark eyes.

"Is she. . . ?" She didn't complete the question, but Paul understood.

"I'm afraid so. Perhaps an attack of the heart?" He was no physician. That's why he'd called for Meera. He didn't like those two teacups on the table. "Were you having tea with her when it happened?"

She shook her head in reply. A kitten wriggled out of her cloak pocket, and she held it up to her chin, closing her eyes, presumably in grief. The kitten mewed pitifully.

"Sergeant Russell, along with the tea, see if there's anything for a kitten, please," he called back to the kitchen. "Perhaps you would like to go to the kitchen until the physician arrives?" That would give him the opportunity to poke about a bit.

The widow squeezed the kitten tighter. "No. I will stay with

23

her. I wasn't there when she needed me. I am here now." She burst into tears again.

Paul had the impression of a strong-willed woman behind the cascade of tears, one who might have been pushed to a brink but not over, not yet.

Minerva rushed in the front door just as the ginger-haired Sgt. Russell returned with a tea tray and a fresh pot. The burly soldier ought to look awkward holding the delicate china, but he slid the tray onto a tea table with expertise, then pulled up two chairs near the empty hearth.

Paul's betrothed was a petite whirlwind. Minerva tested the prone governess's eyelids, her pulse, then briskly turned to the weeping widow on the sofa. "Up you go, let's have a spot of tea. Oh, look at the lovely marmalade kitty! What's his name?"

"Marmie," the widow whispered, unable to resist the tempest that was Minerva. She took the seat the soldier held out for her.

"Marmie! Is that a male name? Aren't all marmalades male?" Minerva took the opposite seat and offered the sugar.

While the women conversed about cats and performed the tea ritual, the soldier gestured toward the kitchen. Paul followed him back.

Closing the door between the rooms, Sgt. Russell nodded at the open kitchen door. "There's a muddy footprint on the doorstep, and the door wasn't closed proper. I'm thinking as neat and tidy as everything is, that the footprint would have been swept up if the lady had time to notice it."

Paul refrained from expressing surprise but stepped outside to examine the doorstep and garden. "It's been dry lately. The ground is hard. There's a stream runs back of that hedge." He stepped down to examine the neat flagstone path through the rows of vegetables and herbs. "More muddy steps. So someone came in through the hedge gate."

"Did the lady make herbals?" The soldier picked a few of the green leaves edging the vegetables and sniffed them. "Thyme and rosemary. There's mint and oregano in those pots. That's lavender and foxglove—those two aren't for cooking, but she has them planted close, with the herbs."

A soldier who knew herbs and cooking? And who also spoke with educated, if not aristocratic, accents. Jack had interesting friends.

"She may have. Minerva will know." Paul examined the footprints, but it wasn't a full outline, just the edges where dirt had fallen off. He'd say male, simply because ladies usually didn't clomp through mud unless they wore boots or pattens. The maids though. . . He hated thinking like this. Some poor girl could have delivered eggs.

Returning to the kitchen, neither of them spoke their thoughts. Sgt. Russell opened a pantry door and found a tin of fresh biscuits he added to a plate. Paul carried them into the front room, where Meera Walker had arrived to examine the deceased.

The manor's physician/apothecary glanced up at their entrance. Stoic Meera seldom expressed alarm, but the line on her brown brow warned she wasn't happy. "I cannot do anything." She waited until Paul was closer before murmuring, "There are signs of irritation in her mouth. It was an herbal tea from the smell of it. I will take the teapot back to the manor. One teacup was empty and the other spilled."

"You might want to leave by way of the back garden. Sgt. Russell noted plants he thought might be used in herbals and not cooking. Perhaps she treated herself?" That was Paul's hope, although the extra teacup and the muddy footstep. . .

Perhaps in other, more normal towns, this death would have passed as natural. Here in Gravesyde, after a few too many incidents, they'd all learned to be suspicious. Perhaps ignorance was bliss, and one could believe crime didn't happen if it wasn't detectable, but that didn't make murder any less criminal.

Who would want to kill an unassuming maiden lady?

FIVE: RAFE

Rafe had spent these last years of war following orders, thinking only for himself when he sought food to feed hungry troops or had time to find a willing woman.

Survival had been his only plan for so long, that food and shelter were always his first instinct. He had a few dreams, but planning had been impossible under the daily threat of dying.

Without funds, he didn't see how that could change now.

From habit, he took orders from strangers who knew the circumstances better than he. The only dead ladies he'd seen lately had been shot by enemy troops, and the cause of death had been obvious. A lonely spinster keeling over after drinking tea. . . Just after a widow lady arrived. . . Not his bailiwick.

"No, I cannot leave her," the widow quietly insisted when the other ladies tried to persuade her away. "She was always there for me. I must do the same for her. Please, I will pay for all the arrangements, if you'll tell me what I must do. I just can't. . ." She sobbed into her handkerchief again.

Rafe could tell the others were flummoxed by her insistence. It didn't seem rational to him, either. Death was just another stage of life as far as he was concerned. Still, he hated seeing a woman in distress.

He waited until he could pull the curate aside again. "Is it safe to leave a woman alone here? Is there some chance the death was other than it seems? I can set up a guard post in the garden, if that's your concern."

That wasn't overly rational either. He needed to go begging with Fletch. But he wasn't ready for that step yet, and so he did what he always did, followed instinct.

"Jack could set up some of his stable lads. . ." The curate looked troubled. "But he's not at the manor today. And the men he uses. . ."

"You don't know me either," Rafe acknowledged. "When will Jack return?" He'd known they shouldn't show up unannounced.

"By evening. His wife is the cook at the manor. If he can't vouch for you, then we'll make other arrangements. You're kind to offer for a stranger."

Rafe thought the Honorable Jack's wife was an earl's daughter not a cook. . . "I've naught else to do this evening. I was planning on bedding down in that crumbling inn."

"I still hate to ask it of you. Miss Edgerton lived here for years without trouble." Upton wrinkled his brow in concern. "Although there is reason for doubt about her death. And if this Mrs. Porter. . ." They'd finally pried a name out of the widow. He shrugged. "It's an odd coincidence. Perhaps she's here to rob the place, although I cannot imagine there is anything of value."

Rafe shrugged off any notion that a weeping widow was a killer. "If there's someone to act as chaperone, I can patrol the grounds. Fletch can go up and see Jack, have his dinner, then take a turn later."

The curate rubbed his hand against his trousers, clearly troubled. "What concerns me is that if someone did kill her. . . then Mrs. Porter's arrival may have interrupted them. She says Miss Edgerton was still alive when she entered. Did she disturb a thief? Someone who wished to search the cottage?"

"Should we question the neighbors? Looks to me like they'd

27

all see anyone on the street, like you saw us, and we saw the carriage."

Upton gestured toward the kitchen. "The hedge hides anyone coming along the footpath. I suspect, if Miss Edgerton did dispense herbals, the people who bought them wouldn't use the front door."

Rafe grimaced. "Sadly true."

The plump Indian lady approached, a steely look in her eyes. "I would like to see the garden before the sun goes down. You are the gentleman familiar with herbs?"

Rafe bowed. "My sainted mother once had a garden twice that size." He offered his arm. "May I escort you?"

"If you would. There are plants I do not grow due to their toxicity. Children and animals are indiscriminate about what they taste." The short, black-haired physician took his arm and without glancing in either direction, nearly tugged him through the kitchen and into the yard.

Rafe had never met a female physician, but he wasn't questioning this one's competence. People often dismissed him as a thick-headed lout because of his appearance. He'd learned as a boy to judge by deeds.

Once out of the widow's hearing, he asked, "There is some chance of poison?"

"Some. It is hard to say since I was not here to observe any symptoms. Most poisons cause purging, and I see no sign of that, so if there was anything fatal in the tea, it acted quickly." Once in the garden, the plump physician released his arm and went to work, examining each plant, dismissing the usual, focusing on the less obvious.

The autumn scents of decaying foliage and coneflowers made him homesick. At this time of year, many of the plants were no more than brown stalks and dry leaves. His mother had often left the stalks so she could identify the location of roots. Mrs. Walker evidently had experience. She didn't dismiss brown clumps but examined them the same way as she did the green.

In moments, she gestured him over. "You are familiar with herbs?"

"Only those used for cooking," he admitted. "My parents owned an inn." He eyed the rich soil she pointed out. "Someone's been digging roots."

"I buy my more dangerous herbs in powdered form just so this sort of thing doesn't happen. If need be, will you stand witness of what we see here? Captain Huntley is magistrate, and he's most strict about any evidence he's presented."

An army officer as magistrate. . . not a noble, or at the very least, a lawyer? If an earl's daughter could be a cook. . . Another eccentric bend to this village. "I'll write out what we find. We can have Fletch and the curate witness it."

"Call them now, please. There is more than this one place. It still means nothing, but it's a direction." She sat down on a garden bench to wait while he fetched witnesses.

Returning to civilian life would take some adjustment. He ought to be commanding his few troops instead of following orders from brown ladies in red shawls. But murder in a peaceful village and not a battlefield. . . was beyond his ken.

Fletch raised his eyebrows at Rafe's request but willingly followed, along with the anxious curate.

The little apothecary rose with a long stick that had been leaning against the bench and pointed at a patch of hard ground in the back of the garden. "Mud, perhaps a footstep." She moved the stick to a dug-up patch. "That is monkshood, also called wolfsbane and formally named aconite. The Greeks used it as arrow poison. Someone has dug the root, the most toxic part of the plant."

"Why would she grow poison in an herb garden?" the curate asked in dismay.

"Like people, every plant has a good side and a bad side. Aconite tinctures are used for anything from sciatica to anxiety and headaches. She most likely had formulas already prepared in her pantry or cellar. I spoke with her once when she complained

29

of an irregular heartbeat. She knew a great deal about folk medicine and recognized her symptoms, but she would have used the leaves to treat it. The root taken alone. . . deadly. But that's not all." The lady pointed to a large bush in the back corner.

"Belladonna," Fletch said, surprisingly. "It can kill cattle. That's not natural here, is it?"

Fletch's family owned land, Rafe knew. He hadn't known about cattle.

Mrs. Walker nodded agreement. "Birds sometimes carry the seeds. She may have found it in a hedgerow or ordered it from someone. Women have used it for cosmetic purposes since ancient times, as a means of dilating pupils to make the eyes beautiful, so it's not impossible to find. It's also used in any number of medicines, for wound treatment, gout, anesthetics. . ."

"And it's poisonous?" the curate asked.

"Extremely, every part of it, one of the most toxic of plants. Again, I would not expect it to kill instantly. I cannot tell if this plant has been tampered with. It's much too large." She returned to the path and handed the stick to Rafe. "If she was treating herself for a heart arrythmia, and someone mixed a tincture of belladonna and aconite, it might have been sufficient to stop her heart almost instantly. The human body is a mystery."

"They could very well have expected her to simply pass out while they searched the place," Rafe suggested. "They may not have known that Miss Edgerton had a heart condition."

"Exactly. If you will write up a note that says you observed the footstep, the disturbed roots, and so forth, we may all sign it. It may come to nothing, but if it becomes necessary, I want it to be clear that we all witnessed this."

Rafe's respect for the physician rose a few more degrees. As he found paper and ink and wrote up the summary, his mind toyed with the idea of a village where educated people gathered. . . He'd still starve.

While they signed the statement, Miss Peniston, *Minerva*—

Rafe was trying to learn proper names since the people here seemed to be very casual—joined them in the kitchen.

"I have found someone to sit with Mrs. Porter. There's a box bed in the corner where they can take turns resting." She nodded at what appeared to be a cabinet with painted designs.

The curate hugged her. "Thank you. I don't think she should be left alone." He glanced to Rafe. "Do you still wish to stand guard?"

"Wolfie can guard the front door. I need to bed down my horse and fetch my gear, then I can set up here in the back. Unless an outsider has a key, the gate can be locked. The walls are not easily climbed, but there's an apple tree in that back corner. . ."

"You really think that's necessary?" Miss Peniston frowned worriedly, glancing back at the front room where the widow sat in mourning.

"Yes," the apothecary said firmly. "I have to feed Moses and must go back to the manor or I'd sit with her a while. I advise locking the gates, the doors, the pantry, and gathering all the keys and guarding them, as a precaution, you understand."

"I'll fetch your gear and take the horses up to the manor," Fletch offered. "What time do you want me to take over?"

Rafe had studied the well-supplied pantry. He already knew the village had no inn or pub to provide a meal. It was either the manor or here. Here, he wouldn't have to beg for his supper. "Come down in the morning. I'll pitch my tent where any thief will have to step over me. I can't imagine any will try."

Fletch snorted, knowing Rafe was simply avoiding the inevitable. But hoping for a free meal and bed, the major didn't argue.

The matter settled, Rafe returned to the back garden to check the gate and the apple tree. The latch was unlocked but the key hung beside it. He locked it and pocketed the key, then studied the tree leaning over from the neighboring yard. The limbs were old and half-dead.

31

He reckoned he'd hear the branch cracking if anyone attempted entry that way.

SIX: VERITY

Too many shocks in too little time left Verity unable to think. Instead, she fell back on feeble Faith and watched, with no notion of how to behave. While she sat there, her throbbing foot up, the efficient Miss Peniston and church ladies prepared Miss Edgerton for her funeral.

Miss Edgerton had always been a buzz of activity. Verity could not associate this lifeless shell with her beloved governess, but she said the prayers she'd learned after too many deaths. Maybe a lightning bolt would strike her dead and she would not have to worry about the morrow.

A world without Miss Edgerton's wise guidance. . . She swallowed a sob of selfish panic.

Life as she'd known it these past years had been bleak and lonely. The one shining hope on her horizon had been her teacher, who was happy helping others as she'd helped the long-lost Faith. As she may have helped the new Verity. . . The world had lost its sunshine.

If only the foolish child she'd been had listened to her wise teacher, summoned the courage to abandon her father's beautiful home to face the unknown. . .

Now here her adult self was, still lost in the unknown,

although now she had no home or Miss Edgerton to ease her fears. She had the money, the security, she'd wanted to acquire, but cold coins did not warm her heart or buy courage.

Marmie deserted her to go in search of food or the garden. She couldn't even name a cat properly. Male cats shouldn't be called Marmie, but that had been what first came to mind. At least she'd known it was a marmalade cat. She wasn't completely ignorant, but book learning only went so far.

A tempting odor of. . . cooking food?. . . seeped into the front room. She thought everyone had left, except the silent woman knitting in the corner. She didn't know why the woman was here. Perhaps she should ask how she knew Miss Edgerton.

Verity had no particular desire to talk. That required thinking. Which required planning. She hadn't the strength to start over, for the second time in less than two weeks.

Trying to determine what was cooking occupied sufficient cogitation. She hadn't had a real dinner since. . . She didn't want to recall those long-ago days. Belatedly, she realized life had passed her by. In the morning, she'd contemplate the horror of a funeral and where to go next. Right now, she possessed as little ability to fathom what was happening as poor Miss Edgerton—so she thought about food.

She clasped her shaking hands and closed her eyes but realized her belly was empty. When had she eaten last? Breakfast, a lovely porridge at the inn in Stratford. What time was it now? She opened her eyes again. The knitting woman had turned on a lamp. The days were growing shorter.

She didn't think it possible to put a morsel in her mouth. Her tongue was dry and her throat had closed. She'd heard the whispers. They thought Miss Edgerton had been poisoned. That was ridiculous. No one poisoned saints. But she felt as if *she'd* been poisoned. What were the symptoms? How had her governess felt when. . . ?

Not thinking.

The big, ginger-haired man entered the parlor carrying a tray containing steaming bowls of enticing aromas. He needed a haircut and a shave. She couldn't remember ever seeing a man with a beard. The carrot-orange curls stood on end as if he'd been running his hands through them. Attractive, in an odd sort of way. He was quite massive, barrel-chested and tall, but he carried the tray with deftness, arranging it on the table as he had the tea things earlier.

"Not much, just bean soup," he announced to no one in particular. "There's some apple cider. It's a bit vinegary but I spiced it a little. The bread is old, but you can sop it in the soup. Tomorrow will be a long day, so fill up while you can."

The knitting lady finished her row, neatly folded her work, and brushing down her skirt, stood to examine the plain fare. Without a word, she took one of the chairs.

If she didn't have to talk. . . Verity did the same, without the knitting, anyway. She was exceedingly hungry. She shouldn't be. She was supposed to be dead.

She didn't dwell on that thought either. It had crowded in there unexpectedly. She sipped the hot cider to clear her throat. It didn't seem vinegary but soothing.

The bread had been warmed and wasn't at all hard. She dipped it into the soup and nibbled. When it didn't come back up, she tasted the soup. Everything was so delicious that she couldn't stop tasting. It had been so very long since anyone had cared to fix a meal for her. . . Tears stung her eyes all over again. She ought to be cried out.

If she died in the night, she'd almost go satisfied. Except, if someone had. . . simply not possible. Shut the mental door on that notion.

She supposed she ought to ask the carrot-haired man's name.

She wasn't ready to allow the world to intrude.

The meal refreshed her enough to recall all the women besides herself that Miss Edgerton knew and communicated with, women who would grieve as she was grieving. Verity knew how to be useful without a lot of thought. The other women were strangers, so she needn't apply more than the formal words she'd learned after the deaths of her parents—the words Miss Edgerton had taught her.

Knowing her teacher would approve, Verity sat down at the spindly desk after she finished her soup. The chair was a bit narrow for her broad beam, but it didn't creak when she sat. She'd seen people using the pen and ink earlier and saw no reason why she couldn't.

She'd found Miss Edgerton's address book by the time the man returned with tea. It was rather like having a butler. Since she hadn't started frothing at the mouth yet, she trusted that the tea was safe. Or that she wouldn't die until she'd finished the letters.

Her eyes were closing with weariness once she'd finished the final missive and realized the knitting lady had wandered off. She'd found the privy earlier, when the house had been full of people. Now, she'd have to brave the dark garden alone. Or go upstairs to the chamber pot in Miss Edgerton's private quarters. . . She wasn't ready for that either.

Folding the stationery, sealing it, and adding the final address, she added a black crosshatching on the edges so the recipients would know it was important enough to pay the postage. She didn't think a village mercantile would carry appropriate funeral paper.

The kitchen had a small lantern burning so she didn't bruise her shins crossing the floor. Realizing Marmie had abandoned her, she looked for the kitten and found it curled up on a towel near the heat of the hearth. The thoughtful orange-haired man must have done that. Could she afford a butler? She'd love to keep this one.

For the first time all day, she felt almost human. She'd prefer to retreat to frozen statuary, but she needed the privy first. Where had the strange man gone?

A crash and a curse from outside answered that.

Heart in throat, she held the door latch. Did she open it or look for a key to lock it?

A hound howled. More crashing, at a distance.

Shaking, she pulled on a cloak left hanging beside the door and tested the latch. It opened. She peered out.

A lean-to covered the back step. No light illuminated the dark corners of the yard. But it wasn't quiet out there.

She lit a lantern to see beyond the lean-to, but the meager light only illuminated the path to the privy.

A man's voice murmured reassuringly, and a moment later, the huge gray hound loped into the lamplight, then vanished like a wisp of smoke around to the front of the house.

Now what? The garden smelled of unfamiliar earth. The impenetrable dark was too quiet, with none of the usual cacophony of city streets. A whole strange world existed that she'd never encountered and had no notion how to navigate. In London, she knew where to go, to whom she should speak. Here. . .

"It's all right, Mrs. Porter." The carrot-haired man approached, returning a sword to a scabbard. "Probably a thief looking to see what he could find."

She'd have to grow accustomed to her new name. She almost looked over her shoulder for the stout old widow she'd stolen it from. Talking, she knew how to do. "Thank you, sir. People can be wicked. Stealing from the dead!"

"The dead limbs from that old tree should be cut out, but they served their purpose this evening. Might I help you?"

He had been so very courteous. . . "May I have your name, sir?"

He scrubbed his big hand through his thick curls. "Just call me Rafe, please. I'm not an officer anymore, and I'm not much of a mister either."

"Oh." That seemed odd. She didn't know if she could do that. "Rafe? Is that short for Ralph?"

He sighed. "No, ma'am. For Rufus. I just wearied of the snickering when so-called gentlemen thought I was too stupid to know it meant *red*."

37

She understood senseless snickering. "Your parents must have loved your hair to name you so. My father told me that people who laugh behind one's back are too rude to be acknowledged, and that I'm better than they. Which makes me better than most of the population, I suspect. It's lonely at the top." She offered a smile and walked past his rather stunned expression.

Could she do this? Could she become this Verity Porter she pretended to be? A widow with a modicum of wealth and no friends in the world?

And if Miss Edgerton had been murdered. . . *Could she find her killer?*

There was a notion she'd like to cram back in its box.

First, after visiting the privy, she needed to look for loose floor-boards. She hadn't told anyone about her teacher's dying words. There was the reason she was trying so hard not to think.

SUNDAY

SEVEN: PAUL

With the sunlight from the ancient stained-glass windows illuminating his congregation, Paul studied their faces from his pulpit. The tiny chapel couldn't hold all the manor inhabitants. Over the summer, he'd built as many pews as he could with wood ripped from old barns and sheds. Some of his regulars from the village had hauled in ragged sofas and splintery benches. And still, the little chapel overflowed this fine September morning, spilling into the churchyard.

A real-life drama attracted as much of an audience as any theatrical production.

He made mental notes of who attended. Miss Edgerton must have known her killer. He hated thinking that person was among his congregation, but the village was still very, very small.

The majority of his parishioners had remained for the funeral service. Everyone had known Miss Edgerton. She'd taught children their letters and numbers, apparently dispensed herbals upon request, and gladly contributed what she could to the chapel now that it was functional again.

The ladies from the manor faithfully attended, so their appearance was no surprise. But with a potential killer on the loose, the manor's men had accompanied the ladies, as they often didn't. Paul wanted to believe the killer was an outsider.

He thought the stately couple squeezed in beside the manor folk might be the Prescotts, dealers interested in buying some of the former priory's medieval furniture. They remained seated for Miss Edgerton's service. Why would they attend a funeral? Certainly not for the pageantry.

Several of the men visiting the manor had attended Sunday services, also, but were now departing before the funeral. Paul recognized the banker's assistant, a Mr. Smith, who had brought a Mr. Sullivan to look at village properties. Surely, they had not known a local herbalist.

The hired help from the orchard, along with several workers rebuilding the manor's tower, generally didn't attend but were here now. Curiosity seekers, no doubt.

He'd been introduced to the Blackwells, father and son, who were restoring the tower to some of its former glory. Had the teacher talked to them about repairs?

Even Clement, the drunken apple picker, sat respectfully, hat in hand. He had a woman with him. Paul hadn't thought the manor had provided housing for families. The village had always been where the workers stayed. Unfortunately, Gravesyde had been abandoned for so long that most of the cottages were uninhabitable.

A more unlikely collection of suspects couldn't be found. Perhaps he wasn't meant to be suspicious of anyone attending church.

He was relieved to note that his betrothed had taken the newly-arrived widow in hand. One of the many reasons he loved Minerva was that she knew what to do without being asked. A lifetime of following the army with her father had taught her far more than most ladies knew.

Mrs. Porter wore the heavy blacks she'd traveled in, hiding behind the enormous, veiled hat, sitting in an alcove where she wasn't visible to the entire congregation.

The big, red-haired soldier sat near her—as guard? He'd shaved and combed his hair for the occasion.

Out of respect, after the service, the gentlemen from the manor carried the coffin to Henri's peddler's cart. Over the last months, the old covered cart had been used as a hearse far too often. The ladies stayed behind to set up tables of food for the mourners. Paul hoped Mrs. Porter would take some comfort in hearing about her friend.

After saying words over the grave and leaving the gravediggers to finish their sad task, Paul walked back to the village. To his surprise, Captain Huntley and former Lt. Jack de Sackville accompanied him, along with the two newly arrived soldiers.

Hunt had been an American army engineer, injured in battle with the British. A baron's son, Jack had fought briefly on the Continent before taking a position in India to make his fortune. Both Hunt and Jack's wives were descendants of the late earl. An American engineer and a British nobleman's son made an unlikely friendship, but between them, they'd been returning the deteriorating estate to functional.

They were the reason Paul's family had a home again. He was proud to walk by their side.

"Walked into a right mess and then attached yourself to a pretty widow before you were even in town a day." Jack pounded the big red-haired soldier on the back as they approached the feast the village ladies had laid out. "You never were one to hold back, Rafe."

"Hard to say if she's pretty," Major Ferguson objected. "She's covered up in veils."

"She's young." The sergeant shrugged. "I talked to her a wee bit last night, in the dark, mind you. Seems a practical miss, just a little overwhelmed. But she had the sense to mail notices this morning to all the deceased's friends and relations."

"I understand there's a sister and some nieces in York. That's a fair way to travel. Did Miss Edgerton own her cottage? Might they be returning here?" Paul asked.

"According to the manor's records, the cottage is old, built on a parcel some earl gifted to one of his henchmen." Captain Huntley swung the walking stick he didn't need anymore. "It's been passed down in the family for over a century, one of the few the bank can't claim, which explains its good state of repair."

"And the inn, captain?" Sgt. Russell asked. "Did you ascertain if the bank owns that?"

"You weren't at dinner last night, Rafe, when we discussed your plans. Told you we needed to talk to Jack instead of playing nursemaid to a grieving widow." Major Fletcher fell back to join his comrade in arms.

"I can't tell you anything," Jack said. "It's all on Hunt, here. Or Walker, more like. As steward, he has to read the old documents and keep tally."

"Most of the village is part of a lawsuit between us and the bank," Hunt explained to the newcomers. "The manor once owned all this land, until the last viscount took it upon himself to mortgage it before he drowned. There is some question about his right to do so since he was only a life owner, and the property reverted to the estate after his death. But more to the point, the survey deed accompanying the mortgage was for that useless hill-side on the road to Birmingham, not for the village."

Paul had heard all this before. He was simply relieved that the chapel and its parsonage was no part of the package. He was doing his best to improve the parsonage so it might be comfortable for Minerva, who had spent these last years living on a duke's estate and now stayed in the manor. He didn't want her to feel as if she were following the drum again.

"So everything in the village sits and rots until the courts decide." The red-haired sergeant grimaced in disappointment.

"It has," Jack agreed. "Because there's been no one to care. But we're here now, and the manor has come into funds recently. My wife also has blunt that her trustees can't control. We're discussing how that might be invested. If we can make an arrangement with

Bosworth to pay a little on what's owed, he might be willing to relinquish some of his control."

Paul knew the manor itself needed enormous improvements, including turning the once-abandoned keep into work areas for some of the inhabitants who needed income. An inn. . . would be an enormous undertaking. Necessary, perhaps, if the village was to grow, but difficult.

"Bosworth? Isn't that the banker who brought Mrs. Porter to town?" Sgt. Russell asked.

"It is. I assume the widow knows him. He didn't come down for the funeral, though." Paul knew about the banker's illegitimate relationship to the earl's family, one that made Bosworth, along with the mortgage, an uncomfortable guest. But the bank was apparently working with a possible buyer for abandoned property—nothing suspicious there. "Perhaps he doesn't know Mrs. Porter or Miss Edgerton well?"

"The clutchfist didn't transport a poor widow out of the goodness of his black heart. She must have money." Jack caught on quickly. "Do we need to consult with her, determine her plans?"

"You want to ask a *woman* to invest in an inn, with no hope of an income for years?" Sgt. Russell asked in horror. "She'd have to be rich as Croesus and just as foolhardy to even consider it."

The captain hummed under his breath and twirled his cane. He was a tall, broad-shouldered, distinctive man, with one blind eye that didn't always coordinate with the other. But underneath that top hat and overlong dark hair, Paul knew, was a razor-sharp mind.

"The two of you are looking for a place to settle, as I understand it?" Hunt addressed the two officers as they reached the bottom of the hill.

"My parents owned an inn. I know how to run one. We've been looking for a position," Russell agreed. "Fletch is my right-hand and can do most anything I can do. But there aren't many openings for more than pot scrubbers, and no one's likely to hire the likes of us to work in their kitchen."

"Gravesyde needs men like you. We also need that inn. All those steam-operated factories in Birmingham are multiplying, drawing entire families away. We need to establish our own industries here, and for that, we need a place to welcome workers, salesmen, buyers. . ." Hunt stopped to watch as the women bustled about tables laden with food. The widow wasn't visible. "Paul, you're the carpenter. How much work do you think it would take to make the inn habitable?"

"The roof ought to be tiled instead of thatched. Or at least covered in tin. The entire interior probably needs plastering. Haven't taken a look at the floors in the upper story. They may need shoring up. Downstairs, we might rip out the worn floor boards, put them to better purpose, and add brickwork or stone. The timber frame seems solid, though. That's all I can tell you." He had earned his way through school doing carpentry. Building inns was substantially above his skill level.

"We're not builders," the sergeant protested. "We might add brute strength, but I couldn't lay a straight brick if my life depended on it. I have a bit of blunt I could put into furniture and glassware and the like. But we'll starve in the meantime."

"You're the one that owns that wolfhound, aren't you?" Hunt asked. "Train it, did you?"

Paul saw the light before the soldiers did. The captain had been on the hunt for someone to train the manor's hounds as guard dogs. He'd wanted wolfhounds but they were rare. And he also needed a bailiff. . .

That was asking a lot of newcomers but needs must. Paul and his small family had been newcomers not so long ago, as had all the manor's occupants. They'd found their niches in a town and manor that needed more hands than were available.

As they emerged into the churchyard, Paul located the widow lingering in the shadows. She had pulled back her veil, revealing a young woman with large, dark eyes shadowed by grief. He didn't think her a killer.

But Meera had said the contents of the teapot had definitely been poisoned.

EIGHT: RAFE

A BAILIFF AND HOUND TRAINER—FAR BETTER THAN A BEGGAR, RAFE concluded after his discussion with Captain Huntley. He had no notion of what a bailiff might do, but he knew dogs. With the dangling carrot of rebuilding the inn, he could do no less than accept.

Fletch had accepted Jack's offer to work training his stable of carriage horses, while both of them oversaw the rebuilding of an *Elizabethan* inn. That's what the captain's wife had called it, least-ways. Fletch called it a rubble pile of history. Neither of them had any notion of where to start rebuilding, but army life had taught them to improvise.

For what it was worth, it seemed Gravesyde Priory Village was Rafe's new home. He'd have to write his parents. Maybe, one day, they could join him here. They knew everything there was to be known about running an inn. Pity they no longer had one.

He filled his always empty belly at the funeral buffet, listening for stories of his new home. The men talked of weather and crops. He heard no tales of the deceased, which he supposed was a good thing. The women might know more, but they whispered among themselves. As bailiff, he'd have to learn about Miss Edgerton somehow.

Because that had been no idle thief climbing the apple tree, despite what he'd told Mrs. Porter. Wolfie had paced the yard, following the culprit as he searched for a way over the wall or through the locked gates. Rafe had known the apple tree was the weak point in the yard's defenses. He'd simply waited for the gent to summon the courage. The breaking branch had sent the thief scrambling, ruining his chance to catch him.

Rafe was rather certain it had *not* been a woman in skirts throwing their legs over that dead branch. He might understand a woman needing her herbals but a man? Had the lady provided elixirs for men? A bailiff should ask, he thought.

A man climbing a tree to break into a dead woman's meager cottage had to have a very strong motive—not that it hadn't taken an even stronger motive to kill the lady. Former governesses generally did not hide secret treasure troves, or even enough coins, to risk burglary.

Miss Edgerton had been killed for a reason and that reason was most likely still in the cottage.

When he noticed the widow slipping out the churchyard gate, Rafe followed.

He only had this one suit of civilian clothes left, and he was aware of their wrinkled state. An officer wore a uniform, so he'd not wasted coin on buying a fancy top hat. He was conscious of his scruffiness as he strode up beside her.

"You should not be alone, Mrs. Porter." As usual, he had not spent much time thinking this through. "Do you have plans to stay in Gravesyde?"

She limped. Her walking stick was not an affectation like the captain's. From what little he could tell, her cloak and bonnet were of decent quality. Her accent wasn't aristocratic but educated. He had the notion that she wasn't poor, just bereaved.

"I have no plans at all," she admitted with a sigh. "I cannot remember the last time I could say that."

He wanted to know more, but if he meant to be presumptuous, it would be for good purpose. "If you plan on staying at Miss

49

Edgerton's cottage, you must be aware that it is not safe. Mrs. Walker has determined that the tea in the pot contained poison. It is possible the culprit was after something in the cottage and your arrival prevented his finding it."

She'd lowered her veil again and he couldn't see her expression, but she eventually nodded, whether with agreement or approval, he could not say.

"Miss Edgerton urged me to visit. She said I might help her set up a school for the young children arriving here as the manor grows." She sounded thoughtful but did not expound further.

"The manor folk appear to be reasonable. Have you spoken with them?" Having grown up in a popular inn, he'd never been particularly awkward around women or anyone, but he couldn't help watching his words with a grieving widow. He wanted to take her arm, help her walk the rutted road, but he was aware her head barely reached his shoulder, and she might possibly be terrified of him.

"I should, I suppose. But there is so much uncertainty. . ." She gestured with a gloved hand. "I would like to know why she had to die. It does not seem reasonable. Was it spite? Anger? Teachers are not wealthy. How can I understand?"

"You want to understand *why* she died and not *who* killed her?" he asked, a little off balance at the path her mind had taken.

She stopped at the garden gate. This time, she removed her veil and faced him directly. She had huge brown eyes with little gold flecks that he'd like to spend more time studying, except she smacked him with words.

"*People* kill. As a soldier, you senselessly killed other men like yourself. My father was a sea captain who fought naval battles and sent countless poor sailors to their watery graves. Someone cudgeled him to death on his way home and robbed him of everything he carried, which was seldom much. I have seen children run over in the street as if they were no more than rats to be eradicated. I have some understanding of why those deaths happened.

But Miss Edgerton. . . If I could only understand. . ." Her voice broke, and she turned to unlock the gate.

He held the panel so she could swing past with her stick, then followed her in and locked it for her. "Miss Edgerton was not a soldier, had no money, and did nothing more dangerous than help the village women and children. I understand what you are saying. But chances are very good that she possessed *something* that someone wanted. You are not safe staying here alone." There, he'd said it.

She halted on the flagstone walkway, with the dead heads of flowers brushing against her black skirt, and turned back to him. "I know nothing of you except that you arrived the same day I did."

Sensible lass. He removed his cap and bowed. "I am former Quartermaster Sergeant Rufus Russell, known as Rafe, from Norfolk. I served with Lt. Jack de Sackville in Spain. He can vouch for me. My parents owned an inn until moneylenders took it away. I can provide references that I never harmed anyone in the serving of apple cakes."

A small smile tilted the corner of her full lips. "I love apple cakes. I haven't had them in ever so long." The smile faded. "But it is not done. I brought no maid. I knew Miss Edgerton had little room."

"I can pitch my tent in the yard as I did last night. I can rummage food and cook with the best of them. If I make inquiries about a maid, can you pay her?" He hadn't come this far without being rude and crude. He had never pretended to be a gentleman.

If possible, those big eyes widened even more. "You would do that? Why? You don't know me. You owe me nothing."

"Does someone need to owe you before offering to be of service? Although, in this case, you are helping me. I have nowhere to stay. I could, conceivably, sleep in that crumbling inn, but I'd still worry about your wellbeing. I have to eat. There is no reason we can't share our resources. Miss Edgerton has a fine garden." Always establish a home base with food and water sources—he'd learned that early on. Once he was fed, he could handle whatever happened.

"Oh. I hadn't thought of that. I've never been much interested in food. I don't even know how to cook a potato, although I suppose I might learn. There are books about such things, are there not?" Her pale brow puckered.

"You don't know how to cook a potato?" That jarred him from complacency. A woman who couldn't cook? She had definitely been gently reared, and he'd better quit admiring those fine dark eyes.

His confidence reasserted itself. "Then you need me. Let's verify that all the gates and doors are locked. Then give me a key, and I'll be off to find a maid, and to see what the village offers in the way of provisions. I'll try not to be gone long, and Wolfie is here to protect you." He followed her into the yard and snapped his fingers at his hound, who came over, floppy tail wagging, for a shaggy head scratch.

"He's a beautiful animal," she said, almost wistfully. "I've never been able to keep one."

"I'll teach you his commands when I return. First, let us be certain no one has attempted to visit while we were gone." Readjusting his thinking, he treated her as he would a lady stopping at the inn, placing her gloved hand on his arm and leading her to the front door. It would be tough remembering how to behave in civilization, but this was good practice.

She'd actually locked up. In the country, folk seldom did. She produced a key ring and entered the now empty house.

Yesterday, it had been full of people. Today, the loneliness had seeped in. Rafe had never lived alone and had no desire to start now. A maid was a good place to start.

As promised, he checked all the locks. The widow had even shut all the windows and knew to hold them closed with sticks—she must have come from the city. He opened the window in the kitchen a bit to air the place out.

She was still standing in the middle of the front room where he'd left her, her gloved hands clasped in her skirt as she studied her surroundings with tears in her eyes. They might both be thrown out on their heads when the heirs arrived, but until then. . .

"Wolfie will patrol the grounds. The kitten needs to be let out." He handed her the key ring. "Keep the doors locked."

He'd lost friends in battle. He knew the pain. It would take time for her to recover from loss. He couldn't offer comfort, yet.

But he hadn't had a woman in much too long and longed for a friendly hug and kiss. The widows he'd known had acknowledged the same loneliness. They were often welcoming on chilly, lonely nights. In the dark, it didn't matter if he was nobody.

NINE: VERITY

QUARTERMASTER SERGEANT RUFUS RUSSELL—KNOWN AS RAFE, Verity smiled a little at this insistence—was the most deliberately aggressive man she'd ever encountered. Most men she had known, however vaguely, had been polite, bowing and scraping if they wanted something and ignoring her existence otherwise.

Rafe just walked in, declared himself at home, and went to work proving it. *Obnoxious*. But right now, she felt like a fluffy seed blowing on the wind. She needed grounding—and a roof over her head. How many homes could one lose in a lifetime? Rafe gave her confidence that all might be well, if she developed a plan.

She wasn't at all certain she was ready to think. It brought back too many fears. . .

She fed Marmie—Manny? Marmot?—some ham and cheese from the larder, then let him out. She couldn't even decide on a name. How could she possibly decide what to do with her future? Evidence that she wasn't thinking at all— she should have picked up scraps from the buffet for the kitten.

She fixed tea for herself. Then, while the sergeant was out, she returned to studying the floorboards in the front room. The kitchen was flagstone, so she was reasonably certain if Miss Edge-water had said *boards*, she meant the front room.

How did one pry up floors? She crouched down and pushed and pulled at a wide plank. She knew so extremely little of life outside of her father's books and her uncle's counting house. . . She stood again and brought her heel down on a board. It creaked but didn't move. Were boards laid over dirt? On joists, she thought, to raise the floor above rainwater. She tried to recall treatises on architecture she'd removed from her father's library. Had she packed any of those in the crates she'd ordered delivered here?

The original cottage floor had probably been dirt or stone. The boards most likely had been added later. She started at the kitchen end of the parlor and systematically stomped on each board with her good foot. All she did was make the broken one hurt.

Had she been wrong about Miss Edgerton's last words? It wasn't as if she'd been clear. It had just made sense to assume that *Papers. Under. . . bor. . .sssss* meant she'd hidden something under the floorboards. She couldn't imagine what kind of papers, but they must be important. A will, perhaps?

She'd also said *tea*. Had she known she'd been poisoned? Why had she not named her killer instead? Because the papers would reveal the killer?

Shudder. *There* would be a reason for someone to break in. How long would it take to find out who the killer and would-be thief was? The poor sergeant couldn't live in a lean-to in the yard forever.

And she couldn't occupy a house not hers for very long at all. She needed to find the papers before she was thrown out.

She let Marmie in, locked the door, and faced the inevitable.

She couldn't sleep on the sofa forever any more than Rafe could sleep in the yard. She had to go upstairs, invade Miss Edgerton's personal quarters. She'd done this for her parents. She'd hated every minute of it, the invasion of their private lives, knowing they kept tattered underwear and love letters from their youth. . .

But she knew from her correspondence that Miss Edgerton seldom ever saw her sister and nieces. They were farm folk and weren't likely to find time or means to travel from Yorkshire during harvest or anytime soon. Verity had asked in her letter to them if they wished to direct her in disposal of the cottage.

She'd be doing them a favor to start cleaning out private possessions. Or should she wait until Rafe found a maid?

In either case, she must go upstairs and look for a place to sleep. Staying in Miss Edgerton's home seemed simpler than contemplating setting into the unknown alone—an effort akin to leaping off a mountain into the ocean. The journey here had taken all the courage she could muster.

She took the narrow stairs from the kitchen up to the wide loft over the parlor. The kitchen had been added on and had no second floor. The centuries-old cottage loft had probably once held hay for the animals kept below. People used to sleep with the animals, she'd read. She couldn't imagine anything more unpleasant. . . Well, except for murder.

The loft was enclosed but not divided. A heavy drapery hung between the front and back walls, with a rope to pull it forward to create a separate room. She knew Miss Edgerton had company occasionally, since there were two beds on either side of the curtain, and she'd invited Verity to visit.

The larger side of the loft held a simple bed covered in an artistic patchwork quilt adorned with rings of blue roses. The smaller side had a cot with a folded blanket. Both sides had chests of drawers and a washstand. The larger side had a wardrobe and small mirror.

Verity thought she might sleep on the cot. It appeared virtually untouched. She opened the chest on that side and found it empty. The meager belongings she'd purchased after the fire would fit in there just fine.

There were even shelves for the small library she'd hidden in the shed and had crated up before she left. After her mother died, she'd worked her way through all her father's shelves, saving books she wished to re-read, selling the boring ones. She had some lovely geographies she'd love to see again.

Uncle Warren had never missed the beautiful volumes. She'd tidied his office by stacking his ledgers in the empty spaces. She'd hoped that one day, she'd save enough coins to leave home and support herself, but she'd have been dead before that happened.

Now, she had her savings, plus much more. How much did cottages cost? More than she had, she supposed. But at least she was thinking a little bit again.

Reluctantly, she opened the tall wardrobe. Miss Edgerton had been tall and slender. Her clothes wouldn't fit Verity. She'd not have felt right wearing them, anyway. She laid out each piece separately, checking for pockets and folding everything neatly. As she'd expected, the fabric was of good quality, but well worn. The quilt had probably been made of pieces too worn to wear. Miss Edgerton wore a lot of blue.

She emptied the drawers, finding nothing of value there either. She'd have to ask the church ladies if anyone could use the clothes.

She should search the desk and bookshelves downstairs next. Had Miss Edgerton known her killer? Known what he or she wanted? Her last words made it seem so, but she might be imagining what she wanted to believe.

Verity was about to head downstairs again when she noticed the rag carpet on the floor. *Floorboards*. The entire loft had floorboards, and there would be a ceiling below the joists, creating a space.

The hound barked a greeting. She peered out the narrow, mullioned window. The sergeant was returning already, a basket over his arm. Had she ever seen a man carrying a market basket? But he was so huge, no one would dare mock him for it. She realized she'd lived a narrow, if not sheltered life. Men who cooked. . .

Did she dare trust him with Miss Edgerton's last words? Not

yet. She didn't know exactly when he'd arrived in the village. She had only his word for it.

She despised suspecting everyone, but after her uncle's venal treachery, and all she'd seen of London's cruelty, she did not trust easily. Or at all.

But she needed to eat and knowing a very large man and his dog stood guard at her door somehow made her feel a little safe. Foolish, she supposed, and how Miss Edgerton had gotten herself poisoned.

Since, at the moment, she was a perfectly worthless bit of flotsam, did it matter if anyone poisoned her? Who would miss her? No one. To the world, she was already dead. That was a very sad commentary.

Now that she had freedom, she needed to determine what she wanted. Since she would never be grand and glamorous and certainly had no interest in marrying, she was fairly certain she ought to aim for useful.

Miss Edgerton had been more than useful but Verity had no formal teacher's training and knew nothing of herbs. Or much of anything else.

She hobbled down the stairs in time to find Rafe unloading his purchases on the kitchen table. "How do I know you won't poison me? Do I need to catch a mouse and test everything on him? I hate tormenting poor creatures." She's saved up a lot of worrying in his absence.

He actually grinned. His was a plain face, with a large square jaw and broad brow and pale lashes. But when he smiled. . . Her insides lurched and she had to look away.

"I'll happily taste everything before serving it to you, if you like. Poisoning good food is a sin. Miss Edgerton's downfall was drinking nasty herbal tea, which tastes like poison even if it's good for you." He set out a loaf of crusty bread and what appeared to be meat wrapped in bloody paper. "I've asked about for a maid. One or two should be showing up for you to interview."

"Thank you." She supposed she should be grateful. She'd never had a maid of her own. At fifteen, when she'd lost most everything that truly mattered, she hadn't even been putting up her hair. She supposed a country maid was more likely to dust and do laundry. She had so much to learn.

Since she was being impolite and exploring, she entered the large larder to examine its contents. Jars of neatly labeled herbs and potions lined half the shelves. The rest contained mundane ingredients like flour and tea. "The man at the mercantile said Miss Edgerton would receive her elixir tomorrow. What exactly constitutes an elixir?" She carried out the tin labeled tea.

Rafe was adding kindling to the fire and already had a kettle heating. "I think of it as a sweet liqueur to be mixed with medicines, but I should think Miss Edgerton could ferment one with honey and any kind of alcohol. Although I suppose, ale and cider are about the only alcohol she might buy here."

"The fermentation process can be complicated, I suppose." She nodded knowledgeably while spooning tea leaves into the pot. If she'd ever read about such a thing, her eyes had probably crossed.

"Not really, if one has the proper ingredients. Birmingham has half a dozen large breweries these days, so the ingredients are available. I'd like to make my own ale and porter." He poured boiling water into the teapot.

He had dreams. She didn't, not anymore.

Verity scooped up the kitten circling her ankles, threatening to unbalance her. She rubbed noses with it, loving the rumbling purr. If she could stay here. . . Even that was too far to plan. She set the kitten outside to roam. "I think I'll see what books are on the shelves. That might give us a better idea of what she's been doing."

He opened the meat paper and began chopping. "Unless she was independently wealthy, she had to earn a living somehow. Although she may have been paid in food."

"Someone knows something. I cannot imagine she let in a complete stranger or that one would have any reason to kill her."

That's what had been bothering her. Miss Edgerton was unlikely to know an army officer and a stranger to town like Rafe. She helped women, mostly, and those would be the ones she'd share tea with.

Horribly sad to think that a woman she'd helped had killed her.

Verity carried her tea to the narrow desk. It only had a few drawers. She checked those first, finding a ledger of expenses and other amounts she assumed to be income. Verity had spent these last ten years in a countinghouse. On long boring nights in an empty counting house, she had taught herself how to read ledgers. But Miss Edgerton's initials and amounts meant very little. She could assume *Bldna 2s* might be a rather expensive herb. The initials of the buyer were meaningless until she learned the names of the locals. She'd seen herbs sold at the market, so such sales wouldn't be unusual.

Setting the ledger aside to study later, she opened a drawer full of correspondence. Miss Edgerton had taught at a girl's boarding school before becoming a governess. It appeared she'd kept up with many of her former students, as she had Verity.

Scanning the letters quickly, her eyes widened, and she started at the beginning to read the veiled inquiries and laments more deliberately. The letters were mostly signed with common names —Mary, Penny—girlhood names a teacher might recognize. But these were no longer girls. They were women asking for help with adult problems—abusive husbands, unwanted pregnancies. . .

Oh, my. This could represent a whole drawer full of men who might want to kill Miss Edgerton.

Outside, the wolfhound barked a vigorous warning.

TEN: RAFE

At the dog's bark, Rafe crossed the parlor where the widow sat at the desk. All the color had drained from her normally rosy cheeks. What had she found in there? Was it any of his business?

"The gate is locked," he explained, opening the door. "Visitors can't knock. Wolfie is letting us know we have a caller."

She nodded and shoved a letter into a drawer as if it might bite.

He trotted into the yard to investigate the intruder, snapping his fingers at Wolfie to stop his barking, while he studied the tall young woman at the half-gate. He recognized her cheerful demeanor from the church this morning but didn't remember being introduced.

Behind her waited a stout older woman who glared at him in disapproval. Perfect. A gorgon to scare off the unwanted.

"You're the curate's sister, aren't you?" Rafe opened the gate. "Sorry, I don't know if I learned the name. I'm Rafe Russell."

"Patience Lavigne, sir, pleased to meet you. I'm Paul's sister and Henri's wife. I believe the two of you discussed fine ales." She stepped into the garden and exclaimed in delight. "Oh, look, the Lenten rose is already sending up shoots! Miss Edgerton had quite a gift."

He assumed she was talking of flowers, a subject which didn't particularly interest him unless he could eat the results. "Will you come in?" He glanced inquiringly at the disapproving female edging past him warily.

"Oh, my apologies. This is Mrs. Wilhemina Underhill. Minerva said Mrs. Porter needs a maid and companion. Mrs. Underhill said she might be interested."

The stout lady bobbed a brief curtsy but didn't acknowledge him otherwise.

Rafe opened the cottage door and made the introductions to Mrs. Porter. One of these days, he'd learn her first name. The widow appeared uncertain how to react but gestured at the sofas.

"Have a seat, ladies. I'll return with fresh tea." An innkeeper had to know how to make guests comfortable. Might as well get in some practice, just in case.

"I can't live in a house of sin," he heard the old lady state firmly as he prepared the tea. She must be slightly deaf and spoke loudly, or she intended him to hear.

"I'm without family," Mrs. Porter was saying as he carried in the tray. "Miss Edgerton offered to be my companion. Her untimely death has left me bereft."

Rafe thought she winked at him as he set the tray down. He lingered, arranging napkins and cups, to see if she meant to be audacious. The widow might be quiet, but she hadn't struck him as shy.

"There's some said as she was a witch, but I don't take to that ungodly talk." Mrs. Underhill glared at him. "But men, now, they're nothing but trouble."

"Mr. Russell is Wycliffe Manor's new bailiff," the very blond, buxom Mrs. Lavigne said excitedly. She appeared to be the kind of cheerful female who found everything exciting. "He is guarding Mrs. Porter in case the thief returns."

"He also provides the most delicious meals," Mrs. Porter said demurely. "I do not cook."

Ah, the lady didn't do audacious, exactly. She'd simply told the old gorgon she'd starve unless he stayed or she cooked. Checkmate.

He returned to the kitchen to finish supper. A companion would put a crimp in his plans to seduce the widow, but she needed to trust him.

If he was to be a proper bailiff, he should catch a killer first. He'd need to know a lot more about the village. Old Mrs. Underhill looked like a fine source of information. He wondered if she liked a good glass of stout with her meals.

He was setting the lamb pie over the fire when Mrs. Porter and her new maid climbed the stairs to the attic. The pub owner's comely wife stayed behind to speak with him.

"Henri says you know how to operate an inn. That is exciting. We need traveling salesmen for the button factory, and eventually, for the perfumery. And Lavender is eager to test her sewing skills on ladies willing to journey here." Her usual smile faded. "I cannot imagine who would travel for a modiste."

"If she becomes very famous or if she's very good and known to be less expensive than city modistes, women will find her." He sorted through the ingredients on the table to begin the apple cake he'd promised. "I don't suppose I can bribe you with pastry to tell me all the town gossip so I know where to look for malefactors?"

She laughed. "Lady Elsa's pastry is pure heaven, and I eat far too much of it. Now, if you can start a brewery, as Henri claims, he may tell you all *he* knows, which is much more than I do."

"That's worth a thought. But seriously, do you know of anyone who might wish a poor teacher harm? I cannot leave Mrs. Porter unguarded until we catch the villain." He counted on a parson's family to know everyone hereabouts.

She frowned and shook her loose blond curls. "I cannot think anyone from the village would harm Miss Edgerton. She was near enough to a saint. She taught children, provided medicinals for a reasonable fee, and gave the bounty from her garden to the church. She always had flowers for the altar."

"Doesn't the manor have an apothecary? Why would anyone

consult a governess for their medicines?" He cracked eggs into the pottery bowl with the butter he'd melted.

Patience wrinkled her small nose. "Meera is a foreigner to them. She's not white or Anglican. Rural folk have little experience with people different from them and are slow to trust. Miss Edgerton's family has lived in Gravesyde since time immemorial, so they trust her. Whether anyone knows it or not, Meera and Miss Edgerton consulted and exchanged herbs and recipes. When a physician was needed, Miss Edgerton sent them to Meera."

So, competition was no factor, good to know. He liked the plump little physician. "So, you're saying we need to look at newcomers? How many can there be?"

"More than usual," she said with a small frown. "Now that the manor has come into a little money, they have hired a coachman and several footmen. I have hired men to pick the orchard. Hunt and Arnaud are hiring laborers and craftsmen to renovate the tower. Those people are almost all strangers, although some may have lived here years ago, and left when the manor was abandoned. Now that the war had ended, there are many men returning home and seeking jobs. We cannot know everyone."

Footsteps on the stairs warned they were about to be interrupted. He returned to mixing his cake.

Patience smiled at the less than smiling Mrs. Underhill. "Well, will you think about it?"

"My granddaughter's house is very crowded. With the new babe coming. . ." Mrs. Underhill waved her chubby hand vaguely. "This will suit. I'll fetch my things."

"I will do my best to make you feel at home," Mrs. Porter assured her. "Your company is much appreciated."

Rafe figured that was quite a lie but a polite one to reassure an old woman on the brink of making a large adjustment. He was reasonably good at gauging character, but the young widow was a bit elusive. One minute, she was a lost waif unwilling to voice an opinion. The next, she commanded an assurance he would not expect from a young woman faced with a murdered hostess.

Once the ladies had left to fetch Mrs. Underhill's belongings, the widow returned from the front room with a handful of what appeared to be letters, carefully unfolded and flattened. Her confidence had returned to hesitancy, as if she didn't wish to show them to him. She had no particularly good reason to trust him.

As he had no good reason to trust her. They were both stranded in this strange land alone. Rafe poured the batter into a pan and lifted a quizzical eyebrow.

"Motive," she said with resignation. "If you are the new bailiff. . ."

He had no notion what a bailiff did, but if it placed him on the manor's payroll, he'd accept the title. He slid the pan into the bread oven, wiped his hands on a thin towel, and took the papers. Reading quickly, he frowned and handed them back. "I don't understand."

She set them down and opened the pantry. "Abortive physics. Preventives. Possibly even means of rendering a man. . ." She gestured helplessly. "Mrs. Edgerton helped women with female problems." She studied the neatly labeled herbs on the shelves. "I don't know enough. We'll have to ask Mrs. Walker to take a look."

Even married women generally didn't know about such things. What kind of life had she led before coming here? Rafe wasn't certain he wanted to know.

"You think a man would kill her for providing *preventives*?" he asked warily.

"Possibly. But if she used this information to ask for money to prevent scandal. . ." She winced and closed the pantry doors, her eyes speaking wells of pain and knowledge.

"Extortion," he said for her. "People have killed for less."

MONDAY

ELEVEN: PAUL

AFTER A REQUEST FROM THE MANOR'S NEW BAILIFF, PAUL ESCORTED Meera Walker to Miss Edgerton's—apparently now the widow's—cottage on Monday morning. As a curate, he was in a position to know most of the village inhabitants, and he'd like a killer brought to justice as swiftly as possible. He simply could not fathom a motive.

Having been warned by the hound's bark, Mrs. Porter emerged, without her hat but still using her stick, to unlock the gate. The enormous wolfhound sniffed and waggled his tail in recognition, allowing them to pass. Entering the cottage, Paul could hear clomping footsteps and a low mumble overhead that indicated Mrs. Underhill at work.

"She has taken the beds out for airing and has the linen soaking," the widow murmured, leading them back to the kitchen. "I am afraid once she has scrubbed the floors, she will not allow us to walk on them."

"I suspect that is her way of saying farewell to the deceased," Paul explained. "She is sending on the last of Miss Edgerton's spirit. She may claim not to be superstitious, but it's ingrained in rural habits."

She smiled. "Actually, I am grateful. It's been a bit spooky. I hadn't seen my governess in ten years, and all of a sudden I am living with her remains. . . I want to know her soul is content and has passed on. Then, perhaps, I might know how to proceed. I hope."

Dark circles underlined her eyes. Her grief was almost palpable. Paul didn't know her well enough to console her. Keeping busy was most likely the best answer.

"Understandable, you need time. Where is Rafe?" Paul asked as the busy apothecary headed straight for the pantry. The kitchen smelled of bacon and coffee, but the remains of breakfast had been cleared away.

"He is taking his new duties seriously. I believe he has gone to the manor to meet as many people as he can. It can't be easy being a bailiff where he knows no one. I thank you and Mrs. Walker for coming at our call. We don't know enough about herbs to understand what is safe and what isn't." Wearing a dark violet round gown, the widow twisted her hands in a muslin apron that nearly reached her feet—one of the teacher's, he suspected. The widow most likely hadn't carried aprons in her meager bag.

Which made one wonder what circumstances she had fled. People seldom traveled to Gravesyde unless they had no choice.

Meera studied the neatly labeled tins and opened a few to test them. "I don't see anything as a cause for concern. I've already removed the few that might cause irritation if taken in large quantities, but on the whole, these are mostly cooking herbs, tisanes, and teas."

Mrs. Porter produced a letter from her apron pocket. "I found this in her desk, with others. The requests are. . ." She handed the paper over rather than explain.

Paul raised his eyebrows at the contents and handed it to Meera. "I am no barrister, but I believe these type of things are illegal?"

Meera scanned the request and shrugged. "Not necessarily, but some can be exceedingly dangerous." She eyed the cabinet again. "Still, I don't see any. . ."

Paul took her place in front of the pantry door, examined the shelves, the width of the door, and ran his hand over the edge. "This shelf isn't on the wall. It's essentially freestanding. If there is a means to move it out. . ." He found a latch behind the door frame.

"He's a carpenter," Meera explained to the widow. "He knows how things are put together."

"Fitting for a man of cloth," the widow murmured, possibly in amusement. Paul had heard all the jests about Jesus being a carpenter and was happy she refrained from saying more. She gasped as the shelf pulled out, revealing a second set.

Meera pushed him aside to examine the hidden contents. "Bring me a basket, please. Your Miss Edgerton may have been trying to help her former students, but in the wrong hands. . . My word. Some of these are quite expensive. We can't grow them here. She had to have ordered them."

Paul thought the physician sounded more admiring than horrified, one academic to another, he supposed. This was women's territory, and he wasn't even married. Neither he nor Minerva had wealth, so they approached marriage cautiously.

Was Meera saying the governess had a closet full of poison? There was motive, indeed.

"Do you think local women may have come to her?" Mrs. Porter asked worriedly. "Might their husbands have objected?"

"I'd say she's been doing this for a long time to have learned all these ingredients. She knew what she was doing. If so, it's hard to believe she allowed anyone other than her patients to know what she did, and they had their own reasons for not telling. But if one of her patients passed on the powders to someone desperate, someone who might be too far along, or who used them incorrectly. . ." Meera sighed and added more tins to her basket. "She could have killed them."

Which meant both men or women might have wished to eliminate the teacher and her practice. Struggling with the implications, Paul took the heavy basket. "There has been no law in these

71

parts for years, probably for as long as she lived here. If someone, anyone, lost a loved one and suspected Miss Edgerton, they might take justice into their own hands."

"I suppose it is possible." Without her dramatic hat, Mrs. Porter had the appearance of any young woman: fair, unwrinkled complexion, long thick lashes, plump lips, attractive in an ordinary sort of way. "But to have it happen the day I arrive. . ."

"Coincidence does happen," he reassured her. "Although I suppose it is possible this person knew you were arriving and thought they should act quickly."

She visibly shuddered. "Even Miss Edgerton did not know I was coming. Perhaps I am meant to be Job and crushed by a thousand ills."

"That might be a little presumptuous," Paul said in amusement, although he had to wonder what had happened to make her think like that.

She offered a vague smile of agreement. "Sorry, but my life has become more dramatic than the theater. There are more letters and a ledger in her desk. Do you have time to take a look and see if the initials mean anything to you? I can fix tea, and Rafe made scones this morning. They are quite delicious."

Meera shook her head. "I cannot help you with initials, and my baby is still nursing, so I must hurry home. Why don't I take a look at your foot while I'm here? I'm surmising from the bandage that it is injured?"

Paul had deliberately not looked at the lady's limb. "I can leave. . ."

Mrs. Porter shook her head. "Another time, perhaps, but my foot appears to be healing, thank you. It looks uglier than it feels. You need to return to your son."

Meera shrugged. "I'll slip out the back gate and up the footpath. You should come to dinner at the manor, if you will be staying for long. We always need more hands. I'm sure we can find work for you, if you need it."

The widow indicated her plain muslin. "As much as I would

enjoy a useful occupation, I have no dinner gowns. I understand you have a seamstress?"

"Lavender! Paul, you must bring Mrs. Porter up to meet Lavender. I doubt she has much in fabrics for a widow, but she can ask Henri to find some when he's in the city."

The widow blushed. "I am officially out of blacks, but I had nothing else, and they seemed safest for traveling alone. I . . . lost almost everything to a fire."

Ah, the reason for seeking a new home. The widow was becoming less of an enigma. Was the injury a result of fire?

Paul opened the kitchen door. "Why don't I escort Meera back to the manor, and bring Lavender down so you needn't task that foot? I'll have Rafe join us. Then we can ponder the ledger while Lavender takes your measurements. You'll still want to visit the manor to see what she has in stock, but you might feel a little more comfortable if you know her first. She's quite young but a genius with thread."

Meera waited until they were out in the lane before murmuring, "Do you really want to know who among your parishioners is paying to rid themselves of children, possibly because the ones they have are starving? Or who might be raping their daughters? Or if someone is attempting to disable an abusive husband? The list of reasons the deceased might have provided those herbs is long and awful."

Paul's existence was a result of rape, so he did not ponder the question lightly. It was an age-old problem, never spoken of, so the number of victims were unknown. He was grateful his mother had found an alternative to being rid of him, but she'd been in easy circumstances. As a minister, he'd seen desperate women grateful for miscarriages.

He wasn't God and refused to judge, despite his teachings. His vicar might have a word or two to say about his rebellious beliefs, but no one paid attention to this penniless parish. His purpose had always been to give aid to the living.

"There aren't many young women in the village, other than a

few new maids at the manor, and they're under my mother's care. If those herbs are the motive for Miss Edgerton's death, then I'd have to say her former students are the more likely suspects." That would be a relief to him. He didn't want to judge people he knew. "It takes money to pay for an exclusive boarding school. They would come from wealth."

"And might be gently extorted later?" Meera suggested.

As his own stepfather had extorted his parishioners for their sins. Paul pinched the bridge of his nose and prayed this wasn't the situation. The sordidness brushed too close to his own life. "Perhaps we should let this case alone."

Meera snorted inelegantly. "Hunt is already chafing at the bit. He'll want his new bailiff to learn the traces and gallop to the rescue. He's well-pleased at finding someone to do the dirty work."

They met the bailiff in question heading down the footpath. Rafe eyed the basket on Meera's arm with displeasure. "That many?"

"Hidden," Paul explained. "I'm to bring Miss Lavender down to talk new gowns while I go over Miss Edgerton's ledger. We thought you might like to know if I identify any of the initials."

"I had thought to go over the church register, but this will be more pleasant. New gowns? She is coming out of mourning?" The burly, red-haired man seemed pleased.

"I'm not at all certain she's been in mourning," Meera said dryly. "Her gown is nearly a dozen years old. Your widow may not be what she seems."

Rafe beamed. "My conclusion, as well. But I'm reasonably certain she did not murder the governess any more than I did. Mrs. Porter brought her hostess apples and candies. I ate both and didn't die."

"I'd be careful what you eat," Meera warned. "If the killer is still about and wants any of those papers in that desk, they might not care who else dies to get at them."

Rafe's smile vanished. "Perhaps we should remove her from that house."

"Try," Meera said with a hint of grimness. "I have a suspicion that under her gentle demeanor is a soul as old and stubborn as any mule's."

"Gentle? There is nothing *gentle* about that lady. She appears to have been through hell and is hardened like iron on a forge. I said she didn't kill the governess. I didn't say she's not capable of it."

TWELVE: VERITY

With Mrs. Underhill cleaning upstairs and the curate planning on returning, Verity didn't have the opportunity to pry up the loft floorboards. She wasn't given to sitting idle though. It was the reason she'd persuaded her uncle to let her run errands. After her mother's death, she'd picked up his mail, gone to the bank, cleaned his office. . . and appropriated whatever she needed.

By the time the manor party arrived with Rafe, she'd matched the few initials on the correspondence with initials in the ledger and was working through Miss Edgerton's address book.

She had also compiled a list of half a dozen household matters to address, along with the need to inventory the bookshelves in hopes there were enough books to begin teaching children. But she had wished to impress the sergeant and set him on the trail of a killer before she turned to the mundane, so she made the suspect list first.

Wolfie announced their arrival. At his bark, Marmie poked her head out of her warm pillow. The aroma of bubbling stew permeated the cottage. She had been raised in a grand mansion, but Verity thought she might learn to enjoy these cozy quarters, should she ever learn to cook more than eggs. . .

And discovered why Miss Edgerton had died. It wouldn't assuage her grief, she knew. That took time. But it might settle her terror.

Rafe led the visiting party in without knocking, making himself at home. The bold soldier had little respect for the common conventions, but Verity was so far out of her element that his lack of manners seemed trivial.

Before taking the curate back to the kitchen, Rafe introduced their adolescent companion with a casual wave. "Miss Lavender Marlowe, seamstress, Mrs. Verity Porter, my hostess."

Verity hid a smile, recognizing that he treated the cottage as a public inn—of which he was in charge. Interesting that he did not linger to admire the exceedingly beautiful child.

"I do hope you want something more stylish and colorful," Lavender exclaimed as Verity greeted her. "Purple is not a terrible color with your hair, but primrose would look so much better with your complexion! And a high-waisted style is better for your figure, as well as fashionable. You don't need to look like a potato sack. How do you feel about lace?"

"That it is an expensive luxury," Verity admitted reluctantly, even though her vain heart longed for it. A potato sack, indeed! "A kitten would shred it. I would like a nice dinner gown, but I need plain dress more, for every day and for church."

The girl nodded enthusiastically. "I can do that too. I have even created a style that allows you to cover up a nice muslin dinner gown for church. You are in good hands. Shall we go upstairs to take your measurements?"

"Wait, first, I must speak with Mr. Upton and the sergeant." Suppressing her excitement at thought of a new frock instead of second-hand, Verity stuck to the practical.

She carried the ledger, address book, and letters to the kitchen table, pushing aside Rafe's sandwich makings. "You may eat after I explain what I have done. I hope it will start your list of potential suspects."

After her explanations, the curate studied the list. "I have never gone about in society. I'll need to take these names of Miss Edgerton's former students up to the ladies in the manor, see if they are familiar with any of them. But I can take a look at the ledger to see if I recognize any of the unidentified initials as local."

"Just give me names when you have them." The soldier returned to slapping meat on bread. "I don't know a soul but I'll find them."

Verity hoped he wasn't being overconfident. As much as she admired his manner of bluntly pushing through every circumstance, some men were all bluster.

She left them to their food and led the seamstress up the stairs, where Mrs. Underhill was making up the beds with fresh linens she must have manufactured from fairy dust. The old ones were still flapping on a line out back.

The drapery divider had been pulled, neatly dividing the loft, leaving each of them with a single dormer window for light. "It smells beautifully of beeswax, thank you, Mrs. Underhill!"

The older lady grunted in return.

"Not very talkative for a companion," Lavender whispered, entering the larger space Mrs. Underhill had assigned to Verity— Miss Edgerton's bedchamber.

"I'm not accustomed to talk. I've lived alone for a long time." Verity had been struggling so hard to overcome grief and survive, that she really hadn't noticed how lonely she'd become. There had always been market people to discuss the price of a meat pie or a servant or merchant to question. She certainly hadn't attempted to strike up conversations with the sailors on the wharf or the men in the countinghouse. She'd been sadly lacking in society.

"Well, this is not a good place to become a hermit." The girl efficiently took Verity's measurements. "What do you need first?"

"A simple, sturdy, round dress to wear about the house and into the village? Long sleeves for winter? I don't need ruffles or frills. Since I don't envision many dinners at the manor, it would be best to see how much this will cost first." Not that she had many choices for improving her wardrobe. She wasn't likely to buy a carriage and visit shops elsewhere.

"I have a few sturdy fabrics in stock for every day use, and a selection of second-hand dresses that can be made over, although they're quite unfashionable in drab colors for servants. You'll need to come up to the manor and we'll see what you like. I have a lovely lavender cambric that might suit, although I suppose you'll want kerseymere or merino for winter. I assume you have no lady's maid and wish them to fasten in front? And what about stays? These are decent but don't really fit properly. Do you need more?"

Impressed by the young seamstress's knowledge and efficiency, Verity indulged in new everything from the inside out. She'd learned to sew by making over her mother's garments when she'd outgrown her childish ones. She was no expert by any means. With everything she once owned lost, she'd had to buy second-hand after the fire. They'd been the first clothes she'd purchased since her father's death, and she'd been practical, buying dark plain clothes and not the frills and colors she adored.

To buy all new seemed extravagant, but necessary, if she was to step into Miss Edgerton's refined slippers, metaphorically speaking. Her wide feet didn't fit the governess's slender shoes. Which reminded her. . .

"I have bundled up Miss Edgerton's clothes. Do you know if the church takes those sort of things?" Verity fastened her gown while Lavender took notes.

"I can take them. I have an assembly of seamstresses who can refurbish and refit old dresses for any who need them. The manor has been providing uniforms for the maids, because many of them only have one gown of their own. Henri picks up durable garments at the second-hand shops in the city when he can."

"That's a great kindness. I appreciate it." Verity produced a basket that no doubt was intended for the laundry and filled it with the garments she'd gathered. "Do you have many seamstresses working with you?"

"They come and go, depending on the season and circumstances. Illness, children, complaining husbands. . . all interfere. But we have a number of older women who show up regularly. There won't be any problem producing what you need this week." Lavender took the basket, carrying it on her hip as they proceeded down the stairs.

Verity followed more slowly, using her walking stick and favoring her foot. She knew in the city that seamstresses worked in conditions ruinous to their health, but the alternatives for women were few. She liked thinking of the manor providing employment and a healthier work place, while the women could still have homes and families. But if lawlessness prevailed outside the manor's safety. . .

She was no one to talk of lawlessness. She had essentially stolen her uncle's daily funds. She had never pilfered more than a few shillings in the past. Her experience with her uncle's business had been limited to carrying the satchel back and forth and dusting the books. She'd studied his ledgers but had assumed he made frequent deposits during the day. If she'd known how much she carried. . .

She might have stolen the bag sooner.

THIRTEEN: RAFE

ARMED WITH A LIST OF POTENTIAL LOCAL SUSPECTS COMBED FROM THE ledger, Rafe set out down Gravesyde's main residential and commercial street. As a medieval village, it had originally served a priory. Later, he supposed the locals had served earls and their guests. The village had obviously never been wealthy or substantial, but it certainly had seen better days.

There were signs that was turning around. The larger establishments were still abandoned and deteriorating. But some of the small ones had been recently rethatched and repaired. The mud daub often needed paint but walls had been mended.

The mercantile still operated. Farm ladies lined their carts in front to sell their wares. Jams, jellies, gourds, the last of the summer vegetables. . . He stopped at each cart, introduced himself, memorized names, and admired goods. He couldn't expect Mrs. Porter to provide all their provisions, so he purchased what looked fresh and useful and gave a penny to an urchin to deliver them to the cottage.

None of the names matched the names he'd been given.

He had great difficulty believing any of these women would have poisoned the governess. How? Dug the roots in the middle of the night, sliced and boiled them over a kitchen stove along with their children's morning porridge? Then what? Taken the tea visiting? He should have asked the physician how poison was administered. It had seemed basic until he thought about it.

It made far more sense that the former governess had done the digging and boiling.

He met the lieutenant and Fletch at the inn on the far end of town, talking to a few workmen they'd produced from who knew where. The manor?

"How much of this place do we want to restore?" Fletch asked, gesturing at the sprawling dilapidated inn, from collapsed pub to stable.

"You cannot feed guests without a pub or shelter their horses without a stable. And in between one needs rooms with beds," Rafe said dryly. "Which part were you planning on leaving out?"

"The stable's not in bad shape," Jack, connoisseur of horses and stables, remonstrated. "The blacksmith has been repairing it to use for his customers."

"Then we'll start in the middle, shore up the inn floors and thatch the roof, unless we can find tin or tile. Neither is pretty but tin should be cheap. Tile is sturdier." Rafe really wanted the thatch with the half-timbered walls, but practically speaking, that wasn't modern and needed constant repair. The whole place should be torn down to the frame.

"We do thatching," one of the workmen declared. "And we can do the wattle, seal up the outside so you can work inside this winter."

Rafe nodded at the man who'd spoken. "I'm Rafe Russell, the imbecile interested in restoring this pit. And you are?"

"Nate Blackwell. This here's my son, George. We have a small property along the river, but we've been up in Birmingham these last years. Can't live off farming these days."

Most men were shorter than Rafe, but this pair hunched their shoulders to make themselves smaller. Worn caps, old boots. . . they weren't earning a fortune in construction. If they'd lived here before—they knew the teacher. His mind instantly called up the list of suspects Mrs. Porter had given him. One or two had the initials B, not that that meant anything.

"Working inside in winter requires rebuilding the chimneys." Rafe couldn't believe he was even considering hurling his few coins into this sinkhole.

"Hunt is hiring chimney cleaners for the manor. We can ask about them," Jack suggested. "Let's go up and make a few lists, have Walker give us some estimates. He's the manor's steward and good with numbers."

Rafe needed to be interviewing suspects, if only he had some. He couldn't see workmen or apple pickers crawling into the teacher's garden to murder her, any more than he could women, but someone had done it. He supposed he ought to meet everyone he could.

"The manor folk think we can work out a deal with the bank to open this place?" he demanded, just to be certain he wasn't flinging coins down a well.

He didn't grasp finance, but he loved running an inn. If the manor had funds to help. . .

Jack shrugged. "Hunt talked to the banker. He didn't object. Bosworth thinks we're mad, but that's not unusual. Hunt's digging out property maps and deeds. We'll most likely need a solicitor to draw up proper agreements, but an inn can only be a boon to the whole village, making it easier for people to stay and conduct business."

Rafe wasn't much on planning and scheming. He wanted an inn. They wanted an inn. Here one was, such as it was. . . Well, beggars couldn't be choosers.

He turned back to the Blackwells. "Can you start by cleaning out the debris? Give us a clean place to start instead of this giant bird's nest?"

The younger Blackwell grunted at the accurate description, eyeing the rotting straw falling into the interior—coated with guano from nesting creatures. The glum pair agreed and trotted off to look for a starting place. Rafe would suggest a wheelbarrow, but they'd work it out.

He reluctantly followed Jack and Fletch up a footpath to the towering manor on the hill above. "No one will be offended by my slovenly appearance?"

Fletch punched his arm as a form of reply, but they were no longer uniformed soldiers. Rafe's civilian clothes weren't up to society's standards.

A former soldier himself, Jack took long strides up the recently trimmed path. "The Reid ladies won't care. Bosworth returned to Stratford, but his assistant Smith is still here, trying to persuade a merchant to buy one of the bank's properties. Miss Talbot is entertaining a Mr. and Mrs. Prescott who are interested in taking away some of our archaic furniture, possibly to restore it. I'm uncertain how that works. There is an architect drawing up sketches for a perfumery under the instructions of two adolescents. The hive buzzes. Really, you think anyone will even notice your existence?"

Ah, opportunity to learn his new occupation. "How many of your guests were here before Saturday? Didn't the banker arrive then, with Mrs. Porter?"

If she were even a Mrs. Porter. How did he verify that? Rafe feared he was in well over his head.

"Bosworth stops here on his way to Birmingham whenever he feels so inclined. He's the manor's trustee and feels it incumbent upon him to oversee our ramshackle affairs. He didn't arrive until Saturday, but his assistant and the merchant, Sullivan, came on Friday, I believe."

"I suppose it's good to have enough wealth for a banker to worry over. If I'm to join with you and Fletch and whoever else takes an interest in rebuilding the inn, we'll need someone to keep accounts. I can't." Rafe believed in being frank.

"I don't know if Walker will wish to take on another task, but we'll find someone. You're right, though, we need to sit down and work out how much money we have for this task before we start spending it. I've sunk most of mine into building my stable and buying good horseflesh. Not seeing profits yet. Pity we never found the earl's jewels." Jack led the way around to the manor's carriage door.

"Jewels?" Rafe studied the workers roaming in and out of the medieval stone tower at the corner between the grand front entrance and the portico on the side.

"Legend has it the last earl hid the family jewels. Descendants of pirates and all that. He left nonsense notes of their where-abouts, but all we've recovered is a child's necklace and a bag of doubloons that may help build your inn. We're on our own other-wise." Jack strode under the portico, and the side door opened as if propelled by magic.

Rafe had met the ex-prize fighter butler earlier. The man was nearly as large as he but was graying and turning soft about the middle. Rafe hoped the butler acted as guard as well as silent door-opener and hat-handler.

He studied the gloomy hall Jack led him down. The right side sported ugly dark landscapes. To his left, they passed the ball-room/walking gallery where Lavender and her ladies had set up production. Jack stopped to greet Henri, who was taking orders for a purchase expedition in the city.

They introduced him to Arnaud, Henri's brother, and Miss Talbott, Mrs. Huntley's cousin, who were apparently directing the tower restoration. Rafe was beginning to doubt if he could even keep track of the manor inhabitants—except all the related ladies had blond hair, blue eyes, and bewitching dimples. The men mostly appeared large and dark, well-fed compared to the villagers. He'd sort them eventually.

Windows, Rafe decided as they continued to the main corridor. The inn should have windows for natural light. These dark halls lit by sconces and a pair of gaslights did not create the welcoming atmosphere of a proper inn.

The lieutenant led them down the long corridor of the manor's central block to the steward's office, where Walker, the captain's African friend, presided. Rafe had already ascertained that the

PATRICIA RICE

one-eyed Captain Huntley had taken charge of the manor, even if all the heirs owned it. Hunt joined them and suggested they gather in the large study in one of the new wings. The fine details of numbers didn't interest Rafe, but he needed to know these men he might work with for the future.

He'd never meant to spend his life in the army, but he'd not given much consideration to what he'd do once the war ended. An inn of his own had always seemed out of reach.

Huntley produced survey maps, inn measurements, and a monocle for reading them. Rafe raised his eyebrow in surprise.

"Hunt is a surveyor," Jack explained. "Likes to keep his hand in, even if his blind eye makes it difficult."

Another victim of war. Rafe nodded understanding and offered specifications where he could, while Walker took notes. His gut wasn't entirely certain that he wanted to bury ten years of earnings, for which he'd risked his life countless times, into a project that would never be wholly his. But he was learning about his new home and new position in the process, so he'd stick it out a while longer.

Captain Huntley's fair-haired wife bustled into the room carrying her own list and wearing a worried frown. Jack and Walker politely rose at her entrance, but the captain merely set down his monocle and regarded her expectantly.

"I have shown these initials—" She glanced at Rafe. "From Miss Edgerton's ledger, correct?" At his nod, she continued. "Elsa and Thea know society far better than I do. They've made a list of possibilities. Most of Miss Edgerton's students at the boarding school would be about our age now or older, which means many are married. We can't know if the initials represent their married names." She handed the list over to Rafe, who didn't recognize a name on it.

"I appreciate this." He didn't know what the devil he'd do with it.

"Thea believes one of them is currently teaching at Miss Edgerton's former boarding school. I put a mark beside her name.

She may be how former students were finding their teacher. We'll make a few discreet inquiries of acquaintances. But we're reasonably certain none have visited Gravesyde since we've been here these last six months."

"But we might want to look about for their family members or servants," Rafe suggested, relieved he didn't have to distress young ladies.

"Noble family members would stand out." Captain Huntley spoke up. "They'd most likely send servants."

"Revenge doesn't seem likely as a motive for wealthy aristocrats to bestir themselves," Rafe warned.

"Oh, many of them have little better to do and plenty of funds to do it with," the captain's bespectacled wife said with a dismissive wave. "But there is also covering up wrongdoing to consider. If anyone thought their precious daughter or wife had been straying—or that they had told Miss Edgerton of a gentleman's villainy—" She let the thought dangle.

"Or their companions or maidservants might be ordered to cover up any trace of prior indiscretions. . ." Rafe shook his head. "All I can do is question the neighbors about visitors."

"Oh, that might be a problem." Clare, Mrs. Huntley, clasped her hands and smiled too brightly. "Mrs. Holly is the closest neighbor. She called Miss Edgerton a witch and burned crosses in the yard, repeatedly."

FOURTEEN: VERITY

VERITY MET MRS. HOLLY ON MONDAY AFTERNOON WHILE SEARCHING for Marmie among the cabbage leaves. The tall scarecrow of a woman, all in black, appeared like a floating wraith over the hedge. Her harsh, angular face and black eyes under a ridge of dark eyebrows nearly scared Verity half to death.

She assumed her neighbor had a stepstool and wasn't flying.

"If you're another spawn of Satan, you'll meet your fate as surely as the last one. Justice is in the eyes of the Lord!"

"One certainly hopes so," Verity replied uncertainly, after recovering her nerves. "I'm Verity Porter. May I help you?"

Huh. Apparently the new Verity was as servile as the old Faith. Should she have called the old lady a vile name? She'd learned quite a few from sailors in the street. Maybe she'd work up to name calling. But here was a good suspect for murder!

"Burn those wicked weeds! Lock the gates of sinners!" The old witch glimpsed Marmie scampering up the path to hide under Verity's skirt. "A familiar! You have a familiar already!"

Verity stiffened her spine and tried to sound authoritative like Rafe. "I believe your nearly dead apple tree is of more danger than my kitten. Someone fell out of it the other night, trying to break in."

Verity tucked the kitten into her apron pocket. She had always wanted neighbors to chat with, but a potential murder suspect or mad woman? Well, how else did she determine who might be guilty? "Would you care to come in for tea and discuss solutions before anyone is hurt?"

The neighbor—who had yet to introduce herself—seemed unable to formulate a reply to a reasonable suggestion.

Fortunately, Mrs. Underhill emerged from the cottage and noted the confrontation. "Rosie, climb down from there before you hurt yourself, and come over for a spot of tea."

Ah, assertiveness! She should emulate her companion.

Rafe found them in the kitchen when he stomped into the cottage later that afternoon. He frowned at their cozy occupation of his worktable.

Mrs. Holly set down the last of the scones and glared. "Who's he?"

"Sgt. Russell, dearie," Mrs. Underhill said, finishing her tea. "The manor's new bailiff. Sergeant, this is Rose Holly. She's agreed you might cut back her old apple tree."

Verity had to muffle a laugh at Rafe's expression while he worked through the conspiracy of old women to put him to work. She hid her smile behind her teacup.

"Mrs. Holly?" He modified his suspicious tone with a quick bow. "Pleased to meet you. Were you using the apple tree branches for your fiery crosses?"

Fiery crosses?

The old witch appeared pleased at the accusation. "Apple trees give off the best scent. Spawns of Satan can't tolerate pleasant scents."

"Which is why Miss Edgerton has the best-smelling garden I've ever encountered. I'll be out picking greens for tonight's supper. Have a good chat, ladies." He returned his cap to his ginger hair and strode out the back door.

Amazing how a man so broad could fill a kitchen but not feel threatening. Or perhaps dead Faith feared men for good reason, but naïve Verity hadn't learned her lesson yet.

Before her cantankerous neighbor could release the deluge of questions forming on her busy tongue, Verity attempted assertiveness in Rafe's aid. She hastily stood up. "Well, this has been lovely, Mrs. Holly. I'm glad we had a chance to chat. But those rolls won't bake themselves."

As far as she was concerned, rolls appeared like magic on a baker's cart, but it sounded like something a widow lady might say.

Mrs. Underhill blessedly led their neighbor out the front, while Verity sought Rafe in the back.

"Fiery crosses?" she inquired warily as he snipped greenery and flung it into a basket.

He had to bend much too far to reach those plants. He needed a tall planter. . . Or she needed to learn what the plants were. He made her feel almost petite. She didn't have massive, muscular thighs to prevent crouching and could reach the plants easily.

She shouldn't be noticing a man's thighs, but Rafe was so very large, he filled her vision—a veritable wall between her and danger. She hoped.

"Mrs. Holly," he said curtly. "She was on the top of my suspect list. She called your teacher a witch and burned crosses in her yard. Repeatedly."

"She called me a spawn of Satan and Marmie a familiar," she offered, biting back laughter at his snit. Rafe wore his feelings on his face, making him easy to talk with. "And then she drank my tea and ate all your scones. When I used to go to market, there was an old lady who snarled at all her customers, but she had the most delicious meat pies and would sneak in a free biscuit to accompany it if I was polite. Sometimes, one wins with kindness instead of confrontation."

She thought about that for a moment when he didn't reply. "I suppose soldiers look at the world a little differently."

He grunted. "Possibly. But I can't unlearn everything I learned these last years if I'm to be a bailiff. You could have been poisoned! I have to suspect everyone."

"And you don't like it." Verity was charmed that he'd worried about her welfare. It had been a very long time since anyone had done so. "Tell me the name of those herbs you're picking, let me label them so I can pick them for you."

He straightened and she had to tilt her head to see his expression. His broad face didn't give much away. She supposed an innkeeper must learn stoicism.

"You go to the market and buy meat pies but you don't know herbs. Who are you, Verity Porter?"

"Not a lady nor a maid," she retorted, swinging around and returning to the cottage.

He followed on her heels, looming over her, catching the door and holding it open. "Fair enough. I'm neither gentleman nor laborer. I believe the generous term is middle class. That isn't what I'm asking."

This was what one got with familiarity. Perhaps it wasn't a good thing. "Does it matter who I am? Or who I was? Because I don't know who I am right now. I want to be a teacher, but without Miss Edgerton's aid, I am nothing."

Knowing Mrs. Underhill was in the front room, listening to every word, she stormed upstairs.

Who was she, indeed? A most excellent question. She had enough to put food on the table for years, if she didn't have to buy a cottage or rent one. So she was not wealthy. Servants had occupied her early years, however, leaving her with no education in keeping house or cooking. Her mother had expected her to be a lady and marry well, so she knew how to play the pianoforte and dance, although she had never played for anyone or danced with anyone. She was singularly useless for all intents and purposes.

Once in the loft, she didn't know what to do there. Dress for dinner? She snorted. She'd take off her apron and be ready.

Did she dare pry at floorboards with people downstairs? She was unlikely to ever be alone with Mrs. Underhill underfoot. Was she really in danger? Did she need Rafe here? She didn't feel as if she were in danger, not as she had been in the city streets. But then, Miss Edgerton had thought herself safe.

She took off her apron and tidied her hair. Without a maid, she couldn't do anything fancy. She simply rolled it up, fastened it with pins, and let a few wisps escape around her ears so her face did not look quite so square. She'd never be a delicate beauty, but she could look neat.

Not ready to face Rafe yet, she studied the floorboards. None of them appeared particularly loose, but she could start a systematic search. Some of the boards were longer than others. The ones under the bed and wardrobe would be difficult to reach. If Miss Edgerton had hidden papers, did she look at them regularly? If so, then the easier boards were more likely. But if she wanted to hide them. . . Guessing got her nowhere.

Crouching down, Verity started in the outer corner. Nothing wiggled when she pressed on it. She tried every board in the unfurnished corner, without any luck. Surely Miss Edgerton wouldn't have moved a wardrobe?

Rafe shouted that dinner was ready. She'd been smelling delicious odors all day and was famished.

Who did she tell Rafe she was? She couldn't mention her uncle or the counting house that had once been her family's lovely home. Someone might eventually realize Faith wasn't dead. If her uncle knew she had his money—

She wasn't very creative. She didn't want to invent a tissue of lies.

Mrs. Underhill had set the kitchen table for three. She had apparently accepted Rafe as some kind of boarder and decided it was safe to eat with him. Considering how wholly unorthodox her situation was, Verity could see no reason to object.

They were both middle class, he'd said. Equals.

That meant he shouldn't be sleeping in the yard.

Verity took a seat where he pulled out a chair. He'd filled their bowls with a delicious stew and set out plates of bread and salad, and what appeared to be wine. Once he sat, she tasted it and frowned. "Do we know what this is?"

"Found it in the pantry. It's too sweet for vinegar." Rafe shrugged and lathered a roll with butter.

"Elderberry," Mrs. Underhill offered. "There's a few who sell it at the market for medicinal purposes."

"I trust we won't be poisoning ourselves in cleaning out the pantry." Verity was fairly certain Miss Edgerton would label anything deadly—although would they know if something labeled *wolfsbane* was fatal? The bottles Mrs. Walker had carried away hadn't *seemed* poisonous.

"I had a glass before serving it," Rafe said complacently. "I'm not writhing in agony, so one assumes it's safe. I've found no equipment for distilling, so I think she was limited to powders and herbs."

"Oh, I didn't think to ask at the mercantile for her elixir. I wonder who she intended that for?" Verity was relieved at the casual conversation, but the pall of suspicion hanging between them was uncomfortable. She took another sip of wine for fortification. She'd never had spirits of any sort. She couldn't decide if she liked it.

"If anyone wants the elixir bad enough, they'll show up at the door." Mrs. Underhill deigned to contribute to the conversation.

"But we won't know what to mix with it. She should have kept records on who took what." Rafe dug into his stew.

Verify froze, her fork of salad halfway to her lips. "What if she *did* keep medical records? And the killer was after them?"

Rafe stopped eating long enough to swallow.

"The bookshelves," they both said at once.

FIFTEEN: RAFE

AS THEY SEARCHED THE PARLOR AFTER SUPPER, RAFE FORGOT HIS irritation at the widow for avoiding his question about who she was. Mrs.—Verity—was industrious in her search for her friend's killer. Ignoring her skirts, she sat on the floor to work through the books on the bottom shelves, while he scoured the top. He wasn't much of a student, so he passed his volumes on to Mrs. Underhill for further inspection. And to keep her occupied.

"Oh, she has children's stories! Look at the lovely illustrations. I wonder who did this? It's hand painted." Pushing the curious kitten aside, Verity flipped through the sturdy pages.

She had said she'd wanted to be a teacher, he reminded himself. Teachers were harmless.

Miss Edgerton apparently hadn't been.

"These books on top seem to be about plants and herbs. Do you think she was a self-taught herbalist? And these drawings look hand drawn as well." He handed down a watercolor illustrated portfolio.

"Miss Edgerton always had a talent for art. I wonder if she did these herself?" Verity took the portfolio to admire.

"She had fancy friends visit," Mrs. Underhill said. "Come in carriages, bringing baskets. Reckon that's where she got some of

94

these. But her ma and grandma started the garden. They knew a little of everything. She'd of learned from them."

He'd known he should have been talking to old ladies. Trying to look nonchalant, Rafe put a volume back in its place. "Of course, this cottage belonged to her family. I'd forgotten that. How did she become a governess at a fancy boarding school?"

"Her grandma worked for the old earl that was. When he left the manor to his son, he took his own staff to one of his fancier estates. She married above herself, sent her children to school. Anne's mother married well and so forth." The elderly lady went back to holding books under the lamp.

"But they always returned here to visit?" Verity suggested, drawing out their companion.

"Aye, more than visit. Men always manage to get themselves killed, don't they? At least they had a place of their own to go to." Finding a book to her liking, she got up and trundled off to bed.

"There's a story there," Verity murmured.

"Women don't often own property—another story." Rafe started on the next shelf. So, women kept secrets. He almost understood. He'd wager some former Wycliffe had given Miss Edgerton's female ancestors possession of this cottage for a reason. "I haven't heard your story yet."

Verity hesitated, flipping pages of the book she was perusing. He waited.

"My father wasn't gentry but earned his fortune," she finally said in a low voice he almost missed. "My mother. . . was disowned for marrying below her station, even though my father was quite well off. I am their only child. I had every expectation of marrying well, which is why they hired Miss Edgerton."

She was being deliberately circumspect, hiding her identity and that of her parents—but giving him a glimpse of who she was: well-educated and related to gentry. Since she didn't offer, he didn't press to learn what happened. Yet. Obviously, her family no longer had wealth. Or she was running away.

"I was rude," he admitted. "I know you didn't kill Miss Edgerton. I have no right to ask more."

"For what little it's worth, we are living together. We should trust each other. I just don't have much experience at it." She added another book to a small stack growing beside her, then cuddled the kitten for comfort.

He'd rather she turned to him for comfort, but that was currently out of the question.

"I'm afraid there's not much to be known about me," Rafe offered in return. "I grew up the son of an innkeeper, expecting to follow in his footsteps. Except Parliament macadamized the road to London and allowed the lords who owned land along that route to connect a new toll road into Norwich. The lords built a new inn on the new road. All the traffic went around us, our business failed, my father borrowed money he couldn't repay, and we lost it all for far less than it was worth. I went to be a soldier to earn my keep."

"And because you felt like murdering a lord or two?" she asked with that hint of amusement he occasionally detected. She set the kitten down and checked the next book.

Bent over an illustration, hair the color of rich caramel gleaming in the lamplight, she gave the appearance of an ignorant miss, but those glimpses of astuteness were revealing. He'd definitely felt like killing. "Probably. I was only seventeen. My parents now live on my uncle's farm. What happened to your parents?" Now that she was opening up a little, he tried again.

She hesitated as she flipped through pages. Inventing a story?

"My mother developed a lung ailment. London is not the most salubrious place for an invalid, but she refused to leave us for the country, and my father's business required that he stay." She paused to wipe a tear with the back of her hand. "He was killed in the street when I was fifteen. My mother only lived another year."

It sounded truthful, not that he was any kind of judge. She'd been orphaned young. That seldom went well. "And so the governess had to go?"

Straightening, she briskly started on the next book. "After my father's death, any money that might come to me was in my uncle's hands. We did not get along. So, that is who I am—nobody."

An educated nobody who did her own shopping in the dirty street markets, buying meat pies. He suspected that left a gap of some years after Miss Edgerton's departure. Inquiring how Verity supported herself during that time would be truly rude. He'd hope the uncle had provided a roof over his young niece's head.

"*Soldiers* are nobodies, mere cannon fodder. It's a struggle for anyone to become somebody." He'd had to do it over the backs of the men above him who had died. And with hard work and an education that gave him an advantage over others.

"Do not discount good fortune in surviving, although in my experience, bad fortune comes more often, and it's what you make of it that matters." She took down a heavy tome she nearly dropped. "As adolescents, we were forced to make decisions for which we were not prepared."

"And lacked the wisdom to think them through. I liked the scarlet uniform that turned girls' heads, plus the promise of a full belly."

She didn't reply. Rafe glanced down. In the lamplight, he could discern a few strands of copper gleaming among the light brown of her chignon. Her nape looked very frail. "Found something?"

When she didn't reply, he put his book on the shelf and crouched down in front of her.

She slammed the book shut and stared at him wildly. The placid lady did not terrify easily. He held out his hand.

She studied the book, studied his hand, then reluctantly placed one in the other. "She was keeping medical records. For her own use," she hastened to add. "To learn from experience."

He opened the ledger and scanned the fine handwriting. The lady had named names. And procedures. And dates.

"Evidence for extortion," he concluded angrily.

PATRICIA RICE

"And possible reason for murder?" she whispered, staring at the unassuming ledger in horror.

"And reason for the killer to return. This goes to the manor in the morning. Meanwhile, I'm sleeping by the kitchen door and Wolfie will sleep by the front." He stood and looked for a better hiding place than a bookshelf.

"The shelves are the best concealment," she offered. "Look how long it took us to find it. And you should have a better bed than the floor. I know the one in the kitchen is too small. Can you not push the sofas together? Then Wolfie can lay across the kitchen door."

He raised his eyebrows but she'd returned to working her way through the shelves as if she hadn't just invited a complete stranger to sleep inside her house, with no more than an old woman as protection.

The woman had utterly no sense of personal safety—which was why she'd traveled here without even a maid as companion. Fearlessly stupid. . . He hadn't even begun to scratch the surface of her depths. And shouldn't want to.

But as he studied the furniture arrangement and thought about sleeping under a roof, with actual cushions under him, a long-suppressed longing for a real home niggled its way through the bedrock of his soldiering years.

He'd never meant to be a bailiff, but protecting people like the widow had been what he'd been doing for most of his life. He simply had to learn to do it within the confines of civilization. Cannon wouldn't catch a killer.

TUESDAY

SIXTEEN: PAUL

Paul studied the medical notes that Meera showed him after the new bailiff delivered them to the manor. With everyone else occupied, Paul was the only connection between manor and village.

As curate, Paul's duty was to his parishioners, which covered almost anything he chose to do. The apothecary seldom attended chapel—Anglican wasn't Meera's religion, after all—but she had reason to be concerned about her patients and the village's new arrivals.

"I recognize a few of these names," he admitted. "But the notes are cryptic. I have no notion of what Miss Edgerton is saying. If I mark the names I recognize as villagers, can you tell me if her report might cause anyone harm? Would someone kill to hide them?"

Meera bounced her infant son on her shoulder and flipped the pages. "These are mostly reports of female troubles, what she's used to treat them, how the medications worked, notes of formulas. . . The notes may help me treat these same patients if they come to me, but they won't. That troubles me more than any fear of extortion."

"You need an office in the village, where the women can find you easily, the way they found Miss Edgerton. Maybe you could set up in her cottage a day or two a week? But that's getting ahead of ourselves. Someone killed the lady, and until we know who and why, no one is safe. Rafe is too new here to recognize names, so it's up to us to see if the notes contain any useful information."

She nodded doubtfully. "I can try, but do not hold out much hope of my being accepted as physician. If I were male, and they needed their medication badly enough, they might ignore my brown skin, maybe. But a brown female. . . We'll see."

She pointed at a page. "The assistant the banker left here is named Smith. Here is a Sheila Smith. This note is from five years ago. Sheila was only seventeen. If I'm reading the abbreviations correctly, the patient was at least eight weeks gone with child. The prescription was for an abortive. The final note indicates the prescription was successful but requires adjustment based on weight due to its harshness."

Paul frowned. "His daughter? His wife? I cannot imagine Miss Edgerton extorting funds from a seventeen-year-old. And there are too many Smiths to assume the banker is related."

Paul's mother had been even younger when she'd been repeatedly raped. To give her unborn child—him—a name, she'd escaped into a loveless marriage. She'd have ended on the streets and starved otherwise. Without his stepfather, he wouldn't be here today. If she had no money and no husband, he understood this Sheila's desperation. Carry the child—and they both died a lingering death.

But even if this Sheila Smith's family had riches. . . the result was little different. An unwed mother wasn't welcome anywhere and any chance to marry well was lost. Her family might pay to hide her disgrace and end up an extortionist's best target.

What worried him was if the banker was somehow involved. Bankers weren't wealthy enough to pay extortion, especially assistant ones. Might a demand drive him to murder?.

He probably should start preaching about the wages of sin.

Preaching wouldn't have saved his mother from violence. It

most likely would not have helped an innocent miss either. Keeping women ignorant only gave men more advantage over them.

Grimly, he wondered if he could talk the widow or Meera into educating girls.

"So these notes won't help us find a killer?" he asked, returning to the immediate problem.

Meera grimaced as she flipped through the pages. "People are not always rational. Perhaps this Miss Smith can no longer have children and her new husband blames Miss Edgerton. Perhaps Miss Smith told someone about Miss Edgerton, and Miss Edgerton refused to help a stranger. Some of these notes indicate reservations about treating her patients as they wished. Look at this one." She pointed at scribbling in darker ink, indicating the lady had pressed angrily with her pen nib.

"*Patient is hysteric. Gave her placebo.*" Paul frowned. "And we have no knowledge of whether the hysteric died or lives happily ever after."

Meera nodded. "This book might be useful as evidence should we ever discover the culprit, but it is of little use in finding them. If you will mark the parishioners you recognize, it might help me later, if I set up an office. Beyond that, I can't see it making a difference."

"I'll tell our new bailiff. He's going through the orchard, apparently trying to size up the men as a possible culprit for climbing over the widow's wall and breaking the apple tree. He works hard, but I fear he is not a strategic thinker." As Minerva was, Paul thought as he left the infirmary and strode down the central corridor in search of his betrothed.

He found her in the library with Hunt, going over faded historical records and intricately drawn maps of the village. She blessed Paul with a smile at his entrance but returned to pointing out relevant plots on the map.

The captain set aside his monocle to nod greeting. "It seems not all the villagers turned to the bank to buy their lots," he explained. "Despite what he thinks, Bosworth can only claim some of the farmland and the abandoned properties. The others were granted title by the earls or bought them with cash."

"Abandoned properties, like the inn and tavern?" Paul examined the maps but lines and numbers made little sense to him.

"Well, we established the tavern belonged to one of our local families for centuries, like Miss Edgerton's cottage, so Henri is fine. The inn was built on the original priory holding and owned and improved by a succession of earls. A local family ran it until the last Wycliffe died. We see no evidence that it was ever sold. The bank's suit claims the viscount offered to sell off the cottages the estate owned to their occupants, and as a favor to the viscount, the bank loaned those villagers the money to buy them. The bank directly paid the viscount. When the manor closed after the last earl's death and employment died out, the tenants forfeited their mortgages and scattered. So the estate—or the viscount's creditors—received the money and left the bank holding useless properties."

"So no one bought the inn and it's still in the estate's name?" Paul left the rights and wrongs of money to others wiser in the matter than he, but the inn directly affected everyone in his parish.

"As far as we can determine, the inn still belongs to the estate," Minerva assured him. "The last earl did not bother putting money into it. After his son's death, he had no reason to keep up the property when he had no son to leave it to. As we can attest, he rightfully assumed his daughters and sisters had no interest in operating an inn."

"Sounds sensible to me. I'll pass that information on to Rafe when I find him. Your new bailiff covers a lot of territory on his rounds."

After arranging to see Minerva over dinner that evening, Paul retrieved his hat from the butler and took the side entrance nearest the orchard. He raised his eyebrows at the sight of a liveried coachman polishing the manor's slightly used but recently refurbished carriage. Would a new carriage driver be another suspect?

Walker was on the drive, speaking with a gentleman on horseback who had apparently just arrived. A far cry from the abandoned fortress it had once been, Wycliffe Manor was returning to life with the aid of its new inhabitants.

Hunt's invaluable steward waved Paul over, introducing him to the visitor. "This gentleman is a solicitor, regarding Miss Edgerton's estate. Could you show him to the cottage and introduce him to Mrs. Porter?"

Word of the lady's death had traveled swiftly. "Of course. I was going that way shortly. Perhaps you would like to rest and have a spot of tea while I finish my rounds, Mr. . .. ?

"Culliver, Amos Culliver, at your service. Tea sounds most excellent, I thank you. . . ?"

"Upton, Paul Upton, curate. I take it you've met Mr. Walker?" Paul raised his eyebrows questioningly.

"Mr. Culliver was just handing me his reins and stating his business," Walker said dryly.

As estate steward, Walker was garbed in a swallow-tailed frockcoat and embroidered waistcoat, his doeskin breeches and high boots matching that of any gentleman. Anyone with half a brain and eyes in his head would recognize that he wasn't a stableboy—if they looked past his skin color.

Paul's opinion of the solicitor dropped several notches, but he would reserve judgment, for now. He tried to be fair. "Mr. Walker is Wycliffe's steward, practically part of the family. He's a busy man. Young Georgie there will look after your mare." Paul nodded at the young boy running up at Walker's signal. "I'll introduce you to Quincy, the butler, and return directly after I finish my errands to take you to the cottage."

Amos Culliver wore a city man's side whiskers, a tailored riding coat that fit his portliness, and an expensive top hat. He did not appear the least abashed at insulting Walker. "I appreciate that." He removed his hat and followed Paul back to the portico.

By the time Paul had the solicitor arranged and had returned outside, Rafe was striding up the hill from the orchard. He waited for Paul to catch up.

"Mrs. Walker figure out that notebook?" the massive bailiff asked without further ado. For his new position, Rafe had exchanged his soldier's coat for an aging tweed country coat.

"Meera says the records will be of help should she open an office in the village, but they're more useful as evidence than as a means of identifying anyone who might want to steal it. Some of the names are likely false. Miss Edgerton described her patients by weight, height, and age. I might identify the names of locals, but knowing that they asked for headache powders does not get us anywhere." Paul jabbed his worn boot heel into the recently leveled dirt of the drive.

Rafe ran a big hand over his ginger curls. "I'm not learning much from the apple pickers. One of them has a London accent, which is a bit strange, but your sister says he's learning, and he isn't afraid of climbing trees, if needed."

Paul nodded in the direction of the new coachman. "Have you talked with the driver? He's new too. As is the architect working on the tower and the furniture dealers." He glanced at the hedge concealing the lower entrance to a once-abandoned keep. "I think all the tower's construction crew is from Birmingham, but I wouldn't swear to it. And I'm not certain why their homes bear on the case at hand."

"Doesn't, yet," Rafe admitted. "I'm scouting, learning the lay of the land. The captain said the driver just turned up at the door, which is suspicious. His accent is London too."

Paul frowned. "Do we know where Mrs. Porter came from? If Miss Edgerton was her teacher and they lived in London. . ."

Rafe nodded. "She's close-mouthed, but if I put it to her that way, she may tell me. Who is the fancified gent you were just talking with?"

"A Mr. Culliver, solicitor for Miss Edgerton's estate. You and Mrs. Porter may need to move into the manor, unless he's here to make arrangements for the cottage. Oh, and the captain says the inn definitely belongs to the manor. There is no question of paying rent to the bank."

Rafe's broad face broke into a beam. "That's the first good news I've had this week. So Fletch and I just need to work out an agreement with Walker?"

"Appears so. Maybe you can make up an apartment in the ruins so you can oversee the work while living on the premises. Mrs. Porter should be safe enough living in the manor. I need to take Mr. Culliver down to the cottage. Will you be there shortly?"

"Let me take him down," usually genial Rafe said with a touch of grimness. "I don't think the widow is ready to move out. Maybe I can help her work out an arrangement."

"Good idea. He's having his tea. If you'll wait until he's done, that gives me time to warn her," Paul suggested.

"I have a notion she won't be happy. She's settling in and searching for clues. And expecting replies from all those letters she sent. . . She has all the old ladies telling her stories of Miss Edgerton over tea and crumpets." The big man didn't look particularly unhappy about the situation.

Having helped solve a few murders recently, Paul's mind immediately leapt to who benefitted most from Miss Edgerton's death. . . And that appeared to be Mrs. Porter.

SEVENTEEN: VERITY

WHAT VERITY REALLY WANTED TO DO WAS TEAR UP FLOORBOARDS, but it had belatedly occurred to her that Miss Edgerton could just as likely have hidden papers beneath the boards on the side Mrs. Underhill was using. And so far, she hadn't had a moment alone to search anywhere.

Should she trust Rafe with her teacher's last words? Why shouldn't she? Let her count the ways. . . But they all boiled down to not trusting men. Listening to the old ladies currently occupying her kitchen only confirmed her nightmares.

Men had all the power. Women had to work around them. She knew that from wretched experience. She and her mother had been powerless to prevent Uncle Warren from turning their beautiful home into a counting house.

"Well, my Sadie says as her Herb gives her enough to feed the young 'uns, right enough. But she don't want no more babes. It's hard on a body, it is. And what would happen to her childern if she wore out and died?"

Mrs. Underhill patted her friend's hand. "We all understand. Annie's mama oncet helped me when I was having that terrible bleeding and couldn't get outta bed."

Verity really didn't wish to hear these tales, but they thought her a widow and aware of married women's troubles. Surely, if these women talked so freely among themselves, they had nothing to hide? Unless a *man* learned. . .

Wolfie barked at a knock at the door. Rafe had left the gate unlocked for her visitors.

Verity gestured for Mrs. Underhill to stay seated and unfastened the door latch for the handsome young curate. He was a man, but she felt comfortable speaking with him. "Mr. Upton, welcome. I fear you are entering a bit of a hen fest."

He took off his cap and bowed as if she were a proper lady. "Rafe sent me to warn you that a solicitor has arrived about Miss Edgerton's estate. He'll bring him down shortly. I wanted to reassure you that whatever happens, you are welcome to stay in the manor until you decide what to do next."

Homeless, again! Panic was her immediate reaction, but Verity had spent half a lifetime battling demons and suppressing anxiety. She took a deep breath, clasped her hands in her borrowed apron, and spoke as if she were in complete control. "I see. Thank you for the warning and the invitation. But I don't see how we can find a killer from the manor. The people who knew Miss Edgerton are in the village. I will speak to the solicitor."

She couldn't tell if the curate's expression reflected concern or understanding. He didn't seem prepared to leave, so she offered him a cup of tea, as one does. He readily accepted, and she settled him on the worn sofa Rafe had slept on last night. Her house guest had neatly tucked all his gear away before she'd even come downstairs.

By the time she had a tea tray prepared, the gossiping old ladies had departed, and Mrs. Underhill had taken up her knitting in the front room, protecting Verity from the dangers of the attractive, auburn-haired young curate, presumably.

After the tales Verity had heard, she was almost grateful for her companion's presence. Her uncle and his employees had given her reason to have low opinions of men, but they mostly ignored clumsy, dowdy Faith. Had she been in more danger than she'd understood?

Of course, not being wealthy, she had little appeal to her uncle's employees. And when she went out, a footman had accompanied her—guarding her uncle's money. Until that last night. . . Well, Luther was always lazy. She wondered how he'd explained seeing her home, when he hadn't. Another fine example of manhood.

She was in a nervous state by the time Rafe threw open the cottage door and barged in, followed more courteously by a gentleman in a caped redingote and tailored frockcoat, his linen only slightly wilted from his journey. Miss Edgerton had a fancy solicitor?

"Amos Culliver, Esquire," Rafe announced. "He's here about Miss Edgerton's estate."

Comfortable behind the shield of etiquette, Verity introduced the curate and Mrs. Underhill, then gestured for the solicitor to take a wing chair, and offered tea.

Rafe settled onto the sofa beside her and helped himself to the last crumpet. Since he'd baked them, he was entitled. "Culliver here wants to sell Miss Edgerton's family home."

Verity bit her back teeth, hard, before applying a smile and summoning a sensible reply. "That is natural, since her family is a long distance from here. But I don't believe Mr. Culliver under-stands the history of Garden Cottage or the safe haven it has provided the women of the family over the centuries. Have you actually spoken with the heirs, sir?" She had no idea where any of that had come from.

Rafe gave her a long look that said explanations were expected at the cottage name she'd made up on the spot, but he refrained from raising a hairy eyebrow.

"I have only just received news of the lady's death," the solic-itor admitted. "I had an inquiry and thought it expedient to act on it. Selling these old houses isn't easy. I thought if I had an offer in hand, the heirs would act more swiftly, rather than letting the old place rot."

"An inquiry?" Rafe's tone was ominous. "From whom? Isn't this a little premature?"

"From another solicitor. I am not able to say more, client confidentiality and so forth. I have only come to estimate the value of the lady's belongings and report to my clients. If they are not inclined to sell, are you interested in letting the cottage?" He didn't seem bothered by the lady's death or the history of her home.

"Yes," Rafe said definitively, without consulting Verity.

"That would depend on the cost," she added, ever-conscious of her limited funds. "I am interested, but upkeep, as you say, is expensive in a place this old." Apparently, some small part of her was still her father's daughter and prepared to bargain.

"I'll talk to a few folk, determine what's the usual around here, then write to the heirs. If, as you say, the cottage has a family history, then they might be grateful to have someone looking after it. I take it you were living here when she died? Do you know of any personal items she might wish sent to her family?"

Verity did not correct his assumption but gestured at the books. "Those are her most precious possessions, but I doubt they have monetary value."

The curate set down his empty teacup. "My fiancée knows the value of books. I'll have her take a look, if you wish, but I suspect they are mostly a teacher's library, good for educating the local children but not much more. I believe Mrs. Porter hopes to step up to that position once she's settled?" He sent Verity a questioning look.

Yes, yes, please. . . But she replied more circumspectly. "If I am given permission to use Miss Edgerton's collection. . . I do not want to presume," she said, lying through her teeth. One way or another, she meant to stay and keep those books.

Rafe might not think highly of her dishonest intentions, but

Robin Hood had a point. The village children needed books more than a bookseller did.

So, the new Verity Porter was every bit the thief the old Faith was. Perhaps freedom really hadn't changed her much. She ought to be appalled. Her mother would have been.

But her father had been a sailor and a ship's captain. He had not made his wealth by being polite and handing over merchandise he'd acquired if someone asked him to give it back. And she'd listened in on his business discussions with men who wished to take as much as they could for as little as they could—which was essentially what Mr. Culliver was here to do.

She might not be bold, but she knew how to listen, and how to apply what she'd learned.

"Miss Edgerton's sister and nieces are her heirs?" she inquired politely. "It is unusual for a woman to hold property, is it not?"

Mr. Culliver sipped his tea and nodded. "True, but the deed was bestowed in different times, and the family has arranged it so the females of the line may inherit. As you say, Miss Edgerton's sister is the only remaining heir. At one point, there was a small fund attached to the estate, but that's dwindled over the years, as dower portions were parceled out."

And Miss Edgerton had probably been living off her portion. Killing over wealth might make sense, but over an ancient cottage, unlikely, even more so if the heirs were half a country away. The medical records still seemed the most likely motive.

After exchanging pleasantries, the solicitor took his leave. The curate escorted him out, promising to have the library valued. Rafe stood and stamped out to the kitchen. Verity followed, watching him rummage in the larder for lunch.

"Do you not think it odd that someone has already made an offer on the cottage?" she asked, curiosity overcoming timidity.

His head popped out of the pantry so he could study her. "I've been a soldier these last years, so I can't say, but it struck me as peculiar."

"One of the heirs is anxious to sell?" she suggested.

"Most likely. Not much we can do, if so." He returned to rummaging, producing a loaf of bread, pickled onions, and smoked cheese. He let Wolfie out the back door and returned with a handful of greens. He slapped everything together and shoved a sandwich in her direction. "Eat. You're pale as a ghost."

She'd spent the last years living in a cellar. Of course she was pale. She didn't tell him that, as she wasn't telling him many things. She cut the sandwich in half to share with Mrs. Underhill.

"What if. . ." She needed to know this man better before revealing why she asked. "What if there is something in here that someone wants, and they think it easier to buy the entire cottage and empty it out?"

"Meera says the record book we found is a poor excuse for murder." He poured ale into a mug and studied her quizzically. "Have you found aught else?"

"No," she said slowly, thinking fast. "But women hide things. We don't normally have banks and solicitors at our beck and call. What if the thief in the apple tree meant to dig in the garden?"

"For bones?" he asked dryly. "A teacher strikes me as unlikely to possess gold."

Painfully true. But riches weren't everything.

"She died for a reason," Verity daringly insisted. "Did you ever ask Mrs. Walker how the poison might have been administered? How would a killer prepare belladonna or whatever she thinks caused her death?"

"She doesn't know. Miss Edgerton may have been the one who dug up the monkshood or snipped leaves of the belladonna. She had an entire pantry full of infusions and powders. For all we know, she may have wished to poison her guest." He stopped and thought about that.

Verity finished the thought for him. "She may have been *treating* her guest with the roots, made a single cup of normal tea for herself, and the guest switched cups with her?"

That meant anyone could have killed her, if they knew what the plants could do and how it might affect her heart.

Or it could just have been an accident. . .

Except for Miss Edgerton's last words, which Verity hadn't told anyone about.

EIGHTEEN: RAFE

RAFE PACKED A SUPPER BASKET WHILE VERITY GLARED ICICLES AT HIM. She hadn't taken to the idea of her teacher killing anyone and was even less enthused about accompanying him.

"Mrs. Underhill wants to have supper with her grandchildren," he admonished. "You cannot stay alone, and I want to see how they are progressing on the inn. We will make a picnic of it."

"It is growing dark and the wind is picking up. We'll freeze." She let him drop her cloak over her shoulders but glanced longingly at the kitten curled by the fire.

The fool woman needed someone looking after her occasionally. Traveling all the way to this outpost of nowhere with only a cat for companion. . .

"I won't freeze. This is nothing compared to the Pyrenees in winter. You can't hide behind four walls forever." He pulled the hood over her hair and picked up the basket.

Wolfie obediently followed.

Verity dragged her feet. "If it won't take long, then I can wait here. No one will know I'm alone."

Rafe took her elbow and dragged her out the door. "Humor me."

She might be stubborn, but she was a lady born and bred,

despite her protest otherwise. She knew she owed him, even if just a little bit. He could hope she also respected his advice, but he wouldn't push his luck.

The street was mostly empty at this hour, with women preparing meals and the family gathering around the home fires. Rafe wanted that some day, but what he had now suited him fine after years of deprivation.

"No one travels through this village. Who will be your customers?" she asked, studying the empty street.

"They don't travel now because there is nowhere to stop to feed the horses or themselves. Anyone wishing to visit the manor, like today's solicitor, must have an invitation to stay at the manor or risk riding at night with a tired horse." He was trying to convince himself as well as her.

Gravesyde had the same difficulty as his father's inn—the highways had passed it by. The government encouraging shipping and cheap imports had made it difficult for small farms to survive, which was why half the village had moved to Birmingham, where they could find employment.

He was basing his hopes on the manor's wealthy inhabitants and the empty land attracting small industries and businesses, thereby drawing enough population to supply the inn with customers. The manor folk were convinced they could make it happen. They were building a future on dreams.

"Start the inn small, with a few rooms and a stable?" she asked, hobbling a little faster to keep up.

His stride was twice that of hers. He forced himself to take small steps. "And a kitchen. And a place for me to sleep. I'll have to live on the premises." Which meant finding a killer so he could leave the widow alone. He wasn't in a hurry to leave her, but he wanted her safe.

"What about your position as bailiff?" She actually sounded concerned.

"I shouldn't think killers normally haunt the streets. I can handle a few drunkards. Hunt mostly wants me to train his hounds. The soldiers he's hired have been doing a fine job, so there's not much for me to do but finish up. They're good dogs."

"Am I walking too fast?" he asked in concern when he thought he'd slowed to a crawl and she fell behind again. "Did Mrs. Walker treat your foot?"

"It's healing. Broken bones take time," she said dismissively. "I'm trying to imagine this as a real village and not a dead end."

He was inordinately pleased that she was considering his future. "It may never be," he warned. "But this is the best offer I've found."

He glanced in the lighted tavern as they passed. Henri had a crowd. Men stood outside, sipping from their mugs, presumably waiting for Henri's wife to begin singing. Someday, he hoped to have a pub serving his own brew.

They reached the sprawling, aging inn and stopped to study the exterior. Several stone extensions had been added on to the original timber & wattle. The rotted thatch sagged. In the evening gloom, it didn't look promising. Despite that, he was excited about owning his own place. Ideas circled.

"New roof, good coat of whitewash?" she asked dubiously.

It needed far more than that, but he wouldn't discourage her. He took her elbow, led her inside, and lit the lantern so they could study the lobby. Workers had carried off the worst of the debris, leaving the worn floor clean. The tall scarred counter waited for a guest book.

Verity limped to the arched doorway on the left. "The pub? Good trestle tables. Will the rats nibble our toes if we eat here?"

She could speak—when it wasn't about her.

"I have big boots." Rafe set the basket down and tested the sturdiness of the table legs. "Solid oak, I wager. Honest folks around here if they didn't carry these off."

"Too large for most homes. The chairs or benches appear to be gone." She climbed up to sit on the table and poked inside the basket.

"Probably for firewood. Easier to cut up and carry. I'm waiting

117

for a chimney sweep before I look in the kitchen." He handed over a meat pie and opened the cider jug. "I don't even dare start a campfire."

"You've spent years eating like this, haven't you?" She nibbled at her crust.

"This is luxury. Will you come eat in my pub when it's ready?"

"Women will be allowed?" She tasted the cider he handed her. "I'd likely starve unless I hire help. I suppose I must learn to cook if I stay. I was hoping Miss Edgerton would teach me."

If it meant she'd express her thoughts, he should give her alcohol more often. "I might need a separate dining room for ladies," he said through a mouthful of pie. "Why haven't you learned to cook?"

She shrugged. "I was more interested in books than food. I like numbers. I could probably keep your accounts should you ever have income to track."

"I'll feed you for free, if you do. I hate numbers, and if others invest, bookwork will be required." He fed Wolfie part of his pie and watched the hound prowl the corners. Apparently no rats had taken up a home recently.

"You are giving a thief time to break into the cottage, aren't you?" she asked, sipping her cider as if it were tea.

"You're much too perceptive. Who taught you that?" Unconcerned, he finished off his pie and wiped his hands on a cloth he'd brought for the purpose.

"Life, I suppose." She handed him part of her pie. "Or maybe I'm just naturally curious. You left the back gate unlocked—to keep the thief from climbing the apple tree again?"

Damn, but she saw everything—even that he was still hungry. No one had cared about his comfort for a very long time.

He owed her honesty, he supposed. "No point in riling our neighbor by forcing thieves to use her yard. I assume there's nothing of real value in the cottage except you. Just don't know how closely they're watching. This may be for naught. I have Henri taking note of who comes and goes from the tavern, but he looked pretty busy with all these new workers around." He glanced at the enormous pub. "His bar is small. I'll have difficulty filling a place this size."

"He doesn't serve food. People need to eat."

That made sense. And if he had his own brewery. . . "I wish I knew somewhere safe to leave you so I can watch the house from the woods."

Finishing off his piece of pie while she politely nibbled at her portion, Rafe prowled about the pub, picturing a bar and customers. With what he'd learned of brewing, he could have men coming from the city just to buy his ale.

Verity sat silent for a while. Rafe suspected that was a dangerous sign. She had an active mind but seldom spoke it. He really needed to know more of her history, but unlike most women he knew, she was close-mouthed. She had secrets, but he could not see how she might have murdered the teacher.

"If there is anything in the cottage a killer might want, where might Miss Edgerton have hidden it?" she finally asked.

He took a slug of cider and thought about it. "Do we take apart the walls?"

"And what do we look for," she added with a sigh. "What would a maiden lady teacher hide that anyone might want? She did not have riches, unless she was a thief."

He shrugged. "Papers of some sort, if we assume extortion and that she wasn't a thief. Might she have kept documents from some prior position that are valuable?"

"Why now?" She fell silent again, her pale brow pulled down in a V.

That's when the little light in his brainpan woke up. "Who was her last student, do we know?" He tried to remember the dates in the medical records. They'd only been kept over these last years. . .

"Me," she whispered. "She returned here after my father died."

NINETEEN: VERITY

VERITY SHUT UP AFTER HER ADMISSION THAT MISS EDGERTON HADN'T worked as a teacher since Milton Palmer's death—because then she might have to admit that, as far as the world knew, Faith Palmer, Miss Edgerton's last student, had just died. She didn't see how there could be any connection but should Rafe start looking for Miss Edgerton's last employer. . . Deception was much harder than she'd realized.

Verity finished her meal, took a handful of hazelnuts Rafe had caramelized, and climbed down from the table. Rafe could carry the basket and lantern when he was done prowling his drafty inn. She was returning to the cottage. She didn't expect to encounter danger in the village's one street, where she'd meet no more than stray dogs and an occasional cat. If some thief was creeping into her home, she'd take a skillet to his head. She had worse to ponder than thieves.

Why had Miss Edgerton quit teaching after she'd left London?

She limped out, stewing. Moments later, she was aware of Rafe's lantern light following. He could have stayed. He didn't need to hover. She'd walked London's filthy streets at this hour without harm for years. She'd have been in far more danger had she stayed in London.

Which gave her another chill. Why had her father's beautiful home blown up?

That was simply too self-centered and pathetic to consider for long. She was *nobody*. They hadn't even searched for her body, so she was quite literally without a body or a grave. No one had cared enough to look. Charming thought.

But after her safe haven had been turned to rubble, her only friend in the world had died. Bad luck? Coincidence? Either notion haunted her, giving her cold chills.

The tavern was even noisier than earlier. She'd heard that the curate's sister often sang early in the evening. She'd like to listen. She loved music but seldom had a chance for more than the ponderous psalms in church. She never thought she'd miss her piano until her uncle had sold it. She'd only been allowed to attend her first musicale when. . .

She hesitated outside the tavern. Angry voices, not music, carried through the open doorway. The very small building appeared to be packed to capacity. Was that usual?

Before she could walk past, a man flew backward through the opening, hitting the ground at her feet. Since he was cursing and holding his jaw, she assumed he wasn't badly hurt. She stepped away just as Rafe arrived, catching her waist, and setting her behind him.

"Hold these," he ordered, passing her the basket and lantern, ordering Wolfie to stay.

Before she could even think to object, he waded his way into the shouting crowd. His voice of command rang over the noisy argument, and the argument lessened, to some extent.

The tall, scowling young man at her feet staggered up and threw himself back into the brawl.

Luther? Had that been Luther? Her addled thoughts must have conjured memories of home. Her uncle's lazy footman never left London as far as she knew. He liked his pretty uniform too much to take another position. The man on the ground. . . had merely been tall. He wore no gold buttons. Her fear was driving her mad.

121

She strained to see inside the tavern but it was shoulder to shoulder men. If Patience was singing tonight, she was hiding behind the bar.

A tall, broad-shouldered, dark-haired man—Henri, the tavern owner, she thought—carved a path through the melee, followed by two gentlemen. One was Mr. Culliver, the solicitor, the other, she didn't recognize. Once safely deposited outside, they brushed themselves off and warily regarded the tall wolfhound.

"Mr. Culliver," she said, dying of curiosity. "I hope you are not harmed?"

He jerked his head up, and seeing her, bowed. "Mrs. Porter. We are unharmed, thank you."

The other gentleman straightened his neckcloth and offered a hasty bow. "Our pardons, ma'am. There seems to be some quarrel over who was where on the day of a lady's death. I am uncertain of the relevance."

Verity raised her eyebrows expectantly, a trick she'd learned from her mother.

Mr. Culliver hastily gestured at his companion. "Mr. Sullivan, a gentleman pursuing the possibility of setting up a shop in Gravesyde. We were discussing property prices when the fracas began."

"I assume it was established that neither of you were in town on Saturday night?" she asked in amusement.

A shop? What kind of shop would anyone open in a dead-end town?

"Well, actually, I *have* been here this past week," Mr. Sullivan admitted, almost apologetically. "I have done business with Lady Elsa's family for years, and she has suggested that I might expand. I sell hardware, everything from pots and pans to iron-ware made by the local blacksmith. My family was originally from here."

Then he and his family presumably knew Miss Edgerton. She really needed to learn more about the neighbors, didn't she?

Whatever papers her teacher may have hidden would most likely pertain to people she knew. And who knew her.

She rested her hand on Wolfie's head, uncertain if the dog would allow her to leave without Rafe. "Very pleased to meet you, sir. I'm Verity Porter. Do you think Sgt. Russell will be very long settling matters? He was escorting me home."

As if in answer, another man flew out the doorway, skidding shoulders first in the dust. Verity thought he looked vaguely familiar, but faces out of their accustomed setting were often unidentifiable. In church, perhaps?

He scrambled up just as Rafe emerged from the tavern.

"Beat it, Clement. You're a sot. I've told Henri if you ever cross his threshold again, I'll fling you out of town." Rafe loomed like a giant over the smaller man.

Ah, yes, she remembered that name from church.

"I got a wife works here," the worker whined, picking himself out of the dirt. "You can't do that."

Taking Verity's arm, while shoving a long-handled knife into his trouser band, Rafe stepped aside to allow the French tavern keeper to emerge, glowering.

"You are not welcome here or elsewhere, Clement. Walker will give you your last wages. I'll not have the likes of you anywhere near my wife." Henri spun around and returned to the lessening noise in the tavern.

Cursing, the maligned Clement glared at the two gentlemen, spat at their feet, and rounded on Rafe. "That's my knife."

Wolfie growled. Rafe placed a threatening hand on the knife. Disgruntled, Clement staggered off toward the path to the manor.

In the dark, Verity heard echoes of the curses her uncle's coachman had thrown at her the night he'd run over her foot. What set men off like that? She had never ridden in her uncle's carriage. He'd no reason to notice her existence, as she'd barely noticed his. He had merely been a small, grumpy figure on a seat above her head, wearing a shapeless coat, while he waited for her uncle in the evening fog. She had no idea why he'd been angry with her and no idea why she heard echoes of his anger in an apple picker.

Ugly suspicion had made her fearful. That wasn't like her.

"Well, that was enlightening," she said brightly, to cover her nerves. "Shall I see myself home while you gentlemen discuss the evening's excitement?"

The gentlemen raised their hats and the merchant replied, "We'll see ourselves back to the manor. It was a pleasure meeting you, Mrs. Porter." They strolled in the direction of the footpath up the hill.

Rafe was silent as they traversed the village, Wolfie protectively at their heels. Verity used Rafe's arm to support her more than the cane. She couldn't keep up otherwise. She hated slowing him down.

"Can a bailiff really throw people out of town?" she inquired to break his unusual silence.

"Probably only from manor land, which isn't the tavern. But if I can, I will." He retreated into silence again, scanning the houses as they passed.

She hesitated as they neared the cottage. He'd been expecting a killer to search after they left. Had the brawl at the tavern been a distraction?

Rafe opened the gate and gestured at his enormous wolfhound. "Search, Wolf." The dog trotted inside, sniffing the ground.

"Original name," she said dryly, hiding her nervousness.

"Like Marmie for a marmalade cat," he retorted. "I am not well read or imaginative. I should think you would be more so."

"I didn't think I could keep him, at the time." She'd lost so much in her life, that she'd seen little purpose in more than a nickname until the kitten fled and was never seen again.

Wolfie yipped, then howled, from the back of the cottage. Rafe handed her the knife. "Stab first, ask questions later." He dashed off into the darkness, leaving her with the lantern.

She hastily closed the lamp, hoping to be less of a target. The dog howled again. Shouts. Pounding footsteps. How long did she stand here, shivering in terror?

She felt like a fool, holding a knife as if she knew how to use one. Or could. The very notion of sticking it into flesh. . . She shuddered. Rafe had no doubt used bayonets and rifles these past years. *He'd killed people.* The genial innkeeper who baked delicious apple cake was a killer.

What in the name of heaven had she done by leaving the city she knew to come here, where she was a fish out of water?

A cat in water. A frog in a desert. A lady without a home.

Her mind couldn't conjure more metaphors. So, fine, she lacked imagination too. She pushed open the gate and limped into the front garden. She didn't recognize the floral night scents, but they were growing familiar and comforting.

Rafe hadn't unlocked the front door but ran around the side, following his hound. Did she do the same?

He had pocketed the key when they left, so the side it was. She tucked the awkward knife into the basket and left it sitting inside the gate. Wielding her cane in one hand and the lantern in the other, she followed the flagstones through the garden. She need only open the lantern if she wanted to see, but she was hesitant to do so. Instead, she held her hand to the house wall and limped down the walkway, trying to make sense of a puzzle created by too many skittering thoughts.

An apple picker with a London accent. A man who resembled her uncle's footman. A merchant opening a store where there were no customers. A solicitor eager to sell the victim's cottage. A fight over who was here when her teacher died. . . Miss Edgerton's death upon Verity's arrival. . .

Perhaps she would end up like the woman in the market who went about pounding her breasts, crying everyone wanted to kill her.

They had proven that Miss Edgerton had been involved in dangerous practices and poisoned with her own herbs. There was utterly no reason it had anything to do with Verity. Or *Faith.*

Guilt ate at her, making her unreasonable. She'd stolen a fortune, let people believe Faith Palmer was dead, and vanished. No one could possibly have followed her or even been looking for her. Had Miss Edgerton heard of Faith's death? How could that possibly matter? Would she have grieved?

In the back garden, she found only an open gate and Wolfie. The hound loped up to lick her hand. Fine, Rafe had gone chasing after thieves and left his dog as guard. Who was she to worry?

The back door was wide open. Opening her lantern, she scanned the doorstep for bodies or weapons and finding nothing, stepped inside.

"Marmie?" she cried in distress, seeing pots and flour strewn across the floor. The disorder didn't cause as much alarm as her missing pet. "*Marmie!*"

The kitten mewed from the depths of the ransacked kitchen, and Faith staggered in relief, casting the lantern light over Rafe's once-neat work space. The light fell on what appeared to be the pantry contents tossed to the floor, along with all the utensils on the fireplace. The hidden shelves had been exposed. Thank goodness Mrs. Walker had taken all the poisons. Anyone could have walked off with them. Had that been the reason for the break in? The thief had wanted medicine? Poison?

They hadn't needed to make such a muss, if so. Perhaps someone hated her. Or Miss Edgerton, since Verity had very little opportunity to make friends or enemies. Her stomach knotted as she searched for her crying kitten.

In relief, she found Marmie under a soup pot. She wanted to kick whoever had been so cruel, but she supposed they'd done her a favor. With the door left open, a frightened pet might have disappeared into the night, never to be seen again. She cuddled the terrified kitten and fed him a shattered biscuit from the floor.

Clinging to the kitten, leading the dog, she peered into the front room. Wolfie didn't seem alarmed, so she assumed the thief had departed—leaving a mess of this cozy room as well. Cushions and books had been tossed. Cinders coated the fireplace, as if they'd stuck a broom up the chimney. The wood in the firebox had been emptied.

Someone had been searching for something.

The front door latch rattled and Wolfie yipped a warning.

"Mrs. Porter, it's just me," Mrs. Underhill called.

Breathing a sigh of relief, Verity opened the door and stepped aside to let her companion enter. "We have had a burglar. Rafe and I stepped out for a while and when we returned. . ." She gestured at the chaos.

Someone had been watching to know when the house was empty. Surely they would not have broken in if she'd been here. . . ? She shuddered and wiped the notion from her mind.

"Oh, my, oh mercy me." Holding the basket abandoned at the gate, Mrs. Uphill clutched her shawl to her chest and surveyed the damage. "You should come back to my daughter's with me. This won't do. This is terrible. Whatever has become of this world?"

As much as Verity longed to hide in safety, she didn't think sleeping on the floor with children and an infant wailing would be conducive to rest. Besides, she couldn't bear being driven from another home, if she could prevent it. "Rafe has chased off the thief. Let us clean up a little until he returns. Unless you'd rather return to your daughter's? I can certainly understand."

"No, no, I cannot leave you here!" The stout woman released her shawl and began setting cushions back in place.

The lady might be an uncommunicative bore, but she had courage and kindness.

"Thank you, Mrs. Underhill, you are a gem. I will try to restore order to the kitchen so we might at least make tea." She didn't think she'd seen the tea canister tossed.

They were still hard at work when Wolfie yipped again and pawed at the back door.

Terrified to open it, Verity rummaged in the abandoned picnic basket for the knife and held it unsteadily as the latch rattled and the door opened.

Rafe strode in, clutching his arm.

TWENTY: RAFE

"WE NEED TO TAKE YOU TO DR. WALKER!" VERITY CRIED, CUTTING off Rafe's bloody sleeve. "This looks deep."

Her eyes were deep wells of fear. He hated doing this to her. "Don't fuss. Just send Wolfie to fetch Fletch. He's at the tavern." Wincing, he grabbed a dish towel to staunch the bleeding. "Open the door and gate. Wolfie knows what to do. Wolf, fetch Fletch," he commanded.

The wolfhound trotted to the front door.

Clasping her pudgy hands nervously, Mrs. Underhill hastened to follow orders—as Verity didn't.

Mrs. Damned Porter rummaged through the mess of the larder, producing his jug of ale. "We don't have wine or whiskey. Will this do?"

He was actually grateful, which didn't make him any less grumpy. "If you mean for me to drink it, yes." He grabbed the jug and swilled it, drowning the humiliation of being brought down by a damned *woman*—and forcing a genteel lady to endure the consequences.

"Even I know a wound needs cleaning." Glaring like a demented general, she waited for him to return the jug. At least she wasn't keeling over. "How do I go about this? May I dab it on with a cloth or must I pour it? The kitchen is already a mess, so it's not as if a puddle of ale will hurt."

With a sigh, Rafe gestured at the wash basin. "Bring that over here. Heat some water. Find a clean towel. I just need to tie it up."

"I've heard of soldiers losing limbs to infection," she said in indignation, actually following his orders this time. "Do not treat me as an ignorant miss. You're losing a lot of blood and it's *deep*."

Now the quiet widow chose to speak. . .

"The blamed woman was carrying a *pistol*," he muttered in indignation. "I was politely trying not to knock her down, and she *shot* me!"

"Next time, knock her down. Women don't break." She set the tea kettle over the fire. "Even a woman deserves punching for creating this mess."

Rafe stewed over her admonition. "I'm twice the size of any female. I could break bones. I was taught to treat women with respect. They're not supposed to carry pistols! Even I don't own one. The bedeviled things can go off any time!"

"As it did," she said dryly. "Maybe she thought you were going to kill her."

"If I'd known she'd shoot me, I would have," he growled. The pain was setting in.

By the time the water heated, they could hear pounding feet on the walk and Wolfie yipping happily. Mrs. Underhill opened the door to Fletch's knock.

Rafe's large friend bounded in, took one look at the carnage, and started for the back door. "I'll fetch Dr. Walker. You know damned well I can't handle blood. How did you get yourself cut up *after* you left the tavern? Should we be hunting the bastard?"

"Watch your language! There are ladies present." Rafe knew Fletch did not handle blood well, but he couldn't send anyone else out. "Don't take the footpath. The culprit has a pistol and was headed for the manor. I don't need a leech. Warn Hunt, look for a female in old-fashioned black skirts with petticoats. She wore a black hat that looked like Mrs. Porter's. . ." He turned to

129

point out the enormous monstrosity usually hanging by the door.

Verity turned, too, and cried in dismay, "My hat! It's gone! That's the first new hat I've had in years. The witch! If you find her, I'll personally scalp her if she's harmed that brim. The lace alone. . ." She looked as if she'd weep.

Everything the woman had gone through, and she cried over an atrocious hat?

"Give me something that smells like you, ma'am," Fletch asked, waiting in the doorway, ready to escape. "We'll set the hounds after your hat, and maybe we'll find this murderous female."

She handed him the handkerchief from her sleeve, wiping her eyes first. "Send Dr. Walker, please. I cannot stitch this wound."

"I can," Mrs. Underhill said matter-of-factly. "We ain't had a physician here in a pig's years. Bring me the sewing kit."

Fletch turned pale and ran.

Rafe swilled more ale. He'd been knifed, shot, and blown up a time or three. He knew the routine. But to have been brought down by a damned woman in skirts. . .

After he'd been sewn and bandaged up, the ladies insisted he lie down on the sofa and put his feet up. He wasn't pulling off his boots and revealing his holey stockings and stinking feet in their presence. He took the sofa and propped them on a chair. He was light-headed enough to topple and didn't want the women fussing more than needed.

They fixed him meat and cheese on the last crust end of a loaf. There would be no bread in the morning. But the food was appreciated. It might keep him upright until the hounds descended.

"Was she still in the house when Wolfie barked?" Verity asked, sorting through the scattered books and returning them to their proper shelves, cautiously examining each one for damage.

Mrs. Underhill had taken charge of cleaning up the kitchen, muttering about the world coming to an end.

"I caught her running out the back gate, with Wolf on her

heels. Where's Marmie?" He glanced to the empty kitten's basket on the cold hearth.

"He scampered upstairs. He's never done that before, so he must be terrified. Could you tell if the thief carried anything? I'm checking to see if any of the volumes are missing."

"I couldn't even tell she had a pistol," he said in disgust. "I got close enough to grab at her skirts, and that's when she turned and shot me. Next time, I'll break her bones."

"Do that," she said furiously, slamming books into place. "It's better than you getting shot, and if she killed Miss Edgerton. . ." She slammed two more books into place.

Ire looked good on her. Nice to know she wasn't always docile.

"This was my only good shirt," he said mournfully, feeling the ale a little too much and setting his mug aside. Fletch would have the cottage overrun shortly, and he didn't need to be drunk.

"I'll buy you two more. Tell Lavender to make them up." The stoic woman who had watched over her teacher's corpse all night had finally unleashed her fury. Steam emanated from her every gesture and word, even if she didn't raise her voice.

Interesting. Money wasn't a problem? She'd arrived with one bag and cried over her lost bonnet. . . But she'd ordered new gowns. . . He wasn't in any condition to puzzle it out.

Fletch arrived with Captain Huntley and the little apothecary/physician. Rafe tried not to groan as Meera shed her colorful shawl and checked his bloody bandage while Hunt quizzed him, and Fletch prowled the kitchen. . . out of sight but not hearing.

"We've got men and hounds searching the grounds, but that footpath leads to half the houses in the village," the captain said, taking the other sofa and propping his bad leg up on the same chair as Rafe used. They needed a proper footstool.

"If anyone shows up on Sunday with my hat on her head, I'll snatch it right off," Verity muttered. "Did she come in just to make a mess and steal a hat?"

Treating Rafe's arm with some concoction that stung like all

131

the fires of hell, Meera glanced around at the disorder. "Have you looked upstairs? Did she have time to search up there?"

Fletch called from the kitchen, "I'll look. We don't know if anyone is still hiding up there."

The little widow finally collapsed in the chair beside the hearth and buried her face in her hands. "I don't own anything anyone can want. This has to be about Miss Edgerton."

Well, yes, that was a certainty as far as Rafe was concerned. Had she reason to believe otherwise? Had he been a little too simple-minded about the lady because he wanted in her bed?

"No one up here but a cowardly kitten," Fletch called down. "I don't think your thief had time to search." He clattered back down to the kitchen.

With a lot more finesse than a battlefield bonesetter, Dr. Walker finished tying a clean bandage and produced a bottle of powders from her bag. "This is for the pain. I'd recommend it over ale."

Now that the blood was out of sight, Fletch returned to the front room. The teacher's dainty furniture and tiny cottage hadn't been designed for three hulking men. The women practically disappeared into the shadows—except Rafe was painfully aware of them. Verity was mangling her apron and working herself into a state, and the apothecary was watching her warily.

"Shall I give you something to help you sleep, Mrs. Porter?" Meera asked, gathering up her supplies. "You've had a little too much excitement, I fear."

"I may never sleep again." Bereft of handkerchief, Verity wiped her eyes on her apron. "I can't bear that Rafe may have been shot for something I haven't found but others might."

That she hadn't found? What did that mean? Rafe sat up straighter. She knew what to look for and hadn't told him?

Eyes glittering with tears, Verity studied them helplessly. "I don't *know* any of you. I don't know who to trust. I'm terrified of what I might find. But if the killer keeps returning. . ."

"Or thief," Meera suggested quietly. "They may not have intended to kill."

The distraught widow took a deep breath and nodded. "Thief, with a pistol, who shoots people and puts poison in their tea. They're dangerous. And possibly quite mad."

Hunt tapped his boot with his walking stick. "We've dealt with madmen and killers before, Mrs. Porter. Gravesyde appears to attract them, possibly because of the tales of treasure. I cannot think anyone would believe a schoolteacher knew anything about jewels, but one never knows."

Verity appeared calmer after mulling over that notion. "Miss Edgerton's family has lived here for centuries and might have knowledge others do not. I had not thought of that. But I should think, if she had any idea where a treasure was buried, she'd have told someone."

"But if the thief isn't after treasure," Rafe interrupted this little fantasy, "then we must look for other reasons. And that's what you fear, isn't it? Some old woman did not shoot me because Miss Edgerton kept medical records about her. She did not appear wealthy enough for extortion."

Weary and resigned, the lady nodded again. Rafe had the ridiculous urge to cuddle her the way she cuddled her kitten. He stifled that urge once she began speaking.

"Before Miss Edgerton. . . passed on. . . she whispered something that sounded like. . ." Verity hesitated, summoning a memory while everyone hung on her words. "She said *tea*, first. Then, *papers*. Her final words were so faint, I don't know if I heard them properly, but they sounded as if she were telling me *under boards*."

They all sat in silence for a minute. Tamping down his fury that she hadn't told him this, Rafe studied the rug-covered planks, then glanced up at the wooden ceiling of the loft. There would be beams up there. . .

Why the devil hadn't she warned him earlier about the lady's *dying words*? What was *wrong* with her?

"Tearing a cottage apart in hopes of finding valuable papers will not do, gentlemen," Meera admonished, donning her shawl.

"What you might fear is the thief burning the cottage to the ground to destroy them, since it has become quite obvious that they are not easily found."

Hunt reluctantly rose with her. "I'll have men patrol the footpath behind the cottage. Does your hound know not to eat anything given by strangers?"

"It had not occurred to me to train him to avoid poison," Rafe said dryly. "I'll keep him inside. He'll let us know if anyone is at the gates."

"Have Mr. Upton search the cottage walls and floors," Meera suggested. "As a carpenter, he knows best how to find hiding places."

"I'll camp out in the yard," Fletch offered. "Rafe, you need a good night's sleep before you go roaring about."

No one offered a word of sympathy to the young widow who slumped silently in the corner, a keeper of secrets. Rafe could understand that. He wanted to shake her, but his aching arm reminded him that not all wounds were visible.

WEDNESDAY

TWENTY-ONE: PAUL

"We could possibly use the chapel as a schoolroom until something more suitable can be arranged." Minerva, the manor's librarian and the brilliant woman Paul adored, systematically worked through the late Miss Edgerton's meager library.

He'd been a little taken aback when Hunt had told him about the deceased's last words. They could have started hunting for hiding places much earlier. But women took odd notions. He listened as he crawled across the cottage floor, testing planks and pushing aside the curious kitten.

"Are there many children in need of teaching?" the widow asked without inflection. She seemed stunned by their search and merely examined school books as Minerva handed them to her.

Paul had thrown back the rugs and ascertained that the cottage's foundation was built on bedrock, with very little besides ancient timbers leveling the floor. He didn't think much could be concealed beneath the parlor. And the kitchen was flagstone.

"It's hard to say," Minerva admitted. "Only a few children live in town. Once word spreads, others may trickle in, if they can find transportation. We'll need chalkboards, but we don't know how many."

She opened one of the larger volumes and studied the pages admiringly. "These are beautiful, hand-painted illustrations."

"Probably too rare to be in the hands of children," Mrs. Porter suggested. "Perhaps I could read to them and show them the pictures."

"Was Miss Edgerton a painter?" Paul asked. So far, all the planks were firmly nailed and nothing a teacher would spend time prying loose. He saw no evidence of scratches on any of the wood. Unless she had no desire to access the papers and had nailed them up. . .

"Miss Edgerton was a good watercolor artist," Mrs. Porter agreed. "But I wasn't interested in art, so I never saw a great deal of her work. I noticed she signed a few pieces in one of the books, but I found no signature on the others." She flipped pages with more enthusiasm than she'd shown all morning. "Here, this one is hers."

Paul obediently checked the page over Minerva's shoulder. "It's her garden, isn't it?"

"So she most likely illustrated these other volumes with plants and their qualities? This one is not a printed publication, just a folio." Minerva pulled a few sheets out. "I wonder if it could be published? I should think the information would be valuable."

"Would anyone want to steal it?" Verity asked worriedly. "Perhaps there is information about plants that provides proof of guilt that the thief had poisoned others?"

Paul let the women speculate as he worked around the hearth. He checked the bricks, just in case, but everything was neatly mortared. The bricks would have been an expensive addition. The ladies of the cottage had not been poor.

Finishing the parlor, he stood. "Do you mind if I go into the loft?"

Mrs. Underhill appeared in the kitchen doorway, drying her hands. "We've put everything up, we have. But that wardrobe is heavy."

"I'll work around it to start." Paul clattered up the stairs in his boots and studied the two neat beds and accouterments. Sparse, but comfortable, he concluded. It was easy to determine which side would have been the teacher's. He started there.

Apparently ignoring all admonitions to rest, Rafe returned from his rounds and was banging around in the kitchen by the time Paul found the loose board. Not wanting to alert the women, he eased partially down the loft stairs to the kitchen, caught the big man's attention, and gestured upstairs. If the teacher had hidden body parts under the board. . .

Rafe nodded, dried off his hands, and followed him up. "They hear us, you know."

"And they'll question us thoroughly later. I just want a witness before I pry up the floor." Paul removed a small crowbar from his tool belt.

Rafe studied the wide board Paul indicated. "She didn't lift it much, did she?"

"No, that's why it was so difficult to locate. I was looking for evidence of use, but it was the wobbling that gave it away." He pried the bar under the loose end and pulled it up. How had the teacher opened it?

The nails popped easily. Using his uninjured arm, Rafe grabbed the end and yanked, and the whole plank pulled off. They gazed into the dark void between the floor and the ceiling below.

Paul donned his work gloves and stuck his hand inside. He'd learned the hard way about the kind of spiders lurking in dark crevasses. He found a string apparently wrapped around a cloth and lifted it gently. It caught on the other boards, too wide to lift through.

"Anything old is likely to crumble," Rafe cautioned.

"Don't touch it with your hands," Minerva appeared at the top of the stairs. "If it's very old, you'll ruin the paper."

"I don't think it's that old." Paul twisted the bundle upright so it would slide through the narrow opening. "The oilcloth looks almost new." He laid it flat on the rag rug.

Verity arrived after Minerva. Her eyes widened in surprise. "More illustrations?"

The package was, indeed, flat and page-sized. "Would you care to open it, Mrs. Porter?" Paul eased the package across the floor to where she waited, wringing her hands. Her expression was hard to read.

"Verity, please." The widow kneeled and tugged tentatively at the string. It didn't open easily. She had to wrangle with the knot before peeling back the oilcloth.

"A lantern," Minerva suggested. The dark page revealed was nearly impossible to see. "The light from the window isn't sufficient."

"We could take it downstairs," Rafe said dryly.

"Not if we must hide it again." Paul dashed down to grab a lantern. Punching bread dough, Mrs. Underhill glanced at him with curiosity, but he didn't stop to explain.

The lamplight illuminated a watercolor painted in blacks, grays, and browns, with only a hint of color here and there. The red. . .

Verity gasped as she studied the image.

Paul gaped in horror at a nightmare scene of a black carriage racing down a cobbled midnight street—and a man in a dark frockcoat falling beneath the horses' feet.

"My father," Verity whispered in horror.

TWENTY-TWO: VERITY

VERITY'S HANDS SHOOK AS SHE LIFTED THE SMALL, VERY DETAILED watercolor of a rainy night, a racing carriage. . . and a cloaked figure, hands upraised, as if shoving the gentleman under the wheels. The illustrator had brilliantly depicted the action—and the result—of what must have been an instant's work. And the victim's horrified expression as he hit the pavement.

She'd recognize her father's mustache and red pocket hand-kerchief anywhere. As a former sea captain, he'd sported facial hair most of his life. Her mother had made him trim it. Tears rolled down her cheeks at the memories.

Her thoughts spun wildly, leaving her unaware of her audi-ence until pragmatic Minerva examined the rest of the documents.

"Bring the lantern closer, please. This looks like a piece of a letter saved from a fire."

Verity had been told her father had been cudgeled and robbed. Or had she just overheard whispers? She'd been very young and the adults hadn't tried to explain. It was possible no one had explained the horror to her mother either.

Verity only half listened as the others talked around her. She tried to identify the coachman or the cloaked gentleman, but their faces weren't more than a blur in the rain. Had Miss Edgerton

PATRICIA RICE

seen this scene? It was so very detailed. . . The carriage had a gold stripe around the base and gold-painted spokes. The tails of the horses were bobbed and beribboned. The cloak had a fur lining, and the gentleman's hat stood taller than most. He was clean shaven. . .

"Verity," Rafe said gently, trying to remove the sketch from her hands. "You said this is your father?"

She widened her eyes and stared at him in horror. She should never ever have said that. What had she done?

She'd trusted these people with Miss Edgerton's last words and now. . .

They had been about *her*? No, no, Faith was dead. Verity had a future. . .

She shook her head, unable to grasp the implications, the awfulness. . .

"This isn't just a letter," Minerva said. "I think there are pieces of a will in here. The language is formal. It's as if someone threw a wad of documents on the fire and Miss Edgerton retrieved them."

As if sensing her distress, Marmie padded out of her hiding place to bump Faith's. . . Verity's. . . elbow. She lifted the kitten to her face and buried her anguish. She wished she'd never said anything. She'd been right to be cautious. How could she possibly explain? She couldn't. She simply couldn't. She just wanted to be Verity, the schoolteacher.

She wasn't even that.

"Verity, Mrs. Porter," Rafe said gently, "Miss Edgerton may have been killed for these papers. We need to understand what they mean."

"I don't know!" she replied hysterically. "I don't know. I was only fifteen. . . Why would she do this? Why would she paint anything so dreadful?"

"Blackmail?" Mr. Upton suggested tentatively.

Verity set the kitten down and tried to stop her whirling thoughts. Blackmail—didn't that mean *extortion*? She couldn't make sense of it. Miss Edgerton extorting. . . ? "Who? We saw no

142

evidence that she had any extra income. The men are unidentifiable. Who would believe a painting? Why would she want me to *see* this?"

Minerva had produced a pair of spectacles and was reading the burned scraps more carefully. "The letter contains words like *fraud* and what appears to be *embezzlement*. The legal paper contains the phrase *amendment to my last*. . . If this is your father in the portrait, can we assume she saved these papers for you? If so, she may be saying that someone in your life was written out of a will due to illegal activities. Although why she would have hidden them instead of providing them to you or a solicitor or. . ." She shook her head in dismay.

"So her dying words may have just been to Verity, telling her where to look for information she wished to pass on?" Mr. Upton asked. "They didn't indicate who killed her?"

Verity clung to that lifeline. But *tea*. . . Her friend had known she'd been poisoned.

"Are you certain this is your father in the painting?" Rafe asked. "Which man?"

Verity blinked at this suggestion and replied in ire. "My father would *never* commit fraud! My father was attacked by a thief, robbed, and killed over ten years ago!"

"How do you know this?" he asked carefully. "You said you were only fifteen. Might they have hidden the truth from you?"

The large soldier who tramped through the house like an earthquake, had flung a grown man from the tavern, and thundered through the kitchen, spoke with such gentleness, that she wanted to weep.

She shouldn't deceive him, but there was nothing he could do now. Nothing could bring back her father or her home. They were all gone, along with dead Faith.

They had no way of tracing an ancient story. She could give them that much.

"I overheard people talking," she whispered, reluctantly recalling that awful night. "I was in my room when a messenger

143

arrived. I heard my mother weeping and ran downstairs. They didn't know I was there. She and our butler and some stranger were discussing arrangements for a *body*. The next day, she told me my father died at the hands of a thief. I attended the service but I never saw him again."

She didn't have to recall the horrible days that followed. They were etched in her memory with such pain that the words might as well have been carved into her skin.

"And Miss Edgerton was there?" Mr. Upton asked.

Verity nodded and found her handkerchief to wipe her tears. "My mother wasn't well. The physician confined her to bed. Miss Edgerton held my hand and explained what I must do and when. She helped dye my clothes. I don't know what I would have done without her."

"And then she left?" Minerva asked.

Verity didn't want to talk about this anymore. She wanted to fall into bed and bury her head under a pillow. And even she knew that was a childish thing to do. She was *Verity* now, a young woman with a sensible head on her shoulders, no longer that helpless child.

Even if her world *had* exploded once more— She'd survived the last two. She would do so again. The first time, with her father's death, she'd had to fight hysteria, present a calm demeanor, be the young lady her mother needed. . . The second time, with the fire, she'd been left hollow. But even with hollowed insides, she knew how to do this. She simply had to edit the story.

"Some days after my father's funeral, my uncle arrived with solicitors, and told Mother that without Father to operate his company, it would have to be closed. Without income, we had to reduce expenses. I came home from church one Sunday, and Miss Edgerton and almost the entire staff were gone. Mother said she had no choice."

"There should have been funds from selling the company," Rafe argued, sounding puzzled.

"Not if he owed the bank for anything," Minerva suggested.

"I don't know more. My uncle inherited everything and moved in. My mother took to her bed. I looked after her. He started using the ground floor for his business. Life went on, just not as it was before." Verity stared at the painting. "If my father was murdered, why would she not have told me? Perhaps the painting is metaphorical, representing the killing of life as we knew it?"

"Where was Miss Edgerton on the night your father died?" Rafe demanded harshly.

Verity shook her head in denial of the direction of his thoughts. "She couldn't possibly have concealed such an event from us!"

But the memories were there, as clear as the explosion that had rocked her world mere weeks ago. She took them out to look at them again. "It was her day off. She usually went to the shops and bought painting supplies and books." Verity considered what she remembered. "I believe she came in late, probably after the messenger. My mother had taken to her bed. I was sitting on the stairs, crying, when she returned. What does it matter?"

And then she realized. . . Miss Edgerton had been out on those empty, rainy streets when her father had died. She shuddered and shoved the painting away.

"No," she whispered. "She could not have. Why would she not say?"

"Who would she tell? It doesn't look as if she recognized any face but your father's." Rafe studied the painting. "Who would *we* tell? Would it have made you feel better to know your father died by carriage and not by thief? That's just a different kind of murder, and no one did anything about it, did they? Was your mother in any state to hire a thief taker? Would there have been any point?"

Verity shook her head. Her hearty, healthy father had thought he'd live forever. She'd come to terms with the monetary loss long ago. He'd wanted his family to have everything they desired. He'd pampered them, given them luxuries, expected them to go out into society the way her mother deserved. He had not prepared them for a future without him.

"Do you happen to know your father's solicitors?" Minerva asked.

If she did, she couldn't say without giving her father's name. Verity shook her head, even as an ugly suspicion crawled under her skin.

"You said your father left everything to your uncle?" Mr. Upton asked after a whispered consultation with Minerva.

And there it was. For ten years, she'd been grateful to her father's younger brother for moving into her father's house so they could keep it, allowing her and her mother to stay in their home, however diminished. He'd even paid her mother's funeral expenses.

"Father had no other family," she whispered. "Not that I know of. Estates pass to the next male, not to women."

"Does your uncle know where you are?" Rafe asked angrily.

Overwhelmed, she shook her head again. She couldn't do this anymore. Rashly, she declared, "He thinks I'm dead."

TWENTY-THREE: RAFE

Rafe wanted to shoot someone, or beat them up, or anything to release his rage. He'd probably have to start with ducking Verity in a pond.

She still wasn't telling them the whole truth.

"We should take these up to the manor." Minerva began wrapping up the papers. "If the thief decides it's easier to burn down the cottage than find them, they'll be safe. For what little use they are."

Had someone really killed Miss Edgerton to steal these scraps of nothing? And why now? Considering Verity claimed the painting depicted her father. . . The story had more holes than a sieve.

"You'll have to bend them enough to hide in a basket. The cottage may be watched. I'll go up with you." The curate stood and helped his intended to rise.

"I don't want to put anyone in danger," Verity whispered miserably. "I should leave. I just don't know where to go."

"If you're dead, no one is looking for you," Rafe said callously, trudging down the stairs. What the devil did she mean, she was dead? She was alive and looking like all the temptresses in Hades, even in those damned demure widow's weeds.

Which she'd probably worn for ten years, *since her father's death*. Was she even widowed? No husband had been mentioned. The lady was a consummate liar.

And apparently, *dead*.

In the kitchen, he whacked off a slice of ham. He needed his own place. Why was he hovering, worried, over a lying, conniving. . . dead person?

Discussing hiding places, Paul and Minerva departed with the painting hidden in a basket of dirty linen. Fine, maybe the manor's laundress would wash them.

Verity didn't come down. Mrs. Underhill clucked and ladled broth from a kettle she'd started earlier. "You shouted at the poor thing. Hasn't she been through enough?"

"What has she been through?" he demanded, cutting ham into the broth. "Has she told you?"

"Why, her friend was murdered before her eyes! Now she's all alone in the world and that lawyer will sell the cottage right from under her. Men move on, but women want a home." She carried the bowl up the stairs.

Rafe slurped the broth and went looking for heartier fare. He was here for the food, he reminded himself. They'd eaten almost everything. "If you want supper, we have to go to market," he shouted up the stairs. She must keep coins on her person for the thief to merely steal a hat.

Where did *dead* women get money? From a bank. She'd arrived with Bosworth. Did the banker know her? He should question the next time the man stopped in. Rafe had a poor opinion of money men but he might enjoy a lowly soldier like him having the authority to question a banker.

"I don't have a hat." She descended the stairs much quieter than he had, looking defeated but still willing to help.

"Dead people don't need hats." He slammed on his tattered bicorne. "We'll see what Lavender has. Aren't you supposed to visit her?"

Clasping her hands, eyes downcast, she nodded and drifted, hatless, toward the back door.

He felt like an ogre. Either she was an exceedingly good actress —or she was a victim of some sort. Right now, she definitely behaved like a victim, and his stupid Sir Galahad inclination kicked in. He really needed to stifle that antiquated proclivity.

"Is it safe for Mrs. Underhill to stay here?" she asked as he held the door for her.

No, it damned well was not. It wasn't safe for *any* of them to stay here while a killer believed they harbored evidence, if that's what this was all about. He was just a lowly soldier who took orders, not a general who understood strategic planning.

He returned to the stairs and shouted up them. "Mrs. Underhill, would you like to go to market for us? I'm taking Mrs. Porter up to the manor for a fitting."

She slowly emerged from the loft, carrying her soup bowl, a cloak, and a bonnet. "Has Mrs. Porter eaten?"

"I'll eat when we return," she promised, sounding a little stronger in her reassurances. "I arranged for Mr. Oswald to keep track of our accounts, so if you would be so kind as to do the shopping, they'll give the receipts to him."

"Mutton or pork, if they have it. I'll go fishing later. We have carrots and potatoes and greens, so pick up anything that catches your fancy," Rafe advised, pushing the little widow out the door. "We need more flour, if Oswald will have it delivered."

She'd arranged for the mercantile to keep her accounts? She'd been here less than a week and she'd already made herself at home. Rafe supposed money would do that. It wasn't as if he had the experience.

"Mr. Upton gave me stakes for labeling the herbs," Verity murmured as they traipsed through the back garden. "I can use Miss Edgerton's paints to write on them. I just need to identify them."

"The basic plants are right there by the kitchen door. They're

149

probably in her books. The others. . . even I may not know what they are. You'll have to ask Mrs. Walker." He was still furious and spoke curtly.

"I have no family other than my uncle," she said softly, irrelevantly.

Rafe held an overhanging branch out of her way until she stepped past. It was a gray September day and the noon sun didn't add much warmth, but it was pleasant walking along the brook toward the main footpath up to the manor. He studied on what she was telling him until he gathered all the ramifications. He didn't like the result.

"You are hiding from your uncle? The one who inherited everything? Why?"

She shrugged. The dim light through the leaves darkened her caramel hair to a streaked brown she wore in a tight knot. "He is a drunk and not a nice man. It makes both our lives easier if he believes me dead."

Did he want to know more? Men could beat wives without the law interfering. Penniless nieces. . . probably didn't count for much either. Except she didn't seem penniless, which might even be worse if the uncle wanted her blunt.

"You think he may have pushed your father under a carriage?" He had to ask, because it very much affected them now.

"I never would have thought so. My father was a generous man. My uncle worked for him in some capacity. I was confined to the schoolroom and paid no heed. Without the company, I shouldn't imagine my father's estate was worth much. So my uncle essentially lost his position when the business closed and had to start his own."

But a child knew nothing of business, and those scraps of paper Minerva had read. . . Rafe reserved judgment. "If he thinks you dead, then there would be no point in following you here," he agreed. "Or any reason to harm Miss Edgerton?"

"That's what puzzles me," she said as they reached the manor drive. "My father has been dead these ten years or more. No one cared what happened to me after my mother died. Why would they care now that I am dead to the world? It makes no sense."

"Unless Miss Edgerton has more under her floors than that one packet. Perhaps we should have kept looking. If she was in the habit of painting incriminating scenes. . ."

"They might be in any of the illustrations we've already found and we didn't notice. Or buried in the medical records we gave to Mrs. Walker. Or perhaps we're looking at this wrong and someone simply hated her and decided to kill her for reasons known only to them."

"And searched the cottage for what? No, someone believes she hid something. They may be wrong, but they're searching, and it's dangerous. Are you certain they are not searching for you?" Rafe took her arm as they approached the manor's weathered wooden front doors.

Captain Huntley had workmen crawling all over the tower, rebuilding the interior for the expanding Reid family enterprises. Apparently replacing moldering panels wasn't high on his list of repairs. Rafe was relieved when the knocker didn't bring the door down.

Verity was quiet as they waited for someone to answer.

Miss Edgerton had died after Verity had arrived. After discovering the painting under the cottage floors, it was difficult for Rafe to believe it had nothing to do with the widow—who might not really be a widow.

If he was lusting after an innocent miss, he might as well shoot himself now.

Whoever had thought war was difficult? Civilization was an endless swamp in comparison.

TWENTY-FOUR: VERITY

As she tried on gowns, Verity decided she'd told Rafe all he needed to know. He had every right to be angry at her for concealing Miss Edgerton's last words, but he didn't have any right to her past. Whatever had happened to her father, they couldn't prove. She might dislike her uncle for his parsimoniousness, but he'd had no reason to harm her father. And he had no particular reason to harm her.

Except. . . she'd stolen from him. So hiding her identity was necessary and had utterly nothing to do with Miss Edgerton's death.

Except that painting. . .

The carriage had to be the clue, but she'd been too young to notice carriages or her father's visitors. He had been a tough businessman. He could easily have made enemies.

Could someone else identify that carriage?

And what good would it do if they did? Which must have been what Miss Edgerton had concluded. She'd drawn a dreadful scene that had haunted her, but there had been no point in telling the grieving adolescent Verity had been back then.

Believing her father may have been murdered. . . Verity

wished she had never seen that painting. Miss Edgerton would have understood that murder might turn her bitter and suspicious. Grief had been hard enough for the protected child she had been.

In a fog of uncertainty, Verity smiled at the lovely blond—rather young—Lavender and her sewing ladies, thanked them for the lovely gowns, and agreed on all their suggestions. The clothes were second-hand, like the ones she'd bought after the fire, but Lavender had a gift for making them stylish. They might not be her mother's silks, but she'd feel like a lady nonetheless.

Only her stolen hat had been almost new, with fresh lace and ribbons. She described it to the ladies, and they promised to watch out for it. She didn't tell them the thief had a pistol. Was that bad of her too? She didn't have a lot of practice in conversing.

In the meantime, Lavender offered her a simple buff muslin bonnet with black ribbons and a small black ruffled edging. Verity thought she might add a little trim to match her new gowns and was grateful to have a hat again, even if it lacked a veil and wasn't as grandiose as the stolen one.

Now, if only she had good shoes. . .

A handsome blond lady of about Verity's age, Clare Huntley stopped in to ask about a gown she was having made up and admired the only slightly faded primrose muslin Verity was trying on. "That color is very fetching. I'm glad you're coming out of blacks."

"They were all I had," Verity admitted. They were all she'd had *before* the fire, so she'd simply bought more. "I suppose I didn't feel very colorful."

"I understand," the captain's wife said with feeling. "I lost my mother and sister within a year of each other and not long after losing my father. I didn't think I'd ever leave mourning either. You should come to dinner when Lavender finishes that one. Minerva says we must discuss schoolrooms and chalkboards."

"And reading primers," Verity suggested. "Miss Edgerton's

books are a bit advanced for beginners." The ancient primers she'd once used to teach with had been in her cellar home. They were gone now. They'd been in tatters anyway.

"Mr. Birdwhistle might help with primers," Lavender suggested, removing a pin from her mouth to hold up a ruffle. "He is helping me to read and has ordered a few."

Mrs. Huntley seemed surprised to learn that. Who was Mr. Birdwhistle? Verity wanted to know more of the manor's inhabitants. She'd never had much opportunity to make friends and had often wondered about the people behind the windows she passed on her trips to the bank.

But if she was a danger to these people. . .

She simply could not understand how. Or why.

"I'd love that," was all she knew to answer. She'd never been to a formal dinner. The thought terrified her, but she wanted to live as other people did.

Mrs. Huntley blithely sailed on to the construction in the far corner of the immense gallery. Verity's home had been comfortably large, but she had never seen the inside of a grand manor. She thought the gallery's two-story windows and chandeliers indicated this might once have been a ballroom instead of a hive of industrious activity. She'd once dreamed of waltzing around a chamber such as this. Now, she rather approved of the more practical activity. Besides, she couldn't waltz.

"I promised Sergeant Russell two new shirts to replace the one damaged by ruffians," she told Lavender as she tugged on her old gown in the dressing room. "Is that possible?"

"New would be easier than making over an old one," the girl admitted. "He's rather large and finding anything his size might be difficult. I have Henri looking out for a nice large coat I can make over, but shirts are simple to sew. I just need him to stand still long enough to measure."

Verity had no notion of where Rafe had wandered off to. He'd merely deposited her here and gone off on his own errands. That was perfectly understandable. She was simply back to feeling like a fish out of water again. She may as well become used to it.

"Where might I find this Mr. Birdwhistle?" she asked once she was dressed in her drab gown again.

Lavender brightened. "I believe he is teaching the boys mathematics by measuring the tower. Let us see how the renovation commences." She led the way past her sewing ladies toward the corner where lengths of Holland linen hung from ropes to contain the dust. Behind the curtains, stacks of lumber and tools lay scattered about. "This floor of the tower will be Sofia's perfumery, we hope. We need more flowers and gardens but there is not much profit in them until the perfumery is ready."

"Miss Edgerton's yard brims with all sorts of flowers. I am not a gardener, but I've read books. I believe flowering plants are produced by seeds and spread by roots, so when it's time to plant more gardens, you'll have at least one source."

"Is there lavender? Sofia thinks we should start with lavender. Since that's my name, I'm thinking it ought to be on the label." The little seamstress grinned at her own absurdity.

"Well, if it is a lavender scent, then your name will be on the label, won't it? Lavender's Lavender eau de cologne?" Verity studied the activity in the rather dark and gloomy stone tower.

On the far side of the large, circular room, workmen were in the process of removing a wall concealing a stairway. A very tall man with dark hair who resembled Captain Huntley—a French count, Verity thought she'd been told—consulted with a delicate blond lady, their heads bending together in a manner indicating familiarity. After arguing over a piece of paper the lady held, the muscular gentleman in shirtsleeves hauled some of the stones down the stairs, presumably to the cellar.

My word. Verity hoped her eyebrows didn't reach her hairline. She didn't often see gentlemen without their coats. . . She'd no idea how much she had missed while hiding behind books! Would Rafe look like that if he removed his coat?

"I'll ask Thea if the boys have gone back to the schoolroom. Come along, you should meet her." Distracting Verity from her reverie, Lavender made her way across a floor coated in sawdust, holding her hem from the grime. "Thea communes with ghosts."

With little concern for her worn hem, Verity followed. *Ghosts?* And broad-shouldered aristocrats who hauled heavy blocks of stone. What else had she missed while living in a cellar?

Following Lavender, she saw Rafe speaking with construction workers. By the time they reached the blond lady, she was consulting with a fashionably dressed couple in garments much too nice for this filthy workplace. Verity searched faces uneasily, hoping she wouldn't be imagining any more of her past in these strangers.

Relieved that she recognized no one, she bobbed a curtsy at her introduction to a Mr. and Mrs. Prescott, collectors of fine furniture. All her father's fine furniture had gone up in flames, so they didn't hold her interest.

"Mrs. Porter?" The fashionable lady became more animated at the name. "I understand your former governess left some interesting art portfolios. We know a publisher who might be interested. Might we stop by and visit?"

Verity's disinterest immediately converted to suspicion. "The portfolios are not mine to display or sell. You will need to consult with Miss Edgerton's solicitor and heirs."

The lady introduced as Miss Thea Talbot intervened. "I believe Mr. Culliver, her solicitor, is still here. I will introduce you later. Lavender, are you looking for someone?"

Visibly unconcerned with the adults, the young seamstress gestured at the stairs. "Have Mr. Birdwhistle and the boys returned to the schoolroom? We need to ask about schoolbooks."

"I believe they've moved their activities to the next floor. Arnaud says these stairs are not safe for them to use until a stair rail is installed. They've opened up the door into the attic, so they're running up and down." Miss Talbott turned her attention to Verity. "My little brother might benefit from having a larger circle of playmates. I will gladly help should you choose to set up a schoolroom."

"I would love to be useful. Might we climb the stairs to see if the tutor is still there?" Verity's curiosity ate at her. How many people did the manor hold and were all of them this helpful? She hoped they followed through on their promises. She was growing excited by the possibilities—if she were allowed to stay.

"If you cling to the wall, I suppose." Miss Talbott glanced dubiously at the smooth stones. "I cannot imagine how they'll add rails."

The broad gentleman in shirtsleeves returned up the stairs to catch this last. "They're all hoping to find more pirate treasure in the walls, so they'll pound all day to cut through stone." He bowed before Verity. "I don't believe we've been formally introduced?"

He was amazingly handsome, more so than scarred and half-blind Captain Huntley. But even in his graciousness, this gentleman didn't leave her as breathless as Rafe, who was now taking the dangerous stairs upward two at a time. *My goodness, the air in the tower must be affecting her.* She feared she was having heart palpitations watching Rafe's. . . She dragged her attention back to the company.

Lavender hastily performed the necessary. "Mrs. Verity Porter, Arnaud Lavigne. Arnaud is a French count but says titles are meaningless. Let's go upstairs. I want to see what they've done up there."

Verity could have lingered longer talking with these fascinating people—and avoiding Rafe—but she obediently followed in Lavender's wake, aware that they were taking time from her work. She didn't wish to be a hindrance.

"Pirate's treasure?" she asked as they climbed, one hand lifting her overlong hem to keep from tripping and leaning on her cane with the other. She didn't have a spare hand for gripping walls.

"One of the earls was said to be a pirate, but we've already found his treasure. He left doubloons in the wall. It's the last earl

157

who hid the family jewels, or sold them, we don't know. Stories grow into legends, Mr. Birdwhistle says. I think he came here looking for treasure too. Minerva says he isn't really a tutor, but she won't say more." Lavender reached the top of the stairs and surveyed another scene of construction clutter. "There he is."

Verity saw Rafe first, talking with the stoop-shouldered Blackwells. Rafe raised his head when she appeared. He still wasn't smiling at her, and her heart sank. She had come to depend on him too much. She hurriedly glanced to the young man with his students.

The tutor who wasn't a tutor smiled in delight at Lavender's call. Verity could certainly understand why. They were two handsome young people, and in any ordinary circumstance, should be courting, she suspected. She wasn't certain what prospects a tutor and seamstress might have, though.

"This is Mrs. Porter, who is interested in starting a village school." Lavender made an improper introduction. "She will need primers to go with the other books Miss Edgerton left. And Thea thinks Davey might attend to widen his circle of friends."

Verity noted that the young boys paid little attention to the conversation. One was using a measuring string on top of a ladder and calling numbers down to the other, who was drawing lines on a large piece of paper. Despite not looking much older than beginning students, they appeared to be working at a more advanced level than she could teach.

Slender, not over tall, the handsome tutor appeared interested. "That might be beneficial for Oliver as well as Davy, for a short time each day. Perhaps I could tutor a more advanced class during those hours?"

Verity thought she must have died and gone to heaven. She had never met so many kind and helpful people in her life. "I would be honored," was all she knew to say. "We still have a lot of organizing to do, and I'm not certain how to gather the supplies needed. Mr. Upton has offered the chapel until we come up with something better."

"The chapel has no chimney. You will freeze in winter. I've been thinking about uses for the attic storage." Mr. Birdwhistle gestured at the area where workmen were repairing a staircase. "Miss Talbot is removing the old furniture. It has windows for light, and I believe they're opening up a connecting chimney. We should speak to the captain."

"I'm going back to work. I'll leave you to schoolrooms. I never want to see the inside of one again." Lavender abandoned them to return downstairs.

"Your bailiff friend is speaking with the men in charge of the construction. I'll tell them what we we're thinking." Impervious to Lavender's dismissal, Mr. Birdwhistle offered his arm.

Verity didn't think the tutor was so very much younger than she. Wouldn't it be fun to dance around a ballroom on his arm? Well, it would be entertaining to dance anywhere, with anyone, she supposed. She'd missed out on so much. . .

Rafe was practically glaring at her, so she ignored him and turned her attention to the workmen who had returned to hammering doors. Apparently, they were too busy to talk to a tutor. Or to be polite.

"We're discussing opening a schoolroom in the attic. Do you think we might disturb the workmen so I may show Mrs. Porter? Once the stairs in the tower are safe, students should be able to use them, shouldn't they?" Utterly oblivious to Rafe's glare, the tutor studied the work progressing on the doorway.

"I was discussing inn repairs with the Blackwells," Rafe grudgingly admitted. "We've probably disturbed their work enough. You should look for Arnaud. He appears to be directing the plans."

Mr. Birdwhistle sighed. "This is the problem with community projects. One must spend a lot of time looking for the right people to do the right thing. I can't abandon my students, Mrs. Porter. You'll most likely find Arnaud wherever you find Miss Talbot." He returned to assisting the boys in their measurements.

Leaving Verity with Rafe.

Stiffly, she informed him, "The furniture couple want to see Miss Edgerton's portfolio, and I believe the merchant wishing to open the hardware brought Mr. Culliver in to offer for the cottage. I do not know any of them, but they were here when Miss Edgerton died. Should we check Mrs. Prescott's wardrobe for a black bonnet and old-fashioned skirts?"

TWENTY-FIVE: PAUL

PAUL FELT LIKE A JUDGE ATTEMPTING TO SEPARATE WARRING neighbors.

He had no understanding of why the usually genial bailiff was practically growling, or why the demure widow had become adamant about investigating business people who might aid the manor. But they'd asked for aid. He should offer what he was able.

"If the Prescotts are merely interested in art, what question do you wish to put to them?" Paul asked, hoping to clear the air, at the very least.

The sergeant had dragged the widow down to the manor's library to consult with Minerva, who was studying the papers previously hidden under Miss Edgerton's floorboards. As the manor's librarian, she followed the conversation but didn't intervene. Paul knew his intended's fine mind was focused, though.

"Mrs. Prescott is of an age with the students Miss Edgerton corresponded with. I believe Miss Talbot meant to write to a friend who knows some of those students?" Distracted by the enormous library, Mrs. Porter studied the shelves rather than the company.

"She just received a reply this morning." Minerva pointed at a folded letter in another of her paper stacks. "Her correspondent says Miss Edgerton was called Fairy Godmother by the students because she provided headache powders and. . ." She cast a glance at Paul and amended, "Relief for female ailments. She left under a cloud but told them the Gravesyde postmaster would forward her mail, so they knew how to find her."

"Under a cloud? The headmistress didn't like Fairy Godmothers?" Paul surmised.

"Usually, a parent complains. It would explain why she took up tutoring instead of teaching at another school." Minerva studied the widow's back. "Is there a reason to suspect Mrs. Prescott was one of those students?"

"Not any more than anyone else." Reluctantly drawn into the discussion, Mrs. Porter picked up the letter. "Mrs. Prescott was here the day Miss Edgerton died. She's of an age with the students who wrote to her about female ailments, as you call it. She's a furniture collector but oddly eager to look at amateur artwork."

The bailiff frowned and took up the letter after she relinquished it. "And Sullivan? The man owns a hardware store in Birmingham. What could he possibly have to do with a female teacher?"

Mrs. Porter replied more curtly than was her wont. "He was here when she died. He seems to know Mr. Culliver, the solicitor who is oddly establishing the value of the cottage before his client is barely cold in the grave. If Mr. Sullivan buys the cottage, then he can tear it down looking for whatever may be hidden there."

"And you think Mrs. Prescott might be the one who stole your bonnet and shot me?" Rafe sounded incredulous.

"All I know is that she is female and wants to see inside the cottage. I have no notion of how one goes about questioning suspects." In a huff, she returned to examining book titles.

Paul was starting to enjoy the byplay. He and Minerva had suffered similar misunderstandings when they'd first met. A meeting of minds required a willingness to listen and try to understand what the other was saying, which took practice and patience.

"For the fun of it, might we also add Bosworth's assistant, Mr. Smith, to our suspect list?" Minerva jotted notes. "He is the one guilty of bringing Sullivan here last week. One of the ladies in Miss Edgerton's records was called Smith. He does not seem much interested in searching the cottage though."

"Because he hired someone to do so?" Rafe suggested. "I don't believe the woman I chased was tall enough to be Mrs. Prescott. And the person who fell out of the apple tree was wearing breeches and had a male voice. Boarding school ladies are unlikely to crawl about gardens or ransack cottages."

Paul leaned his hip against the enormous library table and reduced speculation to practicality. "Then should we look at men who climb trees? The apple pickers? The construction workmen? The new coachman? And must we consider one of Lavender's sewing ladies as the party stealing the hat? It will be almost impossible to verify everyone was where they should be at the times involved."

The big, ginger-haired sergeant frowned impatiently. "Then we set a trap. We will make it clear that Verity and I will be elsewhere for an extended period of time. Mrs. Underhill can return to her daughter's. Word spreads quickly. The trick will be watching the house day and night without being seen."

"Lampblack," Minerva said, unexpectedly. "Messy, but the stuff is near impossible to wash off."

Paul raised his eyebrows at his brilliant but unpredictable betrothed. "You have our attention."

"Brush lampblack on surfaces any thief has to touch. They obviously don't know where to look, so they'll brush up against tables or shelves or cabinets. You'll just have to go in and do a thorough scrub later."

"And the black will have stained their hands or clothes?" Rafe asked. "How do we notice who has turned black? We have a wide range of suspects."

The widow swung around, clasping her hands but looking excited. "I have read about. . . What if we let it be known we will be at the inn from dawn until dusk, cleaning, thatching, not exactly a barn raising but an inn repair? We ask everyone to attend with whatever tools they have. We can hand out brooms and cleaning supplies. I fear we must ask the manor inhabitants to be there, as well."

Minerva looked interested. "We take note of who is there and who is not. Who disappears and comes back black. Someone can sit in the trees and watch the path behind the cottage. Someone else. . . sits in the tavern to watch the street?"

"And Quincy can check anyone who sneaks back into the manor to wash off while the rest of us are out." Paul nodded, searching for all the ins and outs.

"Hard to guard all the manor doors," Rafe added. "Lock up all but the front and side?"

"Patience can have her apple pickers join us! She says the presses have been cleaned and restored, and they have enough harvest to begin juicing. That should bring out everyone in the area to fill their jugs. They'll have to lend a hand if they want cider!" Paul almost bounced up and down in excitement. This was exactly what the community needed. . . to learn to work together.

Mrs. Porter nodded but stuck with the inn idea. "We'll need lots of brooms. And thatching material?"

Rafe appeared relieved that a possible solution had been found. "I suppose we can hope the culprit will not notice the black or will pretend he got it while cleaning, but we'll know if they slip back and try to hide."

Paul knew that catching a thief wasn't the same as proving a murder, but Hunt was good at obtaining confessions. One could only hope.

TWENTY-SIX: RAFE

"Buying brooms instead of ale will put a dent in my budget," Rafe griped as he took the stewed vegetables off the fire and set up the griddle for the fish he'd caught earlier.

"But if you let people take home new brooms, the gift will endear you to all the local housewives so they won't complain quite so much if their men spend time at your pub of an evening." Feeding the nosy kitten from her palm instead of letting it near the fire, the cautious, quiet widow almost sounded giddy with delight.

A giddy widow was dangerous, especially one whose eyes lit like firelight in excitement—and who might not be a widow. Animated, she was lovely and driving him distracted. Rafe had been a soldier too long to understand the minds of women, but right now, even if she kept secrets, he admired her plotting. Free repairs while solving a crime. . .

He'd rather keep her out of the crime business. He had a niggling suspicion she thought she was catching a killer.

"I suppose, if anyone can actually help with the roof, the free labor will save on workmen," he agreed. Tile would last longer, but thatch was cheaper and more in keeping with the structure. He was afraid to expect much.

Mrs. Underhill sat at the kitchen table, checking off the shopping list they meant to send to the city with Henri on the morrow. "Mr. Oswald might help us with the polishing rags and turpentine. He sent that bottle of elixir Miss Edgerton ordered with the flour he delivered. I don't know what to do with it."

"I'd forgotten about that. Did you put it in the pantry?" Setting down the kitten, Verity opened the door and produced the dark bottle. "Shall I give it to Meera? Looks like one of those patent medicines they sell on the streets."

"Show it to me," Rafe demanded, keeping his eye on the fish.

She held the bottle in front of his face. "Should I open it?"

"Mrs. Bigelow's Vegetable Compound." Rafe screwed up his nose. "I've seen men addicted to those medicines. Why would an herbalist touch such a thing?"

"Miss Edgerton hated compounds," Mrs. Underhill declared. "She warned us of the dangers."

"One more oddity," the widow said in resignation. "I hope we catch the killer and he can explain at least some of this, but I'm beginning to suspect there may be more than one problem here."

"Don't see how, unless they conspired." Rafe flipped the pike and tested the skin. "Set the table, ladies. We're almost ready."

They cleared off their writing materials and laid out plates.

"If I knew the inn had a working chimney, I could cook for the crowd on Friday." He set the grilled fish on a platter. With bountiful catches like this, they could eat cheaply all winter.

Huh, sounded like he actually planned to stay. Plentiful food had decided that. Once he caught the killer, he could hunt better accommodations. A roof on the inn. . . He daren't hope. "I'll have to put together a soldiers' stew in a kettle for the workers."

"Bread," Verity suggested, adding fish scraps to the kitten's bowl before taking a seat. "Lots of bread. Can we order cheese with all the cleaning supplies, or is that asking too much of Henri?"

"It's asking too much of my pockets." Rafe lowered himself in the chair and vowed to buy more substantial seats for his pub.

His pub. He was actually believing this might happen. Probably shouldn't. People would laugh once they saw the enormity of the task.

"Ask Mr. Oswald." Mrs. Underhill spoke up. "We have people here who make cheese. They'll be glad for the sale."

"I can do that." Verity actually looked animated for a change. "Shall I talk to several of the farmers and check prices? You'll need regular deliveries someday."

Rafe studied her with suspicion—much more sensible than admiring her fine smile. "Why would you care?"

That wiped away her smile. "Because you said you might need help with numbers. And I want to be useful. And if there is any chance I can stay in Gravesyde, I'll need to earn my way somehow. I have a feeling teaching won't pay."

Now he felt like a callous rat, but she couldn't exist on fantasies. "You're probably right about that. The village would need to be an official village, with a town council that can pass taxes. Unless the bank lets go of its claim, that won't happen."

Her happiness dimmed as she examined her fish. "I suppose I'll have to wait and see if the heirs sell the cottage or will rent it to me. And how much that will cost. I can still buy the cheese, though. Everyone ought to contribute to the meal. The inn will be for the good of all once it's running again."

They hadn't told Mrs. Underhill about the lampblack or the reason for the sudden inn-cleaning party. Rafe had a suspicion the older lady would enjoy the gossip too much. For her benefit, he added, "I'm hoping we can make some of the inn rooms respectable this week. Then we can each have one for free until we're up and running. You'll have to provide your own bed, though."

"Hardly respectable," Mrs. Underhill grunted.

"You can go with us," Verity suggested. "Although I'd much rather stay here, if all goes well. I fear mice in the inn's beds until the roof is repaired."

Rafe almost forgot the ache in his arm as he fed Wolfie under

167

the table and they indulged his fantasy of a working inn. It had been a very long time since he'd had a permanent place to lay his head and fill his belly. He didn't hope easily. And relying on a woman he'd known less than a week. . .

One who kept secrets. Unfortunately, no law required her to tell him everything.

It just bothered him that she still didn't trust him—because it meant she had reason to distrust people. He wanted to know that reason.

FRIDAY

TWENTY-SEVEN: VERITY

"BROOMS, BUCKETS, CLEANING SUPPLIES UNLOADED IN THE LOBBY," Henri reported, taking off his ragged cap and swiping his handsome brow. "Misty day for this."

As if they had a choice in weather. Verity feared her lovely new bonnet would become soggy and bedraggled before day's end. She hadn't worn a light color in so long, she felt conspicuous, especially since she was still wearing a black gown and ugly black boots. Until Lavender completed refurbishing her new dresses, she had little choice, though. At least the black trim sort of matched.

After this last day of preparation, she was starting to recognize the manor inhabitants. Henri Lavigne might physically resemble his cousin, Captain Huntley, but he was far more outgoing and cheerful. He had spent the better part of yesterday in the city accumulating supplies, then helped them move Miss Edgerton's library to safety with his covered cart.

Through the open door, Verity watched men gathering in the inn yard. The thatchers were already setting up ladders, and apple pickers worked on a press under the directions of the farm steward. The manor's unusual cook, Lady Elsa, excitedly tasted apples, directed kettles, and sorted ingredients she meant to test, impervious to the damp.

Loving every terrifying minute of this new experience, Verity even managed to occasionally forget the *reason* they gathered.

Had the killer left town? Or would they try searching the cottage again?

"Will mist hurt the thatching crew?" she asked, avoiding grim thoughts.

"Mist will keep the crew cool." Henri shrugged and ran off to empty more tools from his cart, stopping to hug and kiss Patience while she fretted over placement of the apple baskets her workers carried down.

Mr. Upton, the nice auburn-haired curate, strode into the yard from the parsonage next door and joined Verity in the lobby. "Minerva has the women gathering in the chapel for instructions. Do we have any order for rooms to be done first?"

She checked the notes Rafe had made. "He thinks the children can start on the lobby and pub. Those rooms have mostly been cleaned of debris and just need scrubbing. We'll need stronger workers for the kitchen—will the chimney sweep be here?"

"Hunt says the sweep should arrive by noon. It might be good if the inn can put him up tonight. He can start cleaning the manor's chimneys tomorrow." The curate eyed the inn's worm-eaten interior with the critical eye of a carpenter.

"Then we should probably clean and arrange the servants' quarters before the upstairs. Can't have guests without staff." Verity could almost hear her mother's voice falling from her lips. She desperately missed her wisdom, but she was relieved to discover it was still there when needed.

Rafe and his friend, Fletcher, wandered in next, carrying odd tools she hoped went to the roof because she didn't know their purpose and hated to reveal her immense ignorance.

"Ladders are up," Rafe declared. "We'll have men on the roof shortly, more experienced than we are, we hope."

"I've worked with thatching crews," the curate said. "Let me take this list back to Minerva and I'll keep an eye on them."

Rafe nodded. "Thank you. We'll go up to look at the attic timbers."

As the curate left with his list, Verity had the inexplicable desire for Rafe to kiss her as Henri had kissed Patience. Appalling notion! She needed to impress him with her efficiency so she could earn a position here, not terrify him. "Lady Elsa and her kitchen staff are showing the manor ladies how to cut vegetables for your stew. She asked if you had a recipe you follow."

Rafe set down his tools. "I'll take a look at what she's brought down from their garden. I don't want any more poison ending up in the pot."

Verity puckered her nose. "I had not thought of that. Surely no one would wish to kill an entire village? Let me go with you so I can see what you recommend and make sure nothing else is added. Lady Elsa has ideas for improving the apple cider. I don't know if she can watch both juice and stew."

Poison! One more of ten dozen things that might go wrong. She must have been mad to suggest this. Not leaning on her cane as much as before, she followed him out to the tables. "Do you have your cottage sentries stationed? There are so very many people coming and going. . ."

"Watching the brook path and the street. We don't have enough people for more," Rafe said, stopping at the cooking table. "Lady Elsa, have you met Mrs. Porter? I'm teaching her herbs." He gestured at the table of weeds women had already started chopping.

Lady Elsa was blond, like all the Reid family, and pleasantly rounded as a good cook should be. She waved at Verity from the other side of the table.

"Knowledge is power," she said cheerfully. "Rafe, do I have what you need or do you add secret ingredients?"

He sorted through the bundles. "These are fine. The carrots, onions, and turnips add most of the flavor. I always salted the broth because we never had enough vegetables to taste."

"Beans, you need," a short, rotund lady asserted, tucking her hat under her arm. "More savory and marjoram."

"You know herbs?" Verity asked, mostly out of curiosity, but also because she suspected anyone who might know poisons.

The woman glanced at her, frowned with what looked like surprise, shrugged and disappeared into the approaching mob of housekeepers.

"Do you know that woman?" Verity asked.

Both Lady Elsa and Rafe turned to watch her leave and shook their heads negatively.

Verity didn't trust her instinct to follow. Half the old women here wore black gowns. She was so far out of her depth here—fish out of water died, didn't they?

She refused to die until Miss Edgerton's killer was found. So she needed to dive into strange waters and learn to swim with everyone else.

Taking up a knife, she took a seat on the bench carried up from the chapel. She needed to stay off her foot anyway. She propped it on the trestle of the table, followed instructions, and learned to maim carrots before tossing them into a boiling pot of broth.

When the pot threatened to boil over, she almost related to the vegetable.

By late afternoon, the mist had cleared and the day grew warmer, giving her new hat a chance to dry. All the food had been consumed and "tasting" the apple juice had depleted a dozen jugs. The chimney sweep had created enough soot to blacken everyone in the village. So much for their lamp black.

Tired, discouraged, but admiring the amount of work completed in the kitchen, Verity went in search of Rafe so he could see the miracles the village ladies had wrought and thank them before they left. She found him on the top floor, holding an enormous timber in place while his soldier friend nailed a brace into the wall. Covered in grime, he looked jubilant—and exhausted.

She knew better than to remind him that he'd been shot and lost a lot of blood. The man was as stubborn as herself. Instead, she brought up a concern that had worried her for hours.

She waited until he'd climbed down from his ladder before whispering, "The woman in black skirts we didn't recognize hasn't returned. I want to check on the cottage."

He frowned. "You can't go back there on your own. We have people in place to watch."

She could go easily, without his permission, but she wouldn't have mentioned it if that was her intent. "It will only take a few minutes. People are starting to leave and it's hard to keep track. Everyone is black at this point, and you said we didn't have enough people to watch the gates."

He grimaced and yelled up at his partner, "Errand. Take a break, taste some apple juice." He followed her wearily, wiping at his face with an already filthy handkerchief.

In the kitchen, she showed him the newly working pump so he could wipe himself off and thank the women polishing the final surfaces.

After genuinely admiring the work accomplished, he strode toward the back door, accepting a mug of juice one of the women handed him. "We need to alert Henri or one of the other men we trust, tell them what we're doing."

"Henri's helping Patience haul barrels of cider back to the manor." She hobbled after him. She'd learned a lot about the town and manor inhabitants this day. "I've told Lady Elsa I'm running back to the cottage for a shawl. I don't want our culprit taking notice."

"Half the people in that kitchen had black on them," he noted.

"We can stop at the tavern and ask if anyone passed by clean going one way and dirty the other," she said brightly, hiding her disappointment. They hadn't really thought this through as they

175

ought. Well, at least she had him resting and taking liquids. Now, if she could only persuade him to put his feet up. . .

"Upton's deacon is an elderly chap eager to sit in the tavern and take notes of anyone passing. He knows everyone. We'll ask about your woman in black skirts. The captain has a deaf-mute helper sitting in the trees behind the cottage. Clever lad has a rope rigged to catch anyone coming and going from the manor path and a bell to sound an alarm, since he can't shout for help."

"I'm glad Mrs. Underhill's daughter could take Wolfie and Marmie for the day. I would never have thought of anyone poisoning innocent animals!" Of course, that was a bird-witted thing to say. The killer had poisoned a lady already.

Verity checked over her shoulder to see if anyone followed. She was more accomplished at slipping down shadowy city alleys than an open village street.

Rafe stopped at the tavern to check with Deacon Jones and his list of passersby. He pointed at one of the items on Jones's list and raised thunderous eyebrows. "Lady in black?"

"Only attended church once," the balding deacon said. "Never learnt her name, but she sat with that lout Clement. Heard the captain threw him out but don't know where he went."

"If it's the same person, she was at the inn earlier, telling Lady Elsa she needed beans and marjoram for the stew. I don't know where she went after that." Verity winced. Had she already failed? She didn't know how to behave outside her cellar walls and London alleys. "I assumed she was one of Lavender's sewing ladies."

"Nope, I know them all," Jones claimed. "If she don't go to church or the tavern, I won't know her. Could be Papist, I suppose."

"Well, if she's the person who stole my hat and shot Rafe, I'll snatch her bald." Guilt at her own failure had made her unreasonable.

Rafe dragged her back to the street. "You'll stay far away from her if she's in the habit of carrying a pistol."

Troubled by her outburst, Verity didn't argue. She never said horrible things like that. Or the old Faith hadn't. Did this new person she was becoming go about making threats on the basis of meager evidence? Irrational or not, it had felt *good* to express her fury after so many years of quiet inconspicuousness.

Her uncle wasn't here. She was allowed to speak her mind, wasn't she? If she still had one, leastways.

"If the thief can carry a pistol, why can't I?" she asked, waiting to see if Rafe would explode at her daring suggestion.

"Because they're unstable and dangerous and you're like to shoot off your good foot. If you want a weapon, I'll find a dirk you can carry. I'd prefer that you ran, but I can see you might be at a disadvantage in a race." He glanced down at her cane. "Although that's quite an adequate weapon if used properly."

They'd arrived at the cottage gate. She halted and stared up at him. He wasn't angry? Or calling her too clumsy? "You would teach me to use the cane?"

He shrugged. "Everyone should be able to defend themselves." He shoved open the gate they'd left unlocked to lure in their suspect and removed a knife from his boot.

"Do you smell smoke?" Verity whispered, letting him shield her. She had wanted him to rest for a few minutes. This was not restful.

He muttered under his breath and started for the side of the house. "Stay here."

"Alone? No, sir." She stayed a length behind, her cane clutched tightly. He ran faster—definitely the smell of smoke. A bell rang alarmingly in the distance.

"He's getting away," Rafe shouted, breaking into a gallop. "Fetch help."

And let her home burn? *Again*?

Shouting, "Help, help, fire!" Verity followed Rafe to the back, where the pump and pails were.

With his long legs, he was out the back gate, racing toward the frantically ringing bell, before she emerged into the garden. She prayed he caught the culprit, but she had to save her home. Leaning on her cane, she searched for the source of the smoke—so many flammable shrubs and brown flower stalks she should probably cut. . . What was burning?

Mrs. Holly's head abruptly bobbed above the hedge. Did she wear springs in her heels? The old lady flung more pails over the hedge. "Back step, dearie!"

Swinging around, Verity discovered smoke billowing from a pile of dead weeds and branches at the back door. Even as she watched, the embers flared into flame in a breeze and licked at the wood, bubbling the paint.

Terrified for Rafe, terrified for her cottage, Verity threw down her cane to pump water into pails. Limping, she lugged them to a fire that had grown in intensity while she pumped. She dumped both pails, sending up clouds of smoke and steam. The flames caught on new fuel.

Striding through the back gate, Mrs. Holly filled two more pails. "Been trying to watch, but I fell asleep. She coulda burned us all down!"

"She?" Verity took Mrs. Holly's pails and stumbled back to dump them on the fire while the old lady filled the empty ones. The elderly and the crippled did not make a good fire-fighting team.

"Stout old worm wearing a hat like yours," Mrs. Holly declared. "Thought it was you."

Her *hat*? She still wanted to snatch the thief bald, but she had her hands full.

The alarm bell had stopped clamoring, and a tall lad raced through the back gate. That must be Ned, the deaf mute. Did that mean they'd caught the culprit? His silence verified she couldn't ask.

While Verity pumped, Ned and Mrs. Holly carried. The stench was dreadful, the flames scorched the door but didn't spread. Verity kept an eye on the thatch, but the embers hadn't carried, thanks to good timing and good neighbors.

As they brought the fire under control, shouting voices had her praying for Rafe's safety. Wearily, she pumped a mug of water for Ned. The poor lad had been sitting in a tree while everyone else ate and drank. She hoped someone had at least fed him. He gulped the water, handed back the mug, and dashed back out the gate, no doubt to follow the shouts. She thought she heard Rafe's voice, but she couldn't make out the words.

She swallowed hard and told herself the sergeant could take care of himself. She offered Mrs. Holly a mug and indicated a garden bench. "Please, sit down. I owe you so much—"

Now that events had settled, tears seeped down her cheeks. She started shaking as she studied the scorched walls and door and saw how close they'd come to losing the cottage. Holding her elbows, she tried to steady herself. She could have lost this home too.

Why her? Was she being punished for surviving?

"Give me a minute to catch my breath, and I'll fetch a broom." Mrs. Holly settled her wide skirts on the bench and shook her head. Her salt-and-pepper hair straggled from its tight bun. "I never saw the like. I thought it would be good to have folks in the manor again, but not if this is the trouble they bring!"

"I don't think the manor folk killed Miss Edgerton. They hired Rafe to find the criminal." Verity wanted to look inside, but the blackened door was too hot to touch.

She needed to go in the front to fetch a broom, but she feared what she might see and lacked the energy to fight any longer. Using her cane, she dropped wearily to the bench beside Mrs. Holly, wishing for the earlier mist.

The shouting stopped. She'd heard no gunfire. What did she do now? Her safe cellar hadn't taught her how to deal with the real, frightening, world.

"Shovel in the tool shed, dear," Mrs. Holly suggested. "Dump the ashes on the burn pile." She nodded at the tall foliage concealing the far corner.

Burn pile. Rubbish had to be disposed of somehow. She should have explored the yard more.

Wearily, she pushed up, found the shovel in the cobwebbed shed, and had started digging up charred rubble when she heard voices approaching. She didn't think she'd be offering anyone refreshments yet, but she glanced up eagerly, hoping. . .

Rafe strode through the back gate, looking even more exhausted but triumphant—and carrying her lovely hat. "We have him! We've caught the b—" He cut himself off to stare at Verity. Only then did she realize she must look like a dumpy, broad-beamed Guy Fawkes figure with her scorched hem and soot-coated face. She leaned against the shovel and wished to disappear into the ground—but at least he was safe.

She didn't know how to express her relief. She eyed her hat, afraid to touch it for fear she'd ruin it with her filthy hands. It looked worse for wear. The lace might be salvageable. But his safety was far more important than a hat.

Studying her charred skirt, Rafe exclaimed in horror, "You could have gone up in flame! Sit down! Let me do that." He took her shovel and wrapped a burly arm around her shoulder, steering her gently, as if she were made of porcelain.

She was so shocked, she actually sat back down, hastily wiped her hands on her skirt, and clung to her once-lovely hat.

His two big companions entered through the open gate, distracting her more, but his words. . . She studied the hat and asked in puzzlement, "You caught *him*? I thought Mrs. Holly said it was a woman? Wearing my hat?" She had hoped they'd caught the poisoner.

"The scoundrel was wearing a woman's skirts and your bonnet," Rafe said in disgust, pumping water into mugs and passing them around.

She was too tired and shocked to ask more. "I hope you're hanging him tomorrow." Bitter, angry, grief-stricken, her runaway emotions worried her. She didn't want to appear weak. Men took advantage of weakness. But only anger prevented another outburst of tears.

"Hunt can't hang anyone." The French count leaned inside the shed and found a coal shovel. "He'll hold court tomorrow, then transport the prisoner to assizes."

Rafe used the shovel to finish her task. "I shouldn't have left you alone. A soldier gives chase. Old instincts die hard."

She nearly wept at his almost apology. He had no reason to apologize to *her*, not for making them safe again. She accepted a clean handkerchief from Sgt. Fletcher while Mrs. Holly scolded the men for not protecting a lady.

Verity was no lady. She ought to correct her and Rafe, but the niceties eluded her on this occasion. "It's over then? We're safe? Who is he?" And why didn't she feel safe?

"Clement, the old sot Hunt turned off." Arnaud carted a shovelful of ashes to the burn corner, then doused them with a pail of water.

"He claims he's innocent, and we only have a deaf mute as witness," Rafe explained. "But the hat alone makes him a thief. Mrs. Holly, you didn't see him enter the yard, did you?"

"I did, but I fell asleep, dear," she said sadly. "I just thought he was Mrs. Porter."

Verity thought she ought to object to this description, but she'd always known she was sturdy and unfeminine.

"Rafe caught him running up the path." Fletch dumped water on uncovered embers by the door, creating a cloud of smoke that had everyone coughing. "Mrs. Holly as witness, and the hat as evidence ought to be enough."

"Won't be for Hunt, not for murder, leastways. Have you been inside yet?" Arnaud carried off the final clump of wet ash, leaving a puddle of dirty water on the step.

"Stay there," Rafe ordered when Verity started to stand. "Let me go first."

"I am not a dog to be told to stay." Anger carrying her on, Verity stood and limped past all the big men except Rafe, who blocked her path. She ached in every bone of her body, but for now, this was her home. She had to see. "Is the door still hot?"

Rafe used a rake handle to push at the charred wood. "At least stay behind me," he ordered.

Since he was twice her size, she had no choice.

The door fell apart at his thrust. Cursing, he shoved the remains aside.

Verity peered under his arm. Clement had ransacked the place. Again.

TWENTY-EIGHT: RAFE

REFUSING TO LET THE FOOL WOMAN INSIDE THE COTTAGE, RAFE forced Verity to accept a ride up to the manor in Henri's cart, clutching her mutilated black hat. She was dead on her—broken—feet and still thought she could stay and clean up the doorless cottage.

She looked so very unhappy. . . He shouldn't let a slip of a woman get under his skin like that, especially one who wasn't telling him all the truth.

He paid one of the village's unemployed ex-soldiers to guard the cottage, then walked up to the manor. He should probably stop and check on the animals, but he couldn't just send a prisoner to Captain Huntley without following up with a report.

The manor ladies took Verity under their wings and led her away, leaving Rafe with the gentlemen and his jumbled thoughts.

"The prisoner claims he's innocent, that he was just out fishing to put food on the table. He even had string and a hook in his skirt pocket." Hunt set a glass of brandy on the table beside Rafe. "I've heard about men who dress in women's clothes, but I've never known one to go fishing in them. Can't be easy."

Since the manor's cook had been at the inn all day, the staff had only put together a cold collation. Rafe's fault. Everyone had been helping him achieve his fool dream. At what cost?

"Lousy fisherman if he couldn't catch anything in that stream," Rafe replied grumpily, before tearing into the beef sandwich. "Maybe stolen hats put the fish off."

"Can't hang anyone for being a bad fisherman," Hunt pointed out. "There might be laws about dressing badly, but I'm not inclined to enforce them. How do I punish a man who steals a lady's hat?"

"He had lamp black on his hands." The curate didn't take a brandy but helped himself to a sandwich. "He was in the cottage."

"That might count as evidence for ransacking," Hunt agreed, "if we don't tell the judge everyone in town was covered in soot."

"Can Ned write a statement about what he saw?" Rafe knew he was in well over his head but he desperately looked for ways to keep the drunken sot locked up. He didn't believe Verity could take much more, and he harbored a strong urge to keep her where he could find her. He didn't try to sort that out.

"Ned can write. I'll have him do that." Hunt paced the large study.

Good thing there wasn't any carpet, Rafe thought, or it would have a path in it by now. "I'd have people write up statements that Clement wasn't anywhere near the inn, except if he was wearing skirts, then he may have been the lady in black."

Lt. Jack strode in, his usually genial expression twisted in anger. "The dastard knifed the mattresses and sofas. I'd say he didn't even know about the painting. One doesn't hide artwork in sofas! You may as well have left the place to burn. Mrs. Porter can't move back in."

"She'll take exception to that," Rafe said gloomily. "She has Lavender looking for old clothes she can wear to clean in. We'd have to refuse to hang a new door, and then she'd no doubt hire someone on her own."

"Thank all that is holy that you had the sense to bring the

books to the library." Upton sipped water to wash down his bread. "And that you have Clement locked up so he can't come here looking for them. Minerva is searching the books more thoroughly, hoping to find something we've missed, but if he was tearing up mattresses, it's not books he's looking for either."

"Does it strike anyone as odd that this medieval void in the middle of nowhere has so damned many books?" Hunt asked, drinking his brandy as he paced. "Oswald says a cart arrived today with a load of crates labeled *books*, addressed to your Mrs. Porter."

Verity had mentioned shipping books. He probably ought to have a look at them. "There's your treasure," Rafe said wearily, standing. "Jewels are useless. Books are far more precious."

They all swung to stare at him.

He shrugged. "That's obvious, isn't it? The books in the library tell us the inn belongs to the estate, not the bank. The ones in the teacher's library tell us what plants are good to eat and which ones to avoid. Books will teach the children how to do mathematics and count their coins so they don't get cheated. Books hold secrets that can open a path to success. The earl's treasure is his library."

Hunt topped off his brandy. "Smart man. We want to keep you around. Take the snifter up to bed and get some sleep. Maybe in the morning you can persuade our prisoner to tell us what he's looking for."

Rafe was tempted. He was very tempted. But he wasn't just rambling when he said books held secrets. He wanted to see the library Verity had shipped. She hadn't brought a maid or clothes but she had somehow saved books from the fire that had destroyed her wardrobe? He hadn't given that puzzle much consideration until now.

The curate followed him out. "Did my mother show you to one of the guestrooms?"

"She did. I don't want to sleep on her clean sheets until I take a dive in the river and see if I can rescue some clean clothes. Mrs.

185

Porter will want fresh garments in the morning, so I need to gather those too." Aiming for a back door, he left the brandy snifter outside the infirmary. He could hear an infant wailing in the apartment he knew the physician and her steward husband occupied.

Someday, he'd like to have wee ones of his own. Maybe when he was old and gray.

"Lavender will provide for Mrs. Porter. The manor has a bathtub with plumbing. I can show you to it." The smaller curate matched him step for step.

"Does Mr. Oswald live above his mercantile?" Rafe nodded at the young footman hurrying to unlock the garden door and offer them a lantern.

"He does." Upton took the lantern and followed him out, apparently determined to dog Rafe's steps. "The books should be safe with him. Henri can haul them up to the manor in the morning. Do you really think they're important?"

"We just caught a man wearing skirts who tried to burn down a cottage and may have murdered a teacher. I don't know what's important any longer." And he didn't. He was acting on an instinct that had saved his life more than once. This might not be war, but it was starting to feel like it.

"Oswald will most likely be at the tavern at this hour. I'll ask him to let us in the store." Accepting Rafe's explanation, the curate followed him down the drive, admiring the chilly autumn night. "I hope there aren't many books. I don't think there are many places left to store them."

"The inn," Rafe said grumpily. "It would be easy enough to start a library at the inn, once it's not leaking."

"One everyone could share?" Paul asked with interest.

"That would be up to the lady, wouldn't it?" Rafe considered the notion while the curate ran into the tavern to talk to old Mr. Oswald.

If Verity wished to be a teacher, she'd need books for the children.

He was getting ahead of himself. He had a murder to solve first.

The curate emerged from the tavern with a ring of keys and proceeded down the empty street. "After today's activities, I'm amazed everyone isn't tucked into bed. That was an astounding amount of work accomplished in one day."

"I haven't had a moment free to appreciate it," Rafe admitted gruffly. "Chasing after crooks in skirts and rescuing ladies from ruined houses takes time. I am more than grateful for all the assistance."

"I think folks are eager to see the village come to life again. Too many young people had to leave to earn a living. They don't like the low wages and long hours in the factories, but with all the imports, farming doesn't pay. No one is happy with the situation. Having an inn offers a glimmer of hope that we might have customers for our local businesses and new ones might find us again. Sullivan's hardware would be an excellent start. We could use a tailor and a shoemaker and a flour mill, perhaps even one of those spinning and weaving factories now that all the wool goes to them." He twisted the key in the mercantile's lock and opened the door.

Three crates sat against the counter. Paul pulled a tool off his belt and pried open the top of the first crate. "I feel like a criminal."

"Well, if I'm what passes as the law around here, you're safe." Rafe opened the lantern so the light fell on the crate contents.

Books, just as she'd said, expensive, leather-bound books with gold writing and gilded edges. He left the curate to pick one out and open it.

"A hand-illustrated geography," Upton said in whispered awe. "A valuable teaching tool." Eagerly, he set that one down and reached for another. "Isaac Newton's *Optics*! Minerva will be in alt."

Relieved that the books were educational volumes, Rafe picked up the geography.

Inside, a printed bookplate ornamented with scallop shells and a ship declared the book belonged to the library of Milton Palmer. Verity must have acquired it from a second-hand store. Or perhaps she really was married, and this was her maiden name.

Intrigued, he opened another crate and examined those volumes.

Every one of them had the same bookplate.

SATURDAY

TWENTY-NINE: VERITY

HAVING SLEPT RESTLESSLY IN HER MANOR GUESTROOM, VERITY ROSE to an overcast Saturday, which didn't improve her mood. Even the lovely morning gown Lavender had hastily hemmed didn't raise her spirits. Her few garments in the cottage had to be laundered to remove the smoke. She needed to pack her bags and move—again.

She'd ruined her only good pair of boots fighting the fire.

She had money to buy more, she tried telling herself as she descended the marble stairs illuminated by lovely new gas lights. Things could be worse. All she had to do was find a new life and home.

Downstairs, after picking at toast and tea, she attended the interrogation led by Captain Huntley. Studying the weeping, protesting Clement, she concluded she couldn't snatch the tosspot bald. He was almost there already.

Where had this chubby, ugly little man obtained a woman's skirts? And why? Had he really thought to pass himself off as her? Did he have knowledge of herbs and poisons?

A pity they couldn't prove he'd set the fire meant to destroy Miss Edgerton's home. Mrs. Holly had seen him in the yard but hadn't seen him set a fire.

Verity supposed she was inclined to believe his guilt because he reminded her of her uncle's mean coachman, the one who had let a horse run over her foot. She hadn't known the man—she wasn't allowed to ride in the carriage, after all. But all coachmen in their greatcoats and tall hats sitting way above her appeared short and lumpy. None wore women's skirts that she was aware.

The painting might arouse her suspicion, but her uncle's coach was old, plain black, and looked nothing like the fancy one Miss Edgerton had sketched. And the painted coachman looked like every other shadowy figure she'd ever seen in a driver's seat. She didn't think there was any connection beyond her own ugly thoughts. She wanted someone, anyone, to blame.

Not knowing what else to do after the interrogation ended, she joined the sewing ladies in the manor's gallery to pick the lace off her once-beautiful black hat.

One thing of which she was certain, after watching Hunt's interview, the balding old man who'd stolen her hat was *not* the lady in black who had suggested marjoram for the stew.

She supposed old ladies in black were fairly common. Most women seemed to outlive their men. It was just odd that no one could name the one she'd seen. Everyone in the village knew one another. Where was this one staying? And was she the one Deacon Jones had reported passing the tavern or had that been Clement? Could there have been two people in black at the cottage?

She wanted to ask where Rafe was, but she didn't know who to ask and wasn't certain it was something a lady might do. He was most likely glad to be rid of her. He had no reason to ask after her when she was surrounded by servants and the comforts of the manor.

Well, actually, her father's much newer, better constructed, and well-furnished home had been far more comfortable than this drafty castle with its rattling windows and ancient, threadbare draperies and counterpanes, but she was in no position to complain.

It would be lovely to have a nice female friend to share her fears with. It wasn't as if she'd ever had close friends, just a few young people her age who had visited with their mothers—before her father died. After that, she'd been in mourning, then forced to give up any form of society when her mother became ill. She was even lonelier now, surrounded by people, than she had been when surrounded only by books.

Everyone was so busy. . . She didn't want to take them away from their tasks, especially after they had spent yesterday cleaning the inn.

That didn't seem to bother anyone else. While she helped picked the black lace from her old hat, the pair of construction workers—the Blackwells—who Rafe had hired to help with the inn, distracted Lavender with questions about some quirk of the tower. She and Sofia ran off to make decisions about the incipient perfumery.

Minerva, the curate's fiancée, came in a few minutes later to divert her from lace picking. Bored, Verity gladly followed her into the L-shaped library, which apparently took up nearly a quarter of the manor's main floor. She had to attempt not to goggle at the seemingly endless walls of books just begging to be perused.

Miss Edgerton's lawyer and the furniture dealers were studying the books from the cottage that Rafe had carried to the manor for safekeeping. Suddenly uncertain, Verity hung back. She didn't know that Miss Edgerton would wish her drawings made public.

"These drawings are works of art," the lady—Mrs. Prescott?—declared, flipping the pages of one of the portfolios. "They could be very valuable."

Verity had to draw closer to see which sketches she perused—the herbal, with all the sketches of dangerous plants as well as useful ones. The books weren't hers. She wanted to keep them, but if they cost a lot, she couldn't afford to pay the heirs what the Prescotts could.

So why had they sought her out?

"Do you believe Miss Edgerton drew these?" Mr. Culliver, the solicitor, asked, studying another open book over the top of his spectacles. When she didn't immediately answer, he glanced up. "Are they part of the estate or might they belong to someone else?"

"Oh." Verity hadn't given it a second thought. She took the portfolio he pushed toward her. "Her former students visited and often left sketches, I believe. Some of the older ones—" she pulled out a yellowed, fading picture labeled hemlock, "—may have been drawn by her mother or grandmother. I've not had time to study all of them, but I did notice occasional dates." She pointed at tiny numbers in the corner that seemed to indicate 1790.

"They would have to be published as a collection, then." Mr. Prescott flipped back a few pages in his portfolio. A tall man of middling age, in a tailed frockcoat and starched neckcloth, he bore the air of a respectable gentleman. "Herbs From Garden Cottage, by the Edgerton ladies."

Verity didn't know why she was uneasy about the watercolors and sketches leaving the cottage. Perhaps it was just the fear of someone else being poisoned using information they might garner from the drawings. It didn't seem right, somehow. But how could she possibly express her concern? She was not the heir.

Minerva, ever the colonel's daughter and stern librarian, said what Verity lacked the words for. "Not all those sketches should be published. I daresay the ladies drew them for their own use, to pass on to the cottage's heirs. They include the knowledge of poisonous plants that should not fall into the hands of scoundrels, as we have so recently learned."

"But even poisonous herbs have valuable qualities," Mrs. Prescott argued. "The hemlock Dorian is looking at can be used for breathing difficulties, especially in children. You need only ask your apothecary. She will tell you."

Another woman who understood the use of herbs. Verity forced herself to think instead of quiver. The well-dressed lady was short enough to have been the lady in black, but certainly not old enough. That didn't make her any less likely to have been Miss Edgerton's visitor that fatal day. Rafe had already ascertained the Prescotts had been in residence.

"Might we call in Dr. Walker and ask her opinion?" Verity asked, stepping out of the shadows she preferred even though she really had no say in any of this.

Mr. Prescott waved a dismissive hand. "What an apothecary has to say is neither here nor there. These are valuable drawings. We would like to purchase them. I don't see that Mrs. Porter," he bowed at her, "has any say in the matter."

"Until we hear from the heirs, none of us have any say in the matter," the solicitor reminded them.

The Prescotts seemed very determined to have the drawings. Were the *drawings* what the thief had sought? The killer?

Bringing the books here may have been worse than leaving them in the cottage. Verity cast a worried look at Minerva. The petite librarian nodded curtly back, donned her spectacles, and began gathering up the portfolios. "If these are valuable, we shall keep them in the vault until we hear from the heirs." Without apology, she carried off the sketches.

"Well, I never. . ." Mrs. Prescott exclaimed. Her charming smile vanished, and a frown formed over her delicate nose.

"Miss Edgerton was poisoned with one of those herbs," Verity reminded her, daring to be assertive. "It is very hard for us to consider those pages falling into the hands of someone who might do harm." She turned to Mr. Culliver. "Please, let the heirs know the danger, as well as the value, if you would? It is the least we can do."

Before the Prescotts could argue further, Verity departed, just as Minerva had. Faith had never had good reason to develop a backbone. Perhaps Verity could learn from others how to strengthen it.

Although the confrontation left her wishing she was back at the cottage. If Miss Edgerton's sketches were valuable, should

195

they have shown Mr. Culliver the horrible painting of the coach? It seemed so very personal. . . But if Miss Edgerton hadn't specified it belonged to Verity, then it probably belonged to the heirs too. She should have asked Minerva. If the librarian wasn't always so busy, Verity would like to think of her as a friend someday.

Lavender had returned to the gallery and finished removing the lace from the crushed widow's hat. She was measuring it with her fingers when Verity entered.

"This lace will go splendidly with the bonnet Henri brought in the other day, the one that suits your Sunday gown." She produced a straw hat with a high crown and long brim. "It's a French style! With the black lace and some primrose-dyed silk flowers, it will be perfect on you!"

Verity widened her eyes and touched the tightly-bound, beautiful cream straw. She'd never owned anything half so stylish. "Lace and a ribbon? As an adornment, not a veil?"

"Exactly. And then there will even be lace left to attach to a fichu for your Sunday gown. You will look *très élégant!*" Lavender slipped the bonnet over Verity's chignon and tightened the ribbons, then gestured at her cheval mirror. "Look for yourself!"

The sight of the splendid bonnet with the new-to-her, high-waisted, tea-colored morning gown finally stirred Verity's feminine vanity.

She wasn't *elegant* she reminded herself. She had all the grace of a milkmaid. Or the cow. But Lavender looked so eager. . . And Verity loved the new garments, which was all that mattered, she decided. Backbones didn't require elegance. And the high waist did look splendid on her stumpy figure. "I will take anything and everything you find suitable. I trust your judgment more than mine. I shall need shoes for all this finery. I don't suppose Mr. Lavigne can find shoes?"

"I'd rather he found a shoemaker," Lavender replied, a trifle grimly. "But I shall ask."

"I really must go back and sort out the cottage to see what

can be salvaged. I cannot keep wearing these poor boots." As much as Verity enjoyed the manor inhabitants, she longed for her own place. And poor Mrs. Underhill and Marmie needed a home as well. Perhaps the destruction wasn't as bad as she remembered?

Verity borrowed a shawl to go into the brisk wind. She didn't need Rafe to escort her. She'd been walking around London on her own for years. Well, she'd had a footman for the bank visits, but this was broad daylight, and she carried nothing valuable. An escort was silly. Admittedly, she'd felt brave in Rafe's company, but he had the inn now. He didn't need her.

Reminded of footmen. . . She glanced toward the stable and the new carriage. She hadn't seen the manor's coachman yesterday. She didn't see him now. She ought to ask after him, though, just to settle her mind. He was much too tall to be the usual sort of coachman, like in the painting. And the possibility of lazy Luther following her here was ludicrous. Besides, footmen did not drive carriages. Still, she should ask when she had a chance.

Not brave enough yet to test a lonely walking path, she took the longer public drive down to the road. She had to pass the inn. . . and couldn't resist stopping to admire the newly thatched roof. Workers were still finishing the older section over the lobby entrance.

Rafe was in the yard, carting a familiar-looking crate. *Could that be?* Lifting her hem and swinging her cane, she hurried excitedly into the trampled yard. "Are those my books?"

"Are you Mrs. Milton Palmer?" he asked coldly, not stopping to wait for her.

Struck by his coldness, she froze with horror as she realized he'd said her father's name. She followed him. "You opened them? You had no right to open those crates!"

"Probably not. But you can't keep them in a doorless cottage, and I thought I'd be helpful, more fool me." He carried the heavy crate through the lobby to the newly repaired stairs.

"Put those books down right now," she ordered, surprising

even herself. "You are not a mule and you will make your arm worse."

She probably ought to kick him, but he'd been too good to her, and she'd lied to him in return. He had every right to be miffed.

So did she. Faith might have cringed, but the new Verity was allowed to be angry at having her privacy intruded upon. She put her hands on her broad hips in her lovely new gown and glared at him.

He set the crate on the sturdy guest counter and glared back. "Where do you want them, then? The manor, Mrs. Palmer?"

"I am *not* Mrs. Palmer. And the books need to be where children can read them. And me. Books are meant to be read. And if I can't have them in the cottage. . ." She stopped and gave it some thought. "Why can't I have them in the cottage? You caught the thief. It only needs a door."

"Because there are no beds and no furniture and it is not safe. I'm moving into the inn. I've hired a few people to sew and stuff new mattresses for a few of the guest rooms. Upton is repairing bed frames. If the heirs want to sell the cottage, I don't want to waste time and coin on it."

He acted so cold. . . Her newly revived spirits dropped.

What he said made sense. She simply didn't want to give up dreams of her own home.

She sat down on one of the benches that hadn't been returned to the church yet and, fighting tears, studied her scorched boots. She was so very tired of being alone. To have still another home ripped from under her. . . She didn't have the strength to do it again. "Don't empty the crates," she said miserably. "I'll ask Captain Huntley if there is another cottage I might use."

No place would be as lovely as Miss Edgerton's, but then, she supposed it wasn't lovely any more. Why had that rotten little man ruined everything?

"I'd let you and Mrs. Underhill stay at the inn until you get sorted, but I like to know who my guests are." He left the books but started for the stairs again.

"I'm dead, remember?" she called, wiping away tears as her anger returned.

"Mrs. Palmer is dead?" he shouted derisively from the next floor.

Obstinate idiot of a man. Who did he think she was, anyway? Well, she'd rather like to know that too. She didn't *feel* like meek Faith Palmer any longer. She was too angry. "Yes," she shouted, pushing up from the bench with her cane. "And so is her husband. I did *not* steal those books."

Well, that might be a lie, but it wasn't as if her uncle noticed their absence. Her idea of the law was a little loose.

Rafe returned to the stairs and glowered down at her. "Did you just shout at me?"

Taken aback, she froze as the familiar timidity raised its ugly head. Then she remembered this was Rafe, not her uncle, and he could not throw her out of a home she did not have. She shouted back, "You shouted first! I can shout if I want to."

"Ladies don't shout! Or was that all pretense too? Don't tell me you were their maid and the Palmers left their library to you." He wasn't shouting any more, just glaring.

She blinked in surprise. She had no idea if ladies shouted and didn't care. But a *maid*? "Why would I say any such rubbish?"

He waited.

She wanted a home. She didn't want to leave Gravesyde. If she wasn't sneaky, invisible Faith anymore, then who did she want to be? Someone who got angry and shouted? That wasn't working so well. She could stomp her foot or beat the big oaf with her cane, but Verity Porter wasn't stupid. Verity Porter could buy lovely straw hats and find her own way. . . with help.

Could she also be someone who trusted those who helped them? Which meant no more lying and sneaking. Which also meant she had to tell the truth, all of it.

Terrified, she clutched her elbows for strength. "If I tell you, I'm endangering your life as well as my own."

That was a trifle dramatic. Her uncle had no reason to kill her, just throw her in gaol. That might kill *her* but wouldn't hurt Rafe. So, it took time to undo a lying habit.

"All the more reason to tell me," he declared. "At least then I'll know who or what to look out for."

She shook her head vehemently. "No, you won't. Faith Palmer is *dead*. Verity Porter does not exist except as *me*, standing right in front of you. How do you protect a ghost?"

There, she'd given him her name, for what little it was worth. *Faith* had been a ghost for years.

THIRTY: RAFE

A GHOST, *DAMN*. RAFE HAD NEVER BEEN A DUPE FOR WOMEN—WELL, maybe the first time or two they'd sobbed until he gave them money and they'd disappeared. But whoever in hell the woman was in his lobby wasn't. . . lost and forlorn any more, but scared and just a wee bit angry. That clenched jaw looked good on whoever in hell she was, as if she'd take a battleax to his head but politely refrained.

This was no delicate lady playing on his sympathies.

He'd lived with her this past week. She hadn't taken his money or beat him with her cane for his presumptuousness. The fool woman had tried to make him comfortable, even attempted to mend him— She was furious with him for taking her books and still tried to stop him from hurting his arm! She'd been nothing but helpful, in her quiet, naïve, stubborn way.

And no longer wearing ugly widow's weeds, she turned out to be adorable in a perky bonnet and high-waisted gown. He ought to smack his head against a wall and be done.

Grudgingly, he ordered, "Come upstairs and tell me which rooms you think worth furnishing." He didn't know what else to do with a terrified female trying to be brave.

Was she saying Faith Palmer and Verity Porter were both her?

Except Faith was dead. He could make no sense of it. But inheriting her *parents'* library might be logical.

Did this mean she wasn't a widow? That ought to send him into a panic. Widows knew what they were about in the bedroom. Virgins required marriage. He didn't need complications, but he'd given up any expectations with this female, right?

"Come to the cottage and tell me if anything is worth saving," she countered, just to prove his point. "I need my clothes. And I want Marmie back."

The kitten, he could handle. "I have him patrolling the kitchen for mice. Don't worry, the doors are shut, and he has food and water. I just let him out for a roam a bit ago. Wolfie is patrolling the yard. Choose a room, and we'll haul your clothes back here."

"I don't want that little worm to drive me from my home!" she argued. "I can sleep on the floor. I want to learn herbs and vegetables and how to cook. I want my own home!"

That was the end of enough. "The cottage is not your home! You can't fix up a place you may lose next week."

He clattered down the stairs. He'd toss her clothes in her bag and carry it here. He already had her cat and books. True, he'd miss that garden. . . "If the worm left a basket or two, I'll carry the pantry items here," he decided. "We bought most of them."

She'd bought most of them, with her account at the mercantile. She wasn't poor, just. . . afraid? And it was his duty to protect, even if the obstinate female objected.

She cast him a sideways look and instead of marching back out the door, she headed for the kitchen. Rafe rolled his eyes and followed her. Why was he even trying? He'd never understand the weaker sex. They all seemed to think they were generals.

She opened the kitchen door and the marmalade kitten came running, practically climbing up her skirt. She lifted it into her arms and cooed over it, stroking its tiny head until it purred. "Let's go see what our house looks like, shall we?"

And carrying the kitten, she glared at Rafe as if he were the thief, and set out for the street.

"So, I should keep calling you Verity, even if you're someone else?" he asked conversationally as he surrendered and followed her through the village, waving to people they were coming to know.

"Yes, please." She didn't explain further.

The woman would make him utterly mad.

He hadn't bothered locking the front gate last night. It wasn't as if there was anything left to protect. He shoved it open for her and led the way into the cottage.

Her gasp of dismay nearly broke his heart. He told himself to toughen up. "I told you so."

The neat satin sofas had been ripped down the middle, their insides scattered across the room. The cottage wouldn't need a chimney cleaner after the crazed thief had run a perfectly good broom up it and strewn soot everywhere. Rafe hadn't thought there'd be anything left in the fireplace after the last time.

The bookcase had been turned over and the walls broken into. Fortunately, the intruder must have decided ripping the legs off the wooden chairs would accomplish nothing, so they'd been left whole.

"I can fetch your clothes," he suggested. "You really don't want to see what he's done up there. He must have started as soon as we left yesterday."

Or when the woman in black had passed by the tavern?

The deacon couldn't have expected her to be a thief, but wouldn't he have noticed if it had been Clement in skirts? Ned had seen no one taking the footpath from the manor, but he didn't have eyes in the back of his head. No one could have predicted anyone risking the rocky terrain on the far side of the hill as Clement had when he'd tried to escape.

Perhaps there had been two people? One who traipsed from the inn past the tavern, and Clement sneaking around the far side of the hill from the direction of the highway?

The fact that they'd actually caught Clement ought to be enough, but Rafe regretted it hadn't been in time to prevent this destruction. They'd been after evidence of a thief and possible killer, not trying to stop one. He needed more manpower for that.

Verity's eyes glistened, but she stuck out that determined jaw of hers, cuddled her kitten, and marched into the kitchen. The table and chairs were still good. What remained of the pantry contents were flung everywhere. It looked as if the bastard had even tried digging into the flour, although that was beyond foolish or just plain mean. Flour mixed with soot on all the surfaces.

Wordlessly, checking to be certain the back gate was closed, she let the kitten down, then picked up a laundry basket, and undaunted by his warnings, started up the stairs.

She stalked past the ripped mattresses and floorboards and began folding Mrs. Underhill's clothes into the basket first.

"At least I didn't leave my new shirts here." With a sigh, Rafe folded quilts and sheets. Apparently Clement's knife arm had grown tired by the time he climbed to the loft.

"Leave those there," she ordered. "I will sleep on the floor until I find someone to sew a new mattress. But Mrs. Underhill may need her clothes. I can't expect her to sleep in this."

Rafe thought pounding his head against hard objects might become his new pastime.

"Do you believe that sot poisoned your governess?" he asked bluntly. He'd been tossing that notion around since he'd caught Clement and simply couldn't see it.

That stopped her madness momentarily. She set down the garment she was folding to stare at him. "I thought we assumed the thief is also the killer?"

"You heard him this morning. He still claims he was out fishing, got wet, and put on his wife's skirt to go home."

"Why would he be walking around with his wife's skirt and where is home? Didn't the captain throw him off the estate?" In the dim light from the garret window, she presented an ethereal figure of tan and cream against the dust motes.

If she smiled at him, he'd probably roll over and ask her to rub his belly. Good thing she wasn't smiling. He needed to reclaim his sanity. "He claims his wife has a place down the road by the river, which would explain how he got past Ned. Upton is asking around. The area is littered with abandoned hovels anyone could move into without being noticed."

"You think the killer is still loose?" she asked cautiously. "And Clement was simply hired to hunt for those papers?"

"That's one theory, yes."

"The woman in black and Mrs. Prescott both know herbs. The woman was seen walking toward the cottage yesterday. I saw her plainly. I'm quite certain she wasn't Clement in skirts. And Mrs. Prescott wants to buy sketches of poisonous plants." She sat down on the window seat. "It's possible they are seeking Miss Edgerton's drawings and not the hidden painting and we've practically put the portfolios in their hands."

"You can't stay here," he said as gently as he could. "They tried to burn the cottage."

She nodded reluctantly. "You have an inn to build. I can't sit idle. I'll do what I can to clean up here. The heirs shouldn't be left with a smelly mess. Tonight—I don't know. I'll think on it."

Rafe kneaded his eyes, shook his head to clear the cobwebs, and partially conceded. "We need what food is left in the larder and the garden. I'll help clean the kitchen, come and go as needed, set Wolfie to guard the yard."

"And watch out for strangers," she agreed with a sigh. "It's not as if I can mend furniture. I wish I knew how to catch a killer. I hate to see the cottage burn if we leave it unprotected."

Devil take it, he should probably be setting guards around the perimeter. How much was the captain willing to pay to protect a cottage that didn't belong to the estate?

"What if. . . ?" She stared down at the front yard while pondering.

Rafe waited. It wasn't as if he had any idea what to do beyond guard the premises. He needed a general to give him orders. There was a sad lack of generals in Gravesyde. Well, there were the women, as previously noted. He didn't know about taking orders from women who had never seen combat.

"Comte Lavigne is an artist, isn't he? Do you think, if I paid him, he might duplicate the coach painting? I'd ask for a few of the plant sketches, too, but I cannot fathom how they are worth killing over, so don't know which to copy."

"Arnaud?" Rafe wouldn't approach the nobility in a thousand years. "We almost got the cottage burned with our last trap. Are you planning another so you can get yourself *killed*?"

He couldn't see much of her expression in the loft's shadows, but he thought he heard desperation in her reply. "What if we hung the duplicate in your inn where everyone could see it?"

THIRTY-ONE: PAUL

CARRYING NEWLY-REPAIRED BEDFRAMES INTO THE CROWDED INN lobby, Paul leaned them against the guest desk. For having no guests, the inn was a hive of activity this afternoon. He accepted the mug Rafe handed him, sipped, and wrinkled his nose. "What is this?"

"I'm experimenting with the raw apple juice and some of the manor's smuggled brandy and a few spices. Is it too strong?" Rafe gestured at the pitcher on a shelf behind the desk.

"Not more than punch, I suppose. What are we doing?" Paul gestured to indicate the company.

Thea, the ghost-talking heiress, and Arnaud, impoverished artist and French nobility, had deigned to leave the manor to study the monstrous painting of a murder and the crumbling lobby walls. Such horror would make a dreadful adornment for a welcoming inn.

Sitting on a bench, Verity anxiously kept an eye on the artwork, while trying to repair an old quilt.

"We are looking to have the inn burned down," Rafe replied gruffly, before picking up the bedframes and lugging them upstairs.

"Not alarming at all," Paul said aloud to no one in particular.

"The painting, it is meant to be a message." Amazingly, Arnaud picked up the dangling threads of Rafe's non-conversation. "We should make many copies, so the arsonist will understand that burning the one will not help. The copies do not need to be this size. I am not fond of these—" He wrinkled his nose. "—watercolors, but they are fast."

Until recently, the French artist had barely spoken for himself and had seldom left the manor. Since uncovering the tower and its horde of doubloons, Arnaud had been more forthcoming. The lovely—haunted—woman at his side might have a bit to do with that. At least she didn't appear to be seeing ghosts in the inn. Yet.

"We will keep the original work in the vault. I'd like to frame the copy we hang here." Dorothea Talbot was the reason the Prescotts were at the manor, acquiring medieval furniture. She had an eye for interior design. "The manor attic has dozens of frames. We could hang copies all over town. I'd like to have a small one to send to friends in London. Perhaps they might recognize the carriage."

They had decided the thief was after the painting? Well, it was one of many possibilities, Paul supposed. Of course, if Clement was the thief, they'd prove nothing.

He gathered they'd decided Clement wasn't a killer. Having more than one villain roaming the street. . . was a possibility, sadly.

"If that is my father in the painting, it is ten years old. Do people keep carriages that long?" Verity asked.

"Depends on how wealthy they are. People who know horse-flesh might recognize the livestock." Arnaud tucked the painting into its portfolio again. "I do not think I have to be as careful with the details as Miss Edgerton. This will not be a showpiece but more of the caricature, as you would see in London printing offices. We might label it, if you wish—*Do you recognize this carriage?*"

Rafe clattered back down the steps in time to hear this last. "I like that idea. Glad to hear some sense around here. We could add a reward—identify the killer for ten pounds."

"A hundred," Verity corrected grimly. "I will gladly go hungry for a year if your work brings him to justice. Except there are two people in the painting—the one who pushes and the one who drives. Either might be the person who killed Miss Edgerton."

Paul finished his punch and grimaced. "I had not thought of that, but it makes a terrible sense somehow. But why now?"

Visibly trembling, Verity set down her sewing and stood. "Because that is my father in the painting. I cannot make any more sense of it than that." She pushed past Rafe and ran upstairs.

Thea and Arnaud turned to the former sergeant, who glanced worriedly up the stairs but lingered to explain. "Her father died when she was young. She'd been told he'd been robbed, not that he was deliberately murdered. And we have no idea how Miss Edgerton knew anything, except she was Verity's governess at the time. And we really don't know that this has anything to do with Miss Edgerton's death, since she dealt in questionable activities and no one was aware that Verity was coming here. But the timing is not fortuitous."

"As magistrate, Hunt knows this, doesn't he?" Paul asked.

"I gave Hunt her father's name this morning. He is asking the solicitors to look into the incident. The dowagers insist on writing their families to see if anyone recalls the details. It's been ten years, so chances aren't good." Rafe ran back up the stairs after Verity.

"I thought we had Miss Edgerton's killer locked in the crypt?" Thea asked, frowning. "Are we looking for more?"

"We don't know he's our killer without proof. The odd thing is. . ." Paul didn't know how much of this he was allowed to tell, but it seemed important. He and Minerva had kept Verity's confidences until now, but no one had sworn them to secrecy. "Verity swears no one knows she is alive. A killer would have no reason to follow her here. Yet that painting ties her father to the governess."

"So the painting is curious but we are no longer looking for this killer? Am I wasting my time?" Arnaud glanced at the portfolio he held.

"We can't know if the painting is connected without trying. Clement stays locked up while Hunt sees his mother off to America. Of course, if we can't prove Clement is a killer or arsonist. . . Well, I suppose we cannot condemn him for running in skirts." Paul was still trying to find the wife the prisoner claimed to have. Clement refused to say where he'd left her and none of Paul's parishioners recognized their meager description.

"Upton, do you know how to make shutters?" Rafe called from upstairs.

"Keep this up, and I'll have to hire an assistant," Paul called back. "Will the maintenance budget cover that?"

"If you find an assistant, ask Walker." Rafe banged down the stairs again. At the bottom, he gestured upstairs and kept his voice low. "I'm afraid she'll flee. Can we keep her busy? She says the bedrooms must have shutters or draperies before anyone can sleep in them. If we start work on a schoolroom. . ."

"Birdwhistle wants to use the manor attic for the schoolroom, but the tower stairs will not be finished soon. Is there a place in the inn or do we use the chapel?" Arnaud asked, crossing the lobby to study the pub.

"Draperies?" Thea peered up the stairs. "There are moth-eaten draperies stored in the attic. If the inn's windows are smaller. . ." Without further explanation, she took the stairs up.

"Shutters," Rafe called after her, apparently attempting to establish order. "I don't have laundresses to clean velvets or silks or whatever fanciness is at the manor."

"Ask the lieutenant and captain how well giving their wives orders works," Arnaud said with a snicker. "Once you involve the ladies, your chance to make decisions is lost." He gestured at the pub. "Until you are prepared to open, this may make the schoolroom. You need benches and chalkboards."

"Perhaps Minerva can take Mrs. Porter to visit families with children," Paul suggested, averting any impending explosion over loss of control.

Rafe looked relieved. "If she would do that, that might help. I want to find this killer, and odd as it seems, my instincts say Verity is at the center of it."

"Have you talked her into staying at the inn?" Paul asked. "Wouldn't she be safer at the manor?"

"She wants her own place. She says if she must rent, she has to work. Let us hope some of the parents are willing to pay for classes." Arms crossed, Rafe studied the pub. "Or, might some of them work at the inn for a few hours for free in exchange for Verity teaching their children? And then I'd pay Verity or provide her a free room."

"You think like a revolutionary." Arnaud paced the large space occupied only by trestle tables. "The fathers might work a few hours at the manor, and the maintenance fund pays their wages to the teacher."

"Minerva can sound out the parents, see how eager they are for a school." Paul eyed the scarred walnut bar skeptically —not a schoolroom accessory—but the days were growing cooler, and this room had a fireplace. The chapel didn't. "Young people might return more readily if we have a school to offer."

"If the inn is able to take guests. . ." Arnaud let the thought trail off as he studied the dusty inn yard outside the newly-cleaned mullioned windows.

Paul followed his thoughts. Customers for the manor's small industries—and Arnaud's paintings—needed a place to stay.

"Until we're fixed up proper, with mattresses and linens and shutters, we'll only have traveling salesmen and chimney sweeps," Rafe said dryly. "But it's a start."

Paul left them to discuss schoolrooms. He had a good excuse to visit Minerva now.

Before he left the inn yard, a wagon loaded with lumber entered, driven by the two Blackwells. He waited to help them unload. . . and to ask questions. The pair were newcomers to the village and had been here the day the governess had died.

"Is Captain Huntley providing you a place to stay?" He hefted a stack of boards and carried them to the stable workshop.

"Aye, we got rooms," the son replied, carrying another stack.

The older Blackwell followed with bags of what Paul assumed were nails and other hardware. "We've got a farm of our own we can fix up if work stays steady."

"The wives are unhappy with us down here without them," the son added. "They think we're out carousing."

"I'm going up to the manor now. I'm sure they have other cottages the estate can repair. Do either of you do interior work, like making shutters?"

"I want to learn," the younger acknowledged. "Ain't got the tools for it."

"I'm building a collection of tools." Paul indicated the workshop. "If the village is to continue growing, you'll have steady employment. I'll teach you what I know, if you stay."

The lanky son, George, if Paul remembered rightly, pulled a forelock and nodded. "Be grateful. Wife, too. We got a young one and another on the way and she wants me home."

"Place got killers and thieves here just like Town," the father, Nate, warned. "They won't like to hear that."

"That's understandable. The captain has hired a bailiff to return order. Were both of you up at the manor the day the lady died? Did you notice anything or anyone odd?" Paul wasn't certain how much Hunt or Rafe had talked to people, but most folks considered curates harmless. He might receive different answers.

"Odd, how?" Nate stacked the lumber and began sorting hardware into bins.

Good question. Paul shrugged. "Arguing or people in places they shouldn't be or looking angry, I don't know. The manor has hired so many new folk, the captain can't watch them all."

"That bloke Clement was arguing with his wife," George said, trying to be helpful for a potential employer. "And the coachman chased them off. They're an odd lot. Don't talk like us and don't have much to do with anyone else."

Paul tried not to look too interested. "We can't find Clement's wife. Do you know where she's staying?"

Both men shrugged. Well, he couldn't expect too much. Thanking them, Paul headed up to the manor and Minerva.

It was high time they started a full search for Clement's wife. She might be dead by now.

THIRTY-TWO: VERITY

THAT EVENING, VERITY STUDIED THE INN GUEST CHAMBERS RAFE HAD attempted to make—*habitable*. That was the kindest word she could summon.

The bubbled glass in the windows had been scrubbed, revealing all the cracks and holes. The mullions had rotted and the glass threatened to fall out in places. The sills had been soaked where the roof leaked and most likely needed replacing. The lack of any privacy covering, much less one to keep out drafts. . .

It really wouldn't do. There weren't enough hours in the day. The sergeant had tried, but he was accustomed to sleeping rough. Even in her cellar rooms, she'd had more comfort than an empty bedframe and an old quilt. She most certainly couldn't ask Mrs. Underhill to stay here.

Before she could find Rafe to tell him she'd rather risk arsonists than undress in a naked room, one without so much as a wash basin or chamber pot, she heard someone calling her name from below.

Relieved to hear a friendly, feminine voice, she hurried downstairs. She was using the cane less but her foot protested. She needed to sit down and put it up for a while.

"Miss Peniston," she said in surprise at finding the busy librarian in the lobby. "How may I help you?"

"Let me count the ways. . ." The librarian gestured vaguely. "We need you at dinner tonight. We have ideas for the school, but we can do nothing without your agreement. And Arnaud needs your approval of his sketches. And Paul has been asking questions about the day you arrived and we need to discuss theories. It is likely to be a long evening, so you are welcome to stay the night. Oh, and Lavender says your Sunday gown is ready."

Verity almost took a seat waiting for the petite lady to wind down. "Rafe wants you to lure me to the manor so I won't return to the cottage?" she asked after the librarian stopped for breath.

"Something like that, most likely, but we really do need you. Hunt and Clare have left with his mother and won't be back for days. Elsa and Jack are taking advantage of their absence to dine in the privacy of their suite. Arnaud and Thea will only argue without guests forcing them to mind their manners. We've asked Rafe as well. You will be doing me a favor." She looked quite earnest.

Verity's choices were few. She hated leaving her father's books but Rafe had locked them in a windowless, dry room. She didn't think they'd come to harm. "May I bring Marmie? I dislike leaving him alone."

"Cats like being alone, but it's your choice. Let's pack your bags. We don't know if the thief will come after them next."

There was an alarming thought, even more alarming than formal dining at the manor with the nobility. Well, as she understood it, the only titled inhabitants, besides a former French count who looked like a penniless artist, were the dowagers who kept a suite to themselves. She tried not to be intimidated by the descendants of nobility.

Later, wearing the exquisite, high-waisted primrose muslin Lavender had trimmed with black ribbons, Verity pulled her second-hand shawl around her at the sound of the dinner bell.

215

She hoped it was a dinner bell. The manor maid who had helped her dress had shooed her out, leastways.

The portly butler directed her to the elegant, high-ceilinged parlor where the family gathered. Feeling self-conscious, she waited until these formally dressed near-strangers were all engaged in argument before entering. But Rafe must have been watching.

Newly pressed, with gold buttons shining, his scarlet uniform coat fit him like a glove. Wearing gleaming white, starched linen, his usual scruff newly shaved, Sgt. Russell looked nothing like the shirt-sleeved man who had cooked for her. Well, except for the carrot-orange curls, and even they had been trimmed and pomaded.

Had her parents lived, she might have learned to be comfortable in formal surroundings. As it was, she longed to turn and flee.

Rafe prevented such cowardice. As if he were accustomed to playing host—of course, he was!—he placed her hand on his arm and led her into the company. "I am trying not to look too hard on your splendiferousness," he murmured.

"Splendifer-what?" Amused at his nonsense, she allowed herself to relax in his large shadow. "And does the word apply to you as well?"

"Naturally." He led her to the grouping of people whose names she was learning, although in evening clothes they were imposing strangers.

Before she could greet everyone properly, Henri's tall, blond wife—who normally wore a leather apron and now appeared bounteously buxom in silk—leaned forward eagerly. "I have polled the apple pickers!"

In formal neckcloth and tailored frockcoat, his dark hair brushed back, looking more noble than a tavern owner should be, Arnaud's brother, Henri, grinned. "Patience is becoming very brave. Once, she dared not speak to men she did not know."

"One isn't supposed to speak to men we don't know," Verity

had to reply in defense of the lovely young gardener, who swatted her handsome husband with a fan. "How does one poll?"

"I ask if they live in Gravesyde, and if they say yes, I ask if they have children. And if they say yes again, I ask if any are ready for school."

Taking the seat Rafe offered, Verity accepted a glass of whatever libation the maid served, if only to keep her hand occupied. "And how many potential students did you find?"

"A dozen," Patience crowed triumphantly.

"I will mention our plans in church tomorrow," the curate added. "I am sure we will find more. Even if you can only teach the rudiments, the benefit to the village of having inhabitants who can read and cipher will be enormous."

The anticipation that had led her here returned. Verity had hoped for the aid of her governess, but here were complete strangers willing to stand in Miss Edgerton's place. She had not had to make so many decisions at once in a long time, and then they hadn't been so momentous. She didn't know how to replicate their enthusiasm.

Before she could reply, the Prescotts entered. Several years older than the rest of the company, they appeared distinguished and comfortable with people they scarcely knew. Verity thought she'd like to learn their confidence. She sipped her drink and tried not to wrinkle her nose at the strong sweetness.

The Prescotts glanced at Verity and Rafe in surprise, then took seats next to Miss Talbot.

"Have you determined what pieces are staying and what is to be removed?" Minerva reached for an interesting plate of nibbles and passed it to Verity. "These are crackers," she explained. "Hunt learned to like them in the army and Elsa has learned to bake them. They're good with cheese."

Verity timidly took one, terrified she'd drop crumbs down her cleavage. She'd never exposed so much flesh in her life.

"We've made a list." Mrs. Prescott took a glass but didn't drink.

"They'll begin looking for more suitable pieces to replace our old ones. It shouldn't cost us anything," Miss Talbot said reassuringly. "The really old medieval pieces that the last earl dumped here should be preserved in castles."

More comfortable with the younger people than the distinguished older couple, Verity attempted to not be a ghost any longer. "Might there be old, lesser pieces, which will suit the inn? Or a schoolroom?"

"Surely you are not planning on remaining, Mrs. Porter? We thought the cottage quite destroyed." Mrs. Prescott raised her lovely arched brows.

"We have no intention of letting Verity go," Patience announced cheerfully. "If we have a dozen students now, just think how many there will be in a few years! We might even need to build a real school."

That was a startling, almost comforting, thought. Feeling useful apparently gave her courage. "The cottage's garden is valuable. We are hoping the heirs will rebuild."

The solicitor, who had been pouring his own drink at the sideboard, returned to hear this. "I have a good offer on the cottage. I doubt the heirs will refuse it. I'm sure Mr. Sullivan will be happy to have you dig up the plants and move them. A hardware store won't need them."

Appalled silence briefly enveloped the parlor, until Mrs. Prescott lifted her glass and toasted the room. "Perhaps the heirs will also be amenable to our offer of a substantial sum for the family sketches."

Verity began to see how a murderer might want to kill someone.

THIRTY-THREE: RAFE

TRYING NOT TO SPRAWL HIS LONG LEGS AS HE WAS WONT TO DO, RAFE sat up straight at the manor's candlelit dining table and practiced reading people. He'd first learned the habit in his father's inn to avert drunken brawls that endangered the furniture. It had served him well in the army where fights among his men had been inevitable. With all the fancy chandeliers, china, and crystal, he didn't believe these polite people would start heaving chairs, although tension mounted. Having potential murder suspects at the table would do that.

Verity had narrowed her eyes and grown dangerously silent at Mrs. Prescott's suggestion that the heirs sell the sketches. The others, more experienced at dissembling, had merely directed conversation to planning.

"Do you have Fletch manning the tavern?" Rafe asked Henri while the others discussed furniture.

The Frenchman nodded. "Patience prefers an escort at dinner when we have visitors. I'm enjoying having the major available to take my place occasionally."

"Good practice for running the pub once we open." Rafe grinned at Henri's grimace. They'd be competitors of a sort someday.

While the company tallied the moldering contents of the manor and their usefulness in a public inn, Rafe simply listened. The inn had been stripped of most of its furnishings over the years, and he'd accept anything offered—if only for firewood. He didn't possess a single sentimental bone about old junk.

He didn't have much to add to the schoolroom discussion either. He'd learned numbers and letters from a vicar's wife and from working at his father's inn. In the inn's glory days, he'd attended boarding school and learned rudimentary history and literature which had served him well when dealing with his more educated officers. He understood that the desire to learn was more important than desks.

When the curate and librarian began conferring over their interviews with the villagers, Rafe finally sat up and took note. They knew people, as he didn't, though he wasn't entirely certain that it was wise to discuss suspects in front of strangers who might also be suspects. The Prescotts might pretend to converse with Miss Talbot, but they listened.

"This coachman you say argued with Clement. . ." Rafe interrupted. "Where is he? I don't remember speaking with him."

"Taking the Huntleys to Liverpool," Upton explained.

"He spends all his time polishing harness and wheels when he's here," Henri said with a laugh. "He doesn't know much about horses though. He's raw."

"I hope he knows how to drive." Patience set down her knife in alarm.

"Claims he used to drive his father's farm cart into the city until he was old enough to earn coin working for a Cit. He likes uniforms." Henri nodded at Rafe. "We can't provide a coat as handsome as yours, sergeant. The lad has asked me to look for tails and tall boots, as befits a proper coachman."

Before Rafe could summon an adequate response, Verity actually joined the discussion. She'd been oddly silent for a while.

"What is the coachman's name, might I ask?"

"Arthur, that's all I know." Henri lifted his wine glass. As tavern owner, he knew more of the male villagers than the curate. "Why do you ask?"

"I understood he's from London, like Clement. It worried me." She did not explain why.

Rafe knew she feared she'd been followed. But he'd already ascertained that the unusual city people had been here well before her arrival.

Boldly, for someone who had barely addressed the company this evening, Verity turned to the Prescotts. "Are you from London?"

"No, actually," the lady said with obvious amusement. "We are from Manchester."

Unsmiling, Verity turned to Minerva. "Wasn't one of Miss Edgerton's students from Manchester? I believe I recollect a Seraphina Littlejohn? It was such an unusual name that I admired it."

Rafe noted reactions with interest.

Miss Talbot gasped, and avoiding the eyes of her new friends, abruptly reached for her wine. So, the heiress recognized the name.

Mr. Prescott cleared his throat. "That is neither here nor there. If we are to leave in the morning, we should retire early, my dear."

Minerva responded as if he had said nothing, turning to Miss Talbot. "Thea, I believe you introduced our guest as Sara Prescott?"

Thea—Miss Talbot—nodded uncertainly. "The Prescotts are friends of my family who helped with the sale of my grandmother's estate. My parents, their parents—you know how it is." She gestured helplessly.

Rafe did, indeed, know how that worked. It was how he'd ended up in Gravesyde—knowing someone who knew someone. It didn't mean they knew them well.

"I cannot see how it matters," Mrs. Prescott said stiffly, ignoring the hand her husband held out. "Yes, my name is Seraphina. Miss Edgerton taught at the school I attended. There

221

were many other teachers and students. It's been nearly twenty years since I left. It is not unusual for friendships to arise from exclusive schools. It is the whole point of them."

Rafe understood that too. Fletch had been one of his fellow students, although their school could scarcely be called exclusive.

Before hair pulling and eye scratching could commence, Rafe intervened. "It matters because you knew Miss Edgerton, you did not mention it, even after her death, and you were here the day she died. That is more than anyone I have interviewed can say."

Having accepted her husband's hand to rise, the lady, looking aghast, burst into tears and raced from the room. Her husband followed her out.

"Well, that certainly didn't turn out as expected." Hurriedly, the heiress left the table to follow her acquaintances.

"She wants those sketches for a reason," Verity said grimly.

The solicitor looked pained. "I suppose now she will not offer for them again. You do the heirs no favor."

"Do the heirs care only for the money or might they desire justice for the death of a beloved family member?" Verity folded her napkin and rose. "If you will excuse me—"

"Sit down," Rafe roared, startling her. He'd been staring at Verity's bosom all evening. Her nervousness drove him over the brink. She'd been raised as a lady, far above his reach, had her father not been killed. And now, the death of her governess had left her bereft again. He disliked coincidence. Worse yet, he disliked the confusion she caused in his normally sensible brainpan. He wanted to shake her or hug her and couldn't do either.

She stared at him in astonishment, as did the others. He'd just behaved as a sergeant with new recruits. No matter. He wanted at the bottom of this confounded mystery so he could go back to life as planned.

Minerva tugged Verity's hand, drawing her back to her seat. "You cannot miss one of Elsa's fabulous puddings. Let us see what the sergeant has to say."

Thank all that was holy, Verity reluctantly sat. Well, at least she'd stay safely in the manor tonight, if only to avoid him.

The solicitor raised his graying eyebrows. "Surely you do not believe one of the heirs is desperate enough to cause Miss Edgerton's demise?"

Rafe gathered his thoughts. He wasn't accustomed to ordering about civilians who didn't work for him. But if he was to be bailiff, however reluctantly, then he needed to order about gentry as well as the lesser sorts. If Hunt wanted to boot him from his position for his offensiveness, Rafe was fine with that.

The reason he wanted his own inn was so no one could cast him out, as the bank and the army had. He needed to remember that.

"I think that you, Mr. Culliver, arrived with a potential buyer in an unholy hurry," Rafe stated. "Have you heard from the heirs yet?"

Instead of looking insulted, Mr. Culliver merely seemed annoyed. "My office is in Stratford, only a few hours away. I was notified of Miss Edgerton's death immediately. Captain Huntley offered me a room upon the request of Mr. Bosworth, a mutual acquaintance. Bosworth also informed me that Mr. Sullivan here was in search of a suitable site for his business. There is nothing mysterious about my arrival."

"Thank you. Have you had any other inquiries about the property?" Rafe noted Verity hiding her surprise at his question. Good. Perhaps she'd stay put and listen. He was convinced she held more clues she wasn't aware of—or hid.

The solicitor also looked surprised and eyed Rafe with interest. "You believe the lady died because of her property?"

"Given that she was murdered so someone might search the place, and then it was set on fire, that seems a plausible assumption." He needed to learn better questioning techniques than shouting. Tricky.

The lawyer nodded. "I see. Indeed, I have had another inquiry, from London, but the person is unknown to me and has not presented himself. The inquiry came through a London solicitor."

"Two inquiries? Is that not odd?" Verity paled. "Do you at least know the person's name?"

He lifted his shoulders. "No, that is not how this is done."

Rafe studied Verity. "Did you have someone in mind?"

"The men in the painting," she answered unequivocally. "Who else?"

He experienced a surge of relief at this sensible reply but still thought she held answers, even if she was unaware of them.

"Former lovers, students, gardeners, and herbalists," Minerva ticked off potential buyers on her fingers. "Miss Edgerton and her garden, presumably, were well known outside the village."

"And other than our drunken apple picker and Mrs. Prescott, none of those folks were here the day she died. If we cannot prove their guilt, we are back to looking at the village folk. Someone must know something." Out of habit, Rafe glared at the servant reaching for his empty plate before he could refill it. The footman quivered and removed the china anyway.

"If someone can vouch for the Prescotts whereabouts at the time of Miss Edgerton's death, I daresay we can exclude them." Rafe glanced around the table.

The French artist at the other end of the table shrugged. "They were with Thea most of last Saturday. They explored the manor attics in search of fabrics that might have survived damp and insects. I do not believe either would have left the manor covered in cobwebs and dust."

Rafe hadn't really expected the sophisticated couple to know poisons, much less visit the humble cottage to kill a teacher. But Verity had shown him that he should not assume anything.

"If Clement murdered the teacher, then his wife might tell us how. She could be staying with relations in the area. I suppose I should start scouring farms." And raise the ire of potential customers for his pub. Rafe was beginning to see the fallacy of believing he could be his own man.

He was also thinking the mysterious woman in black was far more likely to be a poisoner than the clown Clement. Hiding was definitely suspicious behavior.

"Tomorrow is Sunday," Upton offered. "We can start asking questions after services."

Cautiously, Verity suggested, "We might do it under the guise of asking if people have relatives or boarders who look after their children, in the interest of knowing who might help with the school and transportation."

Minerva brightened. "Excellent notion. I will set a few of the church ladies to it. The locals tend to be suspicious of outsiders."

Rafe nodded approval but noted Verity still seemed anxious. "Anything else? Now is the time to speak."

"Not to be annoying, but we should probably question the Prescotts about who actually wants those sketches and why. Former students are likely involved. It's just. . ." She stared at the cake set in front of her and didn't complete the thought until Rafe tapped his knife on her plate. She grimaced. "It is foolish and grasping at air."

Impatiently, Rafe encouraged her. "I am grateful for any and all suggestions."

"Only to cover all possibilities, even the most unlikely. . ." She gave a little sigh. "I don't wish this to be all about me, but just in case. . ."

"Personally, I think this is all about you, so continue, please," Rafe demanded.

That earned him a glare, but at least she gathered her courage. "Captain Huntley's new coachman from London. . . He was here last Saturday. I only caught a glimpse of him, mind you, but he resembles my uncle's footman. Perhaps he is a brother? The servant's name was Luther. . ."

"And the coachman is Arthur," Upton added with a touch of urgency. "The similarity. . . How long will it take a message to reach the captain in Liverpool?"

Rafe understood his concern. The Huntleys might be traveling with a killer, one about to make his escape.

SUNDAY

THIRTY-FOUR: VERITY

AFTER CHURCH THE NEXT DAY, VERITY WAS OVERWHELMED BY parishioners inquiring about the new school. Even one of the farmers asked, although she had a suspicion he was on the hunt for a wife who might take care of his motherless offspring.

She had thought herself plain and dowdy and firmly on the shelf. She was a trifle dazed at the preposterous notion she might not need to spend her life alone. She should have heeded Miss Edgerton's invitations much sooner, instead of clinging to the familiarity of her father's home.

She'd been spineless.

Now that she'd realized it, she was determined to grow a backbone. Did stealing her uncle's money count as an act of courage? Probably not. Returning it might have been. It would have also been stupid. Oh well. So she wasn't simply plain and clumsy but clever and criminal. And homeless, *again*.

"You've attracted a new admirer," Minerva whispered teasingly as the widower walked away.

"I'm not much inclined to mother children half my age." Verity hid a blush that anyone had noticed.

"Ah, I had meant to ask, when is your birthday? We've taken

up celebrating birthdays since we've learned some of us never had parties. Davy's is next Saturday, and we're to decide how to celebrate that won't terrify him into hiding." Minerva indicated one of the little boys leaving with the tutor.

"Oh, mine is that Friday!" Verity exclaimed without thinking. She really was bad at hiding who she was. She hastily bit her tongue. There were disadvantages to being dead. She hadn't celebrated a birthday in ever so long, that she'd quite forgotten about it.

"Then we should have an extra cake made for you! I'll tell Elsa. Come with us and help choose which of our attic artifacts should be transported to the inn."

She resisted. Rafe was intent on questioning everyone in the chapel yard. "It's not my place to make the sergeant's choices," she demurred.

Verity missed sharing meals with him in the cozy cottage. After her quiet life, the manor company was a trifle. . . excessive. She almost longed for her lonely cellar and the company of a good book. But she was done hiding.

Steeling herself, she turned to the gentle Valkyrie of an earl's granddaughter to ask if she wished to gather seeds and roots from the cottage garden, in case Mr. Sullivan bought it. Patience jumped at the opportunity.

"I never properly thanked Mrs. Holly for helping the day of the fire. I'd like to take her some of Miss Edgerton's jams, and since her tree died, perhaps bring her some apples from the mercantile." Following the others from the chapel yard, Verity stopped at the inn where Rafe had squirreled away all the cottage's pantry contents, and she'd left her old clothes hanging out to dry. "I'll need to change first."

"You don't have to buy apples!" Patience cried. "I'll bring down a basket. I'll need one to carry the roots anyway. Let's meet at the cottage in half an hour."

Verity waved the others off and veered into the inn yard. Wolfie ran to greet her, and she rubbed his wooly head. "If only kittens could be trained like dogs!" She had left Marmie in the manor's warm kitchen.

Wolf barked his agreement, and when she had no treats to give him, wandered off.

The bare room Rafe had assigned her had acquired a new mattress, a battered washstand with mismatched legs, and a washbasin, but no chamber pot. The workmen were working on a spacious new outhouse, she knew, but traipsing outside in the middle of the night, in a strange place, with a murderer about, did not appeal.

She'd left her blacks hanging on the bedframe to finish drying. She needed to find a laundress for her new gowns, but this old one she managed to wash on her own. After being scorched, it scarcely needed pressing for digging in a garden.

As she changed, Wolfie barked at some perceived intruder in the yard. She glanced out the window but couldn't see him. The woods were full of animals for the dog to chase. She was amazed he didn't gallop after them.

Rafe had evidently returned here last night. A fresh loaf of half-eaten bread waited in the kitchen. She took a slice for herself, stole a bit of cheese, and added a jar of blackberry jam to a basket. Perhaps Patience could show her which herbs might be moved to the inn.

She met Rafe entering as she left. "I am taking some jam to Mrs. Holly. Patience and I are going to dig up a few roots. Do you think the inn might use some herbs?"

"I've been hoeing a plot out back. Let me change, and I'll join you. Why is Wolfie barking?" His Sunday coat didn't fit him nearly as well as his soldier's garb, but he still looked much too handsome for her overwrought nerves.

"I assumed a rabbit. You'll need him to keep them out of your garden until you can build a wall. I told Patience I'd meet her at the cottage. Come along later, if you like. Bring shovels, if you see any." She hurried out, hoping Patience brought her own tools. She was hoping to use the ones in Miss Edgerton's shed. Between the cane and basket, she couldn't carry more.

She met Minerva and the curate strolling from the chapel gate. They were so obviously engrossed in each other that she smiled and didn't intrude with a greeting.

But even in their cocoon of happiness, they saw her and stopped. She was starting to enjoy being recognized instead of flitting invisibly through the streets.

"I think we have solid support for the school," Mr. Upton said first. "We'll have Walker order at least a dozen chalk tablets. Parents say they will send their children with stools until we can provide better. There will be a scarcity of textbooks until we can assess their needs."

"Mr. Birdwhistle will help with that," Minerva reminded her.

"This is happening so fast!" Overwhelmed for the hundredth time these past days, Verity didn't know whether to be elated or run and hide. "I am grateful for all you've done." The shadow of Miss Edgerton's death darkened her happiness. Her late governess would have loved to have seen this come together. "Do you think Mrs. Walker might be interested in any of the herbs in the cottage garden? If Mr. Sullivan buys it, all those wonderful plants will be lost."

"I'll ask her. Is that where you're going?" Minerva asked.

"I'm meeting Patience there. I know nothing, but she will help me choose for the inn." Verity turned to the curate. "Will your mother mind taking Marmie a while longer? It's so awkward not knowing where I'll sleep from one night to the next!"

"Walker is making a list of vacant properties the estate owns," the curate said. "Until then, I'm sure you and your kitten are welcome at the manor."

Verity couldn't tell these nice people that she preferred a tiny cottage of her own to a towering manor belonging to others. She left them at the manor drive and strolled through the village, studying the few remaining buildings in town. She'd ascertained that most of the habitable ones were occupied by the elderly unable or unwilling to go elsewhere. She understood why the hardware store man considered hers the best-kept cottage in town —or once best-kept.

Perhaps she could find one outside of the village—where everyone feared Clement had left his wife, who might be the mysterious lady in black. Rural properties were so very isolated. . .

She felt a moment's trepidation in opening the cottage gate without Rafe's accompaniment. Reminding herself that she'd traversed London's streets unscathed and it was the unfamiliarity frightening her—and that she wasn't to be spineless any longer— she used her cane to push open the gate. The beautiful garden was already showing signs of neglect.

Avoiding the damaged cottage, she took the side path around back to see if Patience had arrived. Hearing a digging noise, she hesitated. The manor's eager gardener might have begun without her, but too many frightening events prevented dropping all caution. So where did caution become cowardice?

Wishing she'd brought Wolfie with her, she set down her basket, raised her cane, and peered around the back corner.

A woman in full black skirts and a shabby black bonnet chopped at the ground in the back of the garden bed.

Verity's first instinct was to rush in and pound the thief's head with a cane, but her natural wariness overruled rash action. If she waited for Patience to enter by the back gate, together they could trap her.

Fighting fury and the urge to demand answers, Verity froze as she always did. How much longer before Patience arrived? The Valkyrie was too sweet-natured to be much of a fighter, but she was larger and stronger than Verity. Between them, they might overcome one old woman.

Although she didn't appear terribly old. Not young, certainly, but strong enough to wield the spading fork in hard ground with vigor. Verity couldn't get a good look at the intruder's face. She was hunched over her work.

233

Before Patience could arrive, a familiar voice called over the wall, "Yoo hoo, dearie, are you out there?" And Mrs. Holly's gray head popped above the wall.

The woman in black dropped the fork, grabbed a sack, and raced for the back gate.

Shouting in frustration, Verity dashed after her, stumbling on the rough ground with her bad foot. "Stop her! Someone stop her!"

The black skirt swept out the gateway.

Verity practically wept upon rushing outside the wall to see the woman leap into the stream with booted feet. In relief, she heard Patience calling a question from the path.

"The thief is getting away!" Verity shouted as Patience came into view and Mrs. Holly hobbled out the gate in her hedge.

Behind her, she heard Rafe's shouts and almost dropped in relief. "In back, she's running away!"

Carrying shovel and spading fork in both arms like a loaded musket, he burst through the open gateway onto the narrow footpath, looking both frantic and furious. She pointed at the black skirt vanishing into the foliage on the rocky, nearly impassable side of the hill.

Rafe dropped the tools and took off, splashing through the low stream and crashing through brush without a second look back.

That could be the woman who had shot him before! Verity froze and watched them vanish around the bend.

Patience picked up Rafe's tools to add to her own and stood at Verity's side to watch them disappear in the distance. "There's nothing over there but the river. Surely, she can't go far."

Mrs. Holly followed their gazes. "Old Gypsy camp," she said. "Long way over. Ain't had Gypsies about since the old days. River used to flood them out until the captain built that dam upstream."

Gypsies? Furious at herself and everyone else, Verity limped back to the garden. "Patience, you need to warn your husband, ask if he can summon searchers. I'll see who I can find. If there is a camp over there, Rafe could be in trouble."

He'd been shot once. Despite his size and great strength, he couldn't fight an entire encampment. Unlike her, the foolish man dashed into trouble without a second thought.

If only she'd confronted the thief. . . She despaired of ever being bold.

MONDAY

THIRTY-FIVE: RAFE

SETTING OUT EARLY THE NEXT MORNING, WITH WOLFIE TROTTING beside his horse, Rafe returned to the caravan encampment he'd found yesterday, hoping his suspect had returned overnight.

The fire was cold. Maybe the old witch had fallen into the river. He could hope. His failure to locate one old woman infuriated him. He should have had Wolfie with him.

Yesterday, he'd had half the men in town scouring the hillside and fields around the caravan, without success. With nothing of the woman's clothing to give the hounds for scent, they'd been useless.

He'd met the manor's orchardist, Abe Bergstein, whose family land was across the highway from the camp. Abe claimed he only came down to visit when it was time to check the health of the new apple trees, and the manor folk verified it. He hadn't noticed any caravan hidden behind the bend of the river and the trees, but he'd only just arrived.

Rafe had also talked to a pair of former soldiers camping among the boulders on the manor side of river and highway. Yesterday, they'd only acknowledged seeing the caravan, no more.

Today, in the mist of a cool dawn, without a pack of hounds around him, Rafe returned to question them again. At this hour, they'd had time to sleep off whatever they'd imbibed to knock themselves out the night before. He found them groggy and burning coffee grounds over a fire.

Dropping a sack of bread, cheese, and apples by the campfire, he swung down from his gelding and ordered Wolfie to stay. The hound obediently lay down in the grass and looked harmless.

"Old lady didn't return last night?" Rafe asked as the soldiers dug into the bag.

"Not that we saw," the grizzled older of the pair replied. He gestured in the direction of the caravan. "Can't see her from here."

Rafe crouched down, helping himself to an apple. He'd been a soldier recently enough to know how they communicated. "What's she selling? Anything useful?"

The two shrugged and tore into the bread.

"Is her gin good? I almost miss the rotgut."

The younger, with a missing arm, gulped his scalding coffee. "Better. She's got a patent medicine takes away the pain. You gonna hang us for trading a coney or two?"

A patent medicine. Rafe's internal claxons screamed an alarm. Miss Edgerton had ordered a patent medicine and warned others against taking elixirs. Could it be as simple as that? The teacher had threatened the Gypsy over bottled poison?

"Captain doesn't hang people or shoot them either. We're all old soldiers. Manor has an apothecary who can help with the pain." Rafe gestured at his own injured arm. The bandage bulged under his old coat sleeve. "Just have to ask up there. No telling what the Gypsy puts in her medicines. Do you still have a bottle?"

The grizzled soldier looked cagey. "Ain't cheap. You got coins to pay for it?"

He could probably search the caravan and find bottles, but Rafe dug around in his pocket for his meager coin purse and showed them two shillings. They wouldn't take charity, but without coins, they'd sell the shirts off their back for more gin. "It's all I have."

The younger dug into his knapsack and produced a nearly

empty bottle of Mrs. Bigelow's Vegetable Compound. There was barely a splash left in it. "Reckon your apothecary can give us this?"

Rafe put the bottle in his coat pocket. "Better, most likely. I'll have her test this, see what you need. If you'll come up to the manor and ask one of your fellows, they'll fetch it for you. Can probably find a bed for you up there too. Winter is coming."

He'd learned that the captain had been working at housing the former soldiers who'd formed this encampment. A few had gained enough strength to move on. Others had nowhere to go and had taken up the manor's offer of employment and beds. Some still dealt with their addictions. But men who had given everything to serve their country shouldn't have to go cold and hungry once they returned home. Rafe despised the heartless government that had flung them out without a ha'penny, leaving them homeless and unemployed. He could have been one of them.

The pair shrugged and returned to their breakfast. He couldn't force them to save themselves.

Ordering Wolfie to follow, he traipsed a rabbit track to a copse by the river where they'd found the caravan in yesterday's search. The manor's gentlemen had politely refused to enter it when no one answered their calls. Believing the law was all that separated men from animals, Rafe had always followed orders.

But he would chase a fox into its lair after it raided a chicken coop. If nothing else, the old woman had raided a garden and poisoned those men with her narcotics. In his mind, she'd given up her right to a bolt hole.

Wolfie sniffed around the outside with disinterest. Rafe didn't know if that was a good or bad sign.

He'd rather be an innkeeper whose only responsibility was keeping order on his premises, but the captain paid him to protect the village. With only an ounce of guilt, he took the ax he'd deliberately brought and shattered the caravan's meager doors.

No old woman leapt out at him. The place stank of drying

herbs and unwashed flesh. He found men's clothes that might fit Clement and stuffed them in his sack. Confronting the prisoner with them might produce some response.

A smelly batch of what was most likely more elixir filled a pot. He emptied it on the ground. Not trusting the drying herbs, he bundled up a few for Mrs. Walker to examine, then cast the rest into the river.

He broke the assortment of empty glass bottles she must have meant to store the elixir in. Destruction of property and trespassing. . . he was exceeding the law he was supposed to be upholding.

But thinking of all the people who wasted their meager coins on potions that cured nothing and most likely caused more harm than good, he couldn't find it in himself to care. She could apply to the captain for recompense, if she dared.

Mostly, he thought about Miss Edgerton's death and Verity's losses. He couldn't charge an old Gypsy with murder without evidence, just because she knew herbs and he had a suspicious mind. But he could make a thief pay.

Finding nothing to give him any idea of where she'd gone, he returned outside to examine the copse. Wolfie led him to where a horse had been tied recently. The dung was probably a day old, though. The ground was hard enough to resist prints, but the few he found showed shoes. He hadn't thought Gypsies shoed their ponies, but he didn't have enough knowledge to be certain.

He checked with the former soldiers for a description of the horse before he left. They were foot soldiers. The best they could offer was that the horse was dark and tall—not a pony, then.

Unease ate at his gut, the way it had before a battle. If fear of the unknown was cowardice, then he'd freely admit to it. But he thought this was fear for those he'd come to know, respect, and. . . Thinking of Verity's tears and determination, he threw his bag over the saddle and mounted up.

She'd stayed at the manor again last night and come down early with a cart of the manor's rubbish for refurbishing *his* inn.

She wasn't lazy or selfish. He'd left her helping sort the junk and carting it upstairs—with a broken foot. If she stayed put, she'd be fine. The lady had developed a tough hide somehow.

The road around the river and woods wasn't direct, but Wolfie, and Rafe's gelding, enjoyed the run. He arrived in the village as the farmers were setting up their carts in front of the mercantile.

He pulled up short, realizing that half the old women hawking vegetables and bread wore black old-fashioned skirts with petticoats. Poor people wore what they had until it wore out. The Gypsy could be any one of these women, and he wouldn't know it. He'd only been here a week. He had no way to recognize a new one.

Damn, he hated his new occupation already.

Dismounting, Rafe tied up his horse and let Wolfie sniff his way around the carts. When the hound showed no sign of recognition, Rafe entered the mercantile. He had to wait until other customers paid for their purchases before he could speak to Mr. Oswald.

"New faces?" The old merchant peered through his fly-specked window. "They all only showed up this past summer, since the manor folk arrived with their big purses. Takes a heap of food to feed all them people. Good to see the old place lively again."

"Do you know the names of the market ladies? Keep their accounts?"

With suspicion, Oswald regarded him over the top of his spectacles. 'What do you want to know for? I keep proper books. Captain ain't plannin' on taxing them, is he?"

"I'm not a tax collector. I'm looking for a killer and a thief. We saw a Gypsy stealing from Miss Edgerton's garden yesterday. She escaped and I'd like to question her."

"Huh, imagine that, a Gypsy. Used to call the Bergsteins Gypsies, but they ain't. They're Jews. Your Gypsy can't be no kin, I guess. Abe ran outta family."

Rafe tamped down his impatience at the old man's rambling recollections. "So you know all the women selling from their carts and none of them have arrived recently?"

Oswald peered out the window again. "Reckon most attend church fair regular. Can't say any one is exactly new. Who's out there depends on what's in season."

Rafe gave up and headed for the door, then swung around with another thought. "Has anyone tried to sell elixirs?"

Oswald squinted at him. "That's what set Annie off a week or two back. Said she'd heard I was selling them. I set her right. I don't take to them patent medicines. If you want alcohol, Henri will sell it to you the way God meant for it to be drunk."

Rafe didn't question God's commands about ale. "Why did she order a bottle?"

Catching his drift, the old man straightened his stooping shoulders in alarm. "She gave me an address, said she wanted to compare it with what I wasn't selling." He glanced out the window at the few carts. "You don't reckon. . ."

"I have no way of knowing. Just keep your eye on them, if you will. And find the address you ordered from." Rafe stamped out. He'd been here a week, bought vegetables off these carts, and the killer could have been right here all along. She may have handed him carrots.

All old women in black looked alike. He groaned at his stupidity.

THIRTY-SIX: VERITY

STANDING IN THE INN'S MOMENTARILY EMPTY LOBBY, VERITY STUDIED the letter she'd picked up at the mercantile. She'd almost panicked when Mr. Oswald told her she had a post. Who would send *Verity Porter* a letter? The only people who knew that name lived here.

Except the bank in Stratford, she realized, unfolding the official letterhead. Skimming past the formal greeting, she read the contents once, then again. Someone had inquired after her? How? Why? Who could possibly know her new name besides the bank and people living in the village?

It wasn't conceivable. In terror, she studied the writing, the bank's address, the signature. . . The letter seemed very real. *Someone had asked after Verity Porter at the bank.* Panic seeped into her bones, freezing them. This was how she'd ended up living in a cellar for ten years. . ..

Footsteps clattered on the stairs. "Six rooms now have chamber pots and wash bowls," Minerva cried cheerfully. "Cracked, stained, and ugly, but very elegantly trimmed in gold and silver."

When Verity failed to respond, the librarian entered the lobby. Verity unfroze enough to shove the letter into her apron pocket and offer a weak smile. "Thank you. Once we have shutters, perhaps Mrs. Underhill will consent to be my companion again."

"You don't have to live here, you know." Minerva studied her through wise eyes but didn't question. "The manor can house you until you decide where you want to live."

That was an open question—should she flee Gravesyde and seek security elsewhere?

Obstinacy raised its ugly head. She didn't want to be driven from still another home.

Again, that was how she'd ended up in a cellar.

Verity offered a small smile at the suggestion but didn't answer. "Did Lavender think any of the old draperies can be salvaged? The windows will look better if we dress them up."

"By the time Paul teaches his new assistant to build shutters, Lavender should have a few panels complete. She thought she might fashion matching bedcovers of spare pieces. We're about to return to the manor for another load. Come up and see what she has," Minerva urged.

"Maybe later, around luncheon. I still haven't learned to cook," Verity said ruefully. "I hate imposing."

Minerva sniffed dismissively. "You've seen how much Elsa prepares. If she didn't have new victims to try recipes on, she'd be desolate. Will you be all right here alone while we start another load?"

Excellent question, another one she wasn't prepared to answer. Her spineless demon clamored to run far, far away. The demon of obstinacy refused to give up another home—even though she had stayed too long in the last one. She had no idea which fiend to listen to.

Reassuring Minerva that she would be fine cleaning and polishing all the new furnishings, Verity watched the cart roll out of the yard. She most likely didn't belong in an inn either, but this was the home Rafe had chosen. It wasn't cozy, but for now, the sprawling structure was empty enough for her to breathe. Familiar tasks provided an anchor of security.

Wolfie had returned without Rafe, but that wasn't unusual. She set out fresh water and gave him one of the old bones collected from the butcher. Together, they wandered out to the garden Rafe had begun plowing. She had to water the roots she and Patience had dug up and replanted yesterday while the men galloped the countryside in pursuit of the thief she'd let escape. Guilt ate at her for that. She should learn to think and act swiftly, take risks, if she wanted to live freely.

And not just survive. There were the two demons again.

She pumped water for the cuttings. Verity didn't remember what they were, but Rafe had been pleased.

Wolfie growled low in his throat and watched the woods up the hill. The blacksmith had cleared a line of young trees from behind his shop for a storage shed, but the forest still encroached on the inn yard. Rafe had said he'd clear it off this winter for firewood.

He planned on staying in Gravesyde.

She wanted to stay, she decided. She liked the people here. She liked the idea of building a new life with everyone else. She wanted to be useful. Casting aside doubt and caution, she dug in her heels. She was staying.

That decided, she had to work out how to be safe. She should ask Walker if her account at the bank was in good hands or if there were better places to put her savings. The steward was responsible for the estate's funds and ought to have wisdom to impart.

And she'd write the banker to warn him not to reveal her whereabouts. It was good to know he protected her. Refusing to leave her father's home had been a form of cowardice. The new Verity Palmer must be courageous and move forward, one small step at a time.

She returned inside to start building her new life. If the pub was to be a temporary schoolroom, it needed bookshelves. Perhaps books could be a permanent part of the décor. Rafe had mentioned setting up a library for her father's volumes. But some of them were needed in the schoolroom.

Wolfie chose not to follow her. He trotted off to guard the perimeter.

Aware that she was alone, probably for the first time since her arrival, Verity straightened her weak spine and limped up the narrow stairs. She'd seen the book crates toward the end of the hall in the old part of the inn. The first earls must have had a lot of tradesmen visiting that they couldn't house them in the enormous manor. Although, she supposed, the old part of the manor was not so large and the late earl had an enormous family.

Thinking the inn's gloomy oak paneling should be painted or papered, she lit an oil lamp. Like the manor's, this corridor had no windows. Gas lights would be wonderful.

She could almost sense the ghosts whispering from the walls, raising the hairs on the nape of her neck. Perhaps she should wait for Rafe. But she had to learn to do things on her own. . .

A noise overhead startled her. They hadn't spent much time in the attic common room where the inn had once housed lesser sorts on cots. She assumed it was even darker and gloomier up there. She didn't wish to encounter rats or bats in locating the source of the noise. Her courage only extended so far.

Books, she reminded herself. She'd come up to seek the reassurance of her beloved books. She located the room snugged in between two larger chambers—a place for a personal attendant, perhaps. It had no windows but was large enough for a cot and washstand. There might be a connector door behind the stack of boxes and furniture. Setting the lamp on the floor, she searched for the crate with the geographies and histories.

Only when she was holding the volumes did she realize she couldn't carry them, the lantern, and her cane. In frustration, she abandoned the lantern, turning off the wick until she could return for it. The unfamiliar hall might be dark and scary, but she couldn't get lost.

Despite the furniture polish that had been used on the old

paneling, the inn still smelled musty. If the manor grew lavender for perfumes, might they make it into pomanders? She shifted the books in an attempt not to stumble about on the cane.

Speculating on other means of improving the aroma—like baking—Verity didn't pay attention to the first step of the narrow staircase until, in her usual clumsiness, she managed to trip. Emitting an *eep* of dismay, she dropped her books and tried to balance her cane and grab the banister. While she was still off-balance, she felt a shove from behind.

Her bad foot twisted. Flinging herself sideways, she bounced against the wall, hit the stairs with her hip—and tumbled. Screaming, she fell

By the time she finally stopped her fall with her cane, Rafe's frantic shouts resounded from outside. Her shoulder hurt from hitting the wall, but her ample bottom had taken the worst of the fall. It took a moment to orient herself before she regained the sense to understand what had just happened.

Had she *imagined* that shove? Had she simply tripped over her worn boots in her usual awkward manner?

No, no, no. She had no more fallen on her own than she had driven that carriage over her foot. Yes, she had tripped, but then someone had very distinctly shoved her. That someone was still up there.

"Upstairs!" she shouted as Rafe pounded into the lobby.

Even her brave new self wasn't stupid enough to believe she had a chance of catching a scoundrel, but by the time Rafe reached the upper hall, Verity had regained her unsteady feet. Using her cane, she limped past her fallen books and up the stairs. There it was, a feeble thread, barely seen and easily broken. She had *not* fallen over her own feet!

Shaking with as much fury as pain and fear, she clumped down the corridor. No more. This was *personal*. She didn't know what she'd done to anyone for them to want her dead, but this time, she wasn't running and hiding.

Furious, she stomped after the murdering coward. Having

searched this floor, Rafe caught up to her before she could reach the rickety back stairs.

"He escaped out the back, I know he did!" It was the only place an intruder could run, unless she wanted to believe one of the workmen had taken a dislike to her and was hiding.

Amazingly, Rafe didn't even question. "Bar yourself in the first chamber," he ordered.

Coward that she was, she considered it. She couldn't exactly run to give chase.

Who would want her dead?

The old Faith Palmer was already dead. What could the new Verity Porter have done?

If someone wanted her dead, she had to think fast and not freeze into inaction. She couldn't abandon Rafe to take off after a killer alone.

Frantically, she hobbled down the main stairs to the lobby, where the next load of furnishings had just arrived in the yard.

Shouting for their attention, she pointed at the hill Rafe was running up. "Killer!"

To her relief, Henri and his large brother didn't question either but dashed off in pursuit. People believed her here. They *heard* her. Only then did she allow herself to collapse in the arms of the manor's heiress decorator.

She had almost died—a second time. The realization brought terror. No one person could be so prone to misadventure.

Did that mean the explosion in London had been meant for her too?

THIRTY-SEVEN: RAFE

RAFE HAD LOST THE BASTARD AGAIN. HE COULDN'T SHOUT HIS frustration, chop down trees, or shoot squirrels until his temper cooled. He couldn't shake ladies until they told him the truth.

But he could and would question them. Which was why he was in the manor now instead of galloping across the countryside with everyone else. The would-be killer had hidden an infernal horse behind the chapel. On foot, all any of them had been able to do was listen to the bastard ride away.

Knowing it was too late, he'd still sent out men with horses, but he refused to leave Verity this time. The manor ladies had whisked her off to safety, and she was pretending to be brave, but he could see her trembling even as he stalked the floor of the small, well-guarded, withdrawing room. She was the key, even if he couldn't understand how.

"I am not hysterical. I am fine. I am furious!" Verity repeated for the benefit of the anxious people gathering around with smelling salts.

Despite her protestations, she shook like a willow leaf. Rafe hung back, hating to play sergeant, knowing it was his job, once his temper cooled. But he had to ask, "Did you see the man who pushed you?"

She caught her elbows, shivered, but seemed to ponder the question. "No. I think he heard you and fled. He must have been hiding in the attic, biding his time."

Rafe tried to calm his temper at the thought of any man pushing a woman, but one with a cane. . . She could have *died*! This intelligent, caring woman who hadn't had a chance to live could have died. . . on his watch, in his inn. Selfish to think that, but it only made him more furious. Verity deserved far better than she'd been served thus far.

"A little food, a little tea, will be good for all of us," the apothecary said, staving off any shouting. The maids scurried off, obeying Meera's orders as if she were lady of the manor.

Rafe racked up another observation—all the ladies here were sergeants, at the very least.

"Now then," Meera continued, "Rafe is pacing for a reason. I will turn you over to him once I'm assured you're steady enough to resist his browbeating. How is your foot? You were limping more."

Rafe patrolled this less grand chamber at the back of the house. Despite the elaborate ceiling decorations, and artwork, it wasn't completely furnished. The ladies had claimed the sturdiest seats. He refused to occupy one of those frail pieces with fading tapestry and tiny arms that would squeeze him like an unwanted lover. He might smash one against the wall soon if he didn't get answers.

"I twisted my foot when I lost my balance. I'm sure it's just bruised." Verity folded her hands in her lap and appeared resigned to interrogation. "I think I shall carry a cane forever. It's very useful."

Unable to restrain himself, Rafe shouted, "If you're already dead, why would anyone want to kill you again?"

"I looked at the herbs you brought from the Gypsy caravan." Ignoring his shout, Meera pinned him with her dark gaze. "They were mostly harmless. In quantities, the fennel might cause extra time in the outhouse and wouldn't be healthy for people with certain conditions. The elixir in the bottle, however, contained both alcohol and laudanum, addictive and possibly deadly, if the patient was taking other medicine."

"In other words, nothing new," Rafe said in scorn. "The killer might not have needed to mix poison in the tea, they could have used the elixir."

"Miss Edgerton would have tasted it. The killer knew not to use anything so conspicuous. But they took chances with herbs or weren't very experienced."

Waiting for the tea, Rafe pondered poison tea, herb thieves, and a killer who shoved frail, limping women down stairs. Instead of calming down, he grew more furious by the minute.

"I think I need to explain something," Verity declared with quiet determination once the tea tray was delivered. "No matter how I look at it, I cannot see how it matters, but today's incident felt very personal."

Personal? She thought someone *pushing her down stairs* might be personal?

Now that he'd worked up a full head of steam, she was calming down. Rafe gritted his teeth and tried not to shout while young Lavender and elegant Thea protested she need explain nothing.

More experienced and observant, Minerva and Meera sat silent.

Rafe tried not to loom. He was out of his depth in a room full of women, while other men did his work for him. He hated this. But he knew Verity held secrets, and he suspected one had come back to haunt her. He took a scone and tore into it angrily.

She held a cup of tea out to him. "Sit. Have a sandwich. You'll need it."

She'd been nearly killed and she wanted *him* to take nourishment? This was not an experience Rafe recognized. He was the one who gave orders and saw to guests. . . No one ever took care of him. Confused, he couldn't rage at her. He accepted the cup and looked for a place to set it down. He wasn't much at balancing delicate china.

Verity placed a plate of bite-sized sandwiches on the table beside the sofa. Instead of lying down and putting up her injured foot, she eased over so he had room to sit. Rafe figured the other women watched and judged his awkwardness, but they continued filling cups and plates, waiting politely.

In resignation, Rafe settled beside Verity, who he knew to really be Faith. He'd asked Walker to have the solicitor investigate, but it was too soon to expect a response.

Once he grudgingly settled, she took a sip of tea, followed by a deep breath. She had her audience riveted better than any actress. She'd make a good teacher.

"As I said, I cannot understand how this matters, but a few weeks ago," she began, hesitatingly, "I lived in a lovely home in a not very fashionable part of London. You have seen the painting of my father's death. My uncle was his heir. He gradually took over our home and turned it into a counting house. After my mother died, I moved into servants' rooms in the cellar to avoid the strangers coming and going upstairs."

Rafe swallowed his hot tea in two gulps. He knew he wouldn't like this story, and he wanted the china safely out of his hands. He crammed his mouth with bread to prevent shouting. The sandwiches were scarcely large enough to stop him.

Verity sipped her tea as if it were fortifying whiskey. "I was quite young, so I occupied myself by studying my father's extensive library. Once I finished a book, if I didn't like it, I'd sell it. I built a small savings in futile hope that my uncle would move his business, and I would have the house back again. He kept expanding instead."

Rafe tore into another sandwich, if only to prevent his fists turning into knots at the image of a lonely young girl reading in a dark cellar, then painstakingly choosing which volumes to keep and which to sell. Then going out in the dirty streets of the city to sell them.

"When I was old enough to do business with the bank, my uncle introduced me as his assistant and allowed me to run his notes and receipts back and forth, as needed."

She pondered this a moment. "I developed a routine, carrying receipts to the bank just before it closed, exchanging them for the cash my uncle needed to start the next day. I'd hand the money over to him, he'd put it into the vault, and I'd go back to my cellar to eat my supper."

"He lived there too?" Minerva asked. "Did you not share meals with him?"

Verity smiled bleakly, smashing Rafe's heart. "He kept a family elsewhere, in a more fashionable district, and went home to them in the evening. I was not invited. I only met my aunt twice, at funeral services, when I was barely more than a child. I was not pretty or well-connected. I think she forgot me after a while. I rather preferred it that way. I had my books and my home."

Rafe wanted to pace impatiently, hurry this up, but she was finally talking. Perhaps she'd never shut up now that the dam had opened.

She sent him a sideways glance, probably recognizing his impatience.

"The only reason I am reciting this tale is to explain what happened to send me fleeing to Miss Edgerton. My house exploded."

Rafe was off the sofa and stamping his frustration across the uncovered floor before he could detonate like her house. "*Exploded*? How?"

And that's when he saw the connection. "Were you supposed to be inside?" he asked in horror. He glared, waiting for answers.

Despite all that she'd been through, rosy patches stained her fair cheeks and fury lit her huge dark eyes. Demurely, she held her teacup and glared back at him.

Not a frail miss. Not a victim. Just a close-mouthed, obstinate female who had been doing for herself so long, that she didn't

255

know how to do it any other way. Her house had exploded and she'd picked up and moved on! Rafe's mind boggled.

"Yes, I normally would have been in my cellar, eating my meat pie, but I had hurt my foot and was running late. And then I stopped to rescue a kitten. I have no idea what makes houses explode. In the newssheets, my uncle blamed it on gas, but we didn't have gas lines."

"Your uncle survived?" Rafe asked, his suspicious mind racing ahead to the ramifications, not liking any of them.

"Yes. His carriage had left by the time I arrived in sight of the house, so I knew I was late. It had happened before. I know how to use the vault. When I was late, I'd just lock up the coins without his help, and he'd forget about my tardiness by morning. It was only if I arrived late *before* he left that he shouted, so I was in no hurry."

"So he left you in an empty building, in a non-fashionable district, all alone, every night, with no protection?" Rafe asked in incredulity.

She shrugged. "It was my home. The neighbors knew me. Men who used to work for my father were around. Because of the vault, my uncle installed strong locks. I never felt unsafe."

The women muttered in shock and dismay. They weren't naïve. There were reasons for even the most sheltered of women to have chaperones at all times.

Rafe wanted to shake Verity for her naivete—but it had become painfully obvious that she was no widow. She had utterly no experience at being a woman. She honestly thought she was dowdy and of no interest. . . And he choked back his outrage at that idiocy by focusing on the crime.

"The house exploded before you entered, while you were still holding the bank bag?" Rafe knew what he asked and couldn't say he'd have done anything differently.

She met his gaze defiantly. "Because the person I used to be died that night. What else was I to do? It was in all the newssheets. Faith Palmer died and the world didn't stop spinning. I lost everything, my clothes, my home, the rest of my father's library, all that I was."

"I think that's enough for now," Meera said quietly. "Let's get you up to bed, give you time to recover. We are not your heartless uncle. We care about you."

Verity refused to leave but awaited Rafe's verdict. She had stolen her uncle's bank bag. That much was clear. He'd had time to work his way through even more tangled knots. He didn't like what he saw, but he wouldn't force her to look if she wasn't ready. The timing was still off, but he was closer to understanding.

He held out his hand to assist her up. "One more thing, then you can go. You say your uncle was your father's heir. Did the solicitor tell you this?"

Taking his callused hand in her bare one, she studied him in puzzlement. "My mother told me. I assume the solicitor told her. She would never have allowed my uncle to take over otherwise. They thoroughly disliked each other."

A damned innocent. . . Rafe bowed and let the women carry her off.

It was time he started using his brainbox instead of brute strength.

THIRTY-EIGHT: PAUL

ADDING HINGES TO THE SHUTTERS YOUNG BLACKWELL HAD CUT, PAUL heard the carriage driving past the inn to the manor drive. Hunt and Clare had returned! They must have changed horses and drove half the night to rush home and deal with Clement.

He finished and hurried over to the inn's kitchen to wash up. Donning his coat over his dirty shirtsleeves, he heard voices up front, and departed through the lobby to see what was happening.

Arnaud and Thea were hanging the copy of the painting of Verity's father being murdered. *Shoved*—as Verity had been. The copy wasn't quite as detailed as the original and Arnaud had been unable to resist adding a few colorful, dramatic strokes of his own, but it was a terrifying portrait of evil.

"Rafe is chomping at the bit," Arnaud explained, stepping back to examine his handiwork. "If that was Hunt arriving, there will no doubt be an inquisition shortly. Want to take my place?"

"Not particularly." Paul straightened his linen. "I'll join you, though. People are afraid. We'll have a vigilante troop before long, burning anything in sight. That painting will. . ." He didn't want to imagine how a watercolor of evil would affect the superstitious. But he was quite certain if the killer was around, he'd either flee or—try to finish whatever he'd come to do.

Unless he was a madman who simply enjoyed killing. Paul didn't think that likely.

"The sergeant has been interrogating the prisoner this past hour." Thea wiped her hands on a delicate handkerchief and started for the door. "After spending the morning badgering the banker's assistant, Miss Edgerton's solicitor, and the poor merchant who wants to buy her property. I think the solicitor and merchant fled."

"It makes sense to question new arrivals, I suppose. I'll have to keep him away from terrifying the Blackwells." Paul followed them out. "We need good builders, and they have a farm around here. Have the Prescotts fled without buying the sketches?"

"Packing. If any of them attempted to push Verity down the stairs, we have no evidence," Arnaud warned. "What does he hope to learn?"

"Who knew the killer or his whereabouts." Paul understood the need for questioning. "The old woman from the caravan must have found another hiding place. I understand it was definitely a man they chased after Verity was pushed this morning, and he escaped on a horse. Jack and a few men are looking for it."

"All Clement admits to was searching the cottage." Arnaud held out his arm for Thea. "And since he was locked up, he couldn't have pushed Verity. The new coach driver is with Hunt and his carriage and cannot be involved. Presumably, the killer needs to be someone who was in the village when Miss Edgerton died *and* when Verity was pushed, or we have two killers on our hands."

"Ah, that explains why the sergeant is keeping a list of who was where and when. The poor sergeant is very worried about our intrepid schoolteacher. Her story is terrifying!" Thea hurried to keep up with Arnaud's long strides.

Arnaud slowed down for her. "As we have ascertained before, the manor is too large to track who was where and when. The Prescotts, they claim to be in the library, but Minerva, she was loading the cart and cannot give witness. The solicitor and the

259

hardware merchant say they were examining properties, but they could have been studying the inn. And so it goes."

"Well, the Blackwells were with me." Paul stopped and thought about that. "Although I was called away for a while. Confound it, they were right there behind the inn this morning!"

"Motive," Arnaud said tersely as they reached the manor. "No one has any motive."

"Other than hating women," Thea said, almost tranquilly. "Killers are not necessarily rational, correct?"

"So they killed Miss Edgerton because she was female and alone, and then went after Verity for the same reason?" Paul shuddered. He'd dismissed that theory but if others hadn't. . . "I wouldn't blame anyone for abandoning Gravesyde in that event."

Hunt's carriage had already been unharnessed and trunks carried inside by the time they entered the manor. Taking advantage of the last hour of daylight, workers pounded on the walls of the tower. The halls bustled with servants, many of them newly hired. More people meant more could be accomplished. It also meant more problems, Paul realized. Civilization was not always civilized. He and the new bailiff had their tasks cut out for them. Hunt couldn't do it all anymore.

Paul left Arnaud and Thea so he might stop in the library and check on Minerva. Seeing her always raised his spirits. . . and his hopes. As she gathered up her notes, she offered the quick smile that always thrilled him.

"Walker has had a response from the solicitor to our inquiries about Verity's claim to be Faith Palmer. Hunt is bellowing for a meeting in the study. He wants to send Clement off to assizes and expects answers." His fiancée took his arm and squeezed it a little in anticipation. "I like that he doesn't mind me attending."

"He would be a fool not to," Paul offered truthfully as well as gallantly. "You are an astute observer of human nature as well as a most excellent researcher."

"Observation seldom provides evidence, I fear. I can say

Clement doesn't appear to be competent enough to poison anyone, but that doesn't mean he didn't." She hesitated at the foot of the grand staircase and glanced toward the gilded but backward longcase clock on the landing chiming nine. "Should we subject Verity to Hunt's bellows?"

"She needs to be there. Can you be her shield?" Even as they spoke, he could see Verity accompanying the captain's wife, Clare, in the upper hall. They were in earnest conversation, so he assumed the schoolteacher was being reassured that Hunt's bellows were worse than his bite. Except, they weren't, once the captain decided he had the evidence he needed.

Since he didn't hear anyone in the small study, Paul assumed Hunt occupied the larger one in the new wing. With a few more servants to polish and dust, it was seeing more use.

They waited for Clare and Verity to descend, then strolled through the manor together. The schoolteacher wore one of the new gowns Lavender had made up for her. With her caramel hair in a chignon, and wearing a new bronzish colored gown, she appeared as much a lady as any of the earl's descendants. It was hard to imagine her hiding in a cellar all those years. Or anyone cruel enough to leave a young woman there.

Minerva dropped his arm to take up Verity's, and the two women whispered, leaving the captain's wife to take Paul's arm.

"I understand our new bailiff is up to all the rigs, as they say in Town." Clare exuded the confidence that had brought the manor's heirs together and guided them to their current cooperation, doing so with quiet dignity.

"A bit raw but Rafe leaves no stone unturned," Paul agreed. "He'll be a good innkeeper once the place is suitable for use."

"Not if he drives off all his customers shouting at them," she said in amusement. "Elsa has given me all the gossip."

Their lady cook heard all the news first and stirred scandal broth with her delicious meals.

"I don't suppose she has learned who wasn't where they were

supposed to be while Miss Porter was being pushed down the stairs?" Paul let Clare enter the study ahead of him.

"Not that I know of," Clare murmured, gazing upon the full study. "This promises to be entertaining."

In his country tweed, Rafe was pacing angrily up and down along the far wall, next to the mostly empty bookshelves. In counterpoint, Hunt had propped himself behind the massive desk with one booted foot casually flung over the arm of his chair. Walker, as always, preferred the comfortable wing chair in the far corner, where he could set his journals and notes on an empty shelf. Behind his quiet demeanor, the African steward's brilliant brain was a force to be reckoned with.

Per usual, Hunt didn't rise when the ladies entered. Walker, Arnaud, and Henri did. The study didn't provide the same number of seats as the great hall Hunt used for his trials, but over the last months, several leather armchairs and miscellaneous others had found their way in here. Minerva and Verity accepted the two the gentlemen offered. They pulled them right in front of the desk so Minerva could drop her notes on the nearly empty surface. Nothing shy about his intended.

Paul settled Clare in the corner behind Hunt and propped his shoulders against the door jamb to keep an eye on the hall.

"Your tale first, Miss. . . Porter? Palmer?" Hunt leaned back in his chair as if having a chat with one of his friends. A big man with an intimidating scar down the side of his face, he knew how to use his size when necessary. Apparently that wasn't now. Yet.

"Please, I prefer to be called Verity Porter now. Faith Palmer died the night of the fire. I see no need to resurrect her. She had no family or friends. If I am allowed to stay in Gravesyde, I would like to believe that Verity Porter might become someone useful."

Rafe snorted. "In one week she has organized the town into restoring the inn and given a home to a widow, until some wretch destroyed the cottage. Upon my honor, she is furnishing a town library! Had she been a man, she'd be a general by now."

Verity appeared to blink in surprise, then cast her eyes downward, to her folded hands. "I have done nothing but bring trouble. I will understand if you prefer that I leave."

"Stop that foolishness!" Rafe roared. "Captain, this is a waste of all our time. We need to be out hunting the villain who tried to shove her down the stairs. There is good reason to believe he killed Miss Edgerton."

Verity's head jerked up at that. Along with everyone in the room, she turned to stare at the outraged sergeant.

"What makes you say that Sgt. Russell?" Hunt asked implacably.

"Because he tried to murder Verity in London, first."

A gasp ran around the room and Hunt sat up straight. Verity stared at Rafe with eyes so wide that Paul thought they'd come off her face.

Relentlessly, the sergeant continued. "When he thought he succeeded, the killer had someone poison Miss Edgerton, who hid evidence of Verity's father's murder. This man lacks any conscience whatsoever. Once he realized Faith Palmer might not be dead, he tried to have her killed again. Verity, tell them when your birthday is." Rafe quit his pacing to glare at her, as if she should have known all this.

Which, Paul thought, she probably ought to have, except she'd grown up inside of books and trusted the people around her.

"I'll be twenty-five this Friday," she offered tentatively.

Hunt frowned. "That's the age when Lady Elsa came into her trust funds. Thea, did you not say you gain some control of your funds when you reach that age?"

Wide-eyed, Thea nodded. "I was supposed to marry and let my husband take charge of them. Apparently, the law fears women will foolishly marry the wrong sort or spend the funds irrationally unless we are firmly on the shelf."

Verity shook her head. "I have no trust fund, no wealth. There is no one looking after my non-existent funds."

"Except your uncle," Rafe proclaimed ominously. "Who kept you hidden from any possible suitors."

Before anyone could react, boots pounded down the uncarpeted hallway. Paul stepped aside for one of the new young footmen.

"Captain, sir, Adam says as how there's an altercation in the stable yard and your coachman is about to get killed!"

THIRTY-NINE: VERITY

VERITY CLUTCHED HER HANDS AS HALF THE MEN RUSHED OUT TO rescue a coachman. Mrs. Huntley called for tea. Lady Elsa arrived with maids carrying trays. Verity wasn't in the least hungry. Her stomach felt like stone, and her head whirled.

Minerva patted Verity's arm, then stood to confer with the steward and curate in the corner. They whispered between themselves, then sent the footman on another errand. Clare poured tea, but Verity was afraid to hold the cup. She was shivering again.

Uncle Warren? She could not work her mind around Rafe's accusation. If her stout, miserly uncle wanted her dead, he could have pushed her down stairs any number of times these last years. No one would have missed her. Why would he care if she lived or died? He already had everything she'd ever wanted.

Rafe seemed to believe it had to do with the painting. Was he saying the man pushing her father was her *uncle*? Had he taken all she had ever loved as well? Her shivering intensified. It made no sense.

The men returned, shoving and dragging two rather bruised and disheveled. . . prisoners? Their hands were bound anyway. Distracted by this novelty, Verity appraised the new arrivals.

"Luther?" she whispered in dismay, recognizing the insolent

young man who had been assigned to escort her to the bank. He hadn't been a bad sort, just rude and lazy. What was he doing here?

At the sound of his name, Luther quit protesting and went white as any of the manor's ghosts.

The other prisoner was female—the woman in black? Verity considered what little she could see of the personage wrapped in heavy skirts, full sleeves held back with bedraggled ribbons, and an ugly bonnet hiding her hair. Of middling age, middling size, jowls drooping toward her wrinkled neck, mouth pinched and angry, she did not look like anyone Verity knew.

"She was beating him with his own crop," Henri said in amusement as Rafe stationed the prisoners in a corner and placed his massive bulk between them.

Hunt lowered himself to his desk chair and snatched up one of the delicacies Lady Elsa had prepared. He gestured at Luther. "You know him, Miss Porter?"

"He is my uncle's footman. Why on earth is he here?" None of this made sense. Luther could have beat her senseless, stolen the bank bag, and left her in an alley long, long ago. Like her, he was too stupid to do anything more than follow orders.

"He's our new carriage driver, calls himself Arthur." Hunt looked disgusted. "We hired him the week before Miss Edgerton's death."

"I didn't have naught to do with nothing!" Luther protested. "I been taking care of that landau as if it were my own."

"You stupid fool!" the woman cried. "If you'd done what you ought, my man wouldn't be suffering in a dungeon! Now you straighten all this out so I can take him home, where he belongs."

"As far as we are aware, Clement set fire to a cottage and destroyed its contents," Hunt corrected mildly. "He won't be going anywhere anytime soon, unless he cares to recompense the owners for the destruction or someone proves his innocence."

Ignoring the woman's screech of outrage, Luther leaned over to peer at Verity. "Miss Palmer, is that you? You look different."

"You want to see my broken foot as proof?" she asked dryly, pointing her cane at the bandage bulging beneath her open boot. Not that he'd bothered to see her to the physician that night. "Why are you here?"

"Your uncle told us we was to find Miss Edgerton and ask her for his painting back." Not having been offered a seat, he straightened. Ropes prevented him from placing his hands behind his back as he'd been taught to do but seldom had.

"And when she refused?" Hunt asked before Verity could.

Luther shrugged. "I got my post as coachman. I didn't need to go back to Town to be yelled at. I always wanted to be a coachman."

The female prisoner struggled as if she wanted to hit him some more. Verity wished she could remember her, but she didn't.

"You let my man do all the dirty work, you thatch-gallow! All you had to do was sweet talk the old tabby a little, see how much she wanted for the painting, but no, you couldn't get past the back door. You left it to me!"

Rafe interrupted this argument. "Is Mr. Palmer in town?"

Her uncle? Why on earth would her uncle even know Gravesyde existed. . . *Miss Edgerton.* He'd sent Luther to retrieve a painting. He knew where her former governess lived. Why? She'd never in a lifetime cipher all this. People weren't numbers.

Luther shrugged. "Not so's I'm aware. I ain't seen him since I left Town."

The servant was not only too tall to be the man who'd pushed her, he'd been driving the carriage at the time. She couldn't accuse him of anything except laziness.

The woman—Mrs. Clement?—shut up and looked wary instead of answering the question. Could she have worn men's clothes this morning?

"We can lock her in the wine cellar until she talks," Hunt suggested. "I think we've plugged all the rat holes."

Very, very scared, Verity wanted this over now. Uncle Warren?

Here? She could scarcely think about what Rafe was insinuating. If these people somehow killed Miss Edgerton. . .

But they seemed to be saying they were only sent for the painting. Unable to stay silent any longer, she dug her fingers into her palms and demanded, "Are you saying Mr. Palmer, my uncle, asked you to retrieve a painting from Miss Edgerton?"

Luther bobbed his head eagerly. "Sent me and Clem to fetch it. Her ladyship here come along to borrow her family's caravan, said she wasn't letting her man sleep in no woods."

Apparently gathering the seriousness of the situation, Mrs. Clement remained mute.

"Why would my uncle want a painting when he just lost his business premises? He never cared about the paintings on his office walls, and I'm certain his wife would not want anything so evil." Verity still couldn't believe what she was hearing.

Luther shrugged again. Mrs. Clement pinched her lips tighter. At a nod from Hunt, his artist cousin ambled off.

The man she thought was Lady Elsa's husband arrived, shoving a filthy and cowed Clement. Verity studied the prisoner closer but still couldn't place him. He was only a little taller than his wife, rounded, balding, and bandy-legged. He could have been the man who pushed her, except he'd been locked up.

"Thanks, Jack." Hunt reached for a decanter and glasses on a shelf behind his desk. "Is it too early?"

"Stop it, Hunt," Clare said in annoyance. "You're taunting the prisoner, and you don't know for certain how guilty he is."

"I ain't guilty of doin' nothing more than I was told!" Clement protested. "I told you everything I know." He only cast one anxious glance at his wife, then glanced longingly at the brandy decanter.

Arnaud returned bearing an easel and a portfolio. He took out Miss Edgerton's painting and set it up. "Is this the painting you were sent for?"

The prisoners stared at the dark portrait of evil. Their mouths dropped open. Clement, in particular, grew deathly pale. Admittedly, the watercolor presented a shocking image. Tears rolled down Verity's cheeks as she finally accepted what Rafe had been telling her.

"That's my uncle's carriage, isn't it?" she whispered. "It just isn't painted like that anymore."

Cursing and weeping, Clement crumpled to the floor.

"Why?" Verity whispered, taking the handkerchief Minerva handed her.

"Clem didn't mean to do that!" Mrs. Clement cried. "It were an accident! Clem didn't know the old bastard pushed him. It was all of a sudden like. He been holding that over my poor man's head all these years, and it was him that did it! He needs to hang."

Verity concurred, but she didn't know how it would be done and she still didn't fully understand why. Her father's business had failed. The house in its undesirable part of town couldn't possibly be worth killing for. What had her uncle gained?

"Stand up and tell us what happened," Hunt ordered, nodding at Rafe to yank the prisoner back to his feet.

Visibly shaken, Clement shook his head in denial. "It were an accident! They was fighting all the way home. They got out. I was told to go around the block, keep the horses moving. It wasn't a street for fancy carriages. Mebbe I returned a little too fast—"

"You were drunk as usual, you old fool! The gin will be the death of you." Mrs. Clement wept the words.

"I couldn't of stopped!" he cried. "Nobody coulda stopped. He just stumbled right in front of the horses. It all happened so sudden."

"And then you left him there," Verity whispered in horror. "You drove off and left him there. He might have been saved!"

Standing with the aid of her cane, she slapped the weeping coachman as hard as she possibly could. It felt good.

FORTY: RAFE

"VERITY'S UNCLE IS STILL OUT THERE," RAFE WARNED AS CLEMENT was led away, followed by his weeping wife. They'd not been able to pry any confession from her, only imprecations and curses fitting any Gypsy witch.

They'd had to let Luther go back to polishing the carriage. At least Rafe knew the coachman hadn't been around when Verity was pushed. Establishing anyone's whereabouts for Miss Edgerton's death was a knot twister.

He sipped his brandy and paced, trying to think, but he only saw Verity's stricken face as she finally accepted that her uncle had killed her father. Tears streaked her cheeks, but she refused to leave the discussion.

"You don't think Mrs. Clement pushed Verity?" Hunt asked, pouring the brandy into glasses and letting everyone help themselves.

The ladies declined the liquor but sent for more tea.

"She seems more than capable of killing Miss Edgerton *and* pushing Verity," the librarian said, stirring sugar into her cup.

"She apparently has knowledge of herbs." Verity clenched and unclenched her fists instead of drinking tea. "But if that was my uncle pushing my father into the path of horses and *pushing* worked once. . ."

Excellent point. Did killers use the same means every time? That would mean the uncle hadn't killed Miss Edgerton. Rafe wanted to pin it all on her scoundrel uncle. But if Mrs. Clement had knowledge of herbs. . .

Rafe feared Verity might take flight at any moment, but he couldn't deduce her thoughts. The quiet, demure schoolteacher was inwardly raging. Her cheeks had flushed with pink and her normally brown eyes had turned molten gold in fury. If he could paint, he'd portray her as a vengeful goddess—a bit scary but fascinating.

"If he knew your governess had that painting, why would your uncle wait until now to look for it?" Henri asked, sipping Hunt's brandy. "When you think about it, why bother at all? It might serve as a warning, but if everyone thought her student dead. . . I can't imagine officialdom accepting a painting as evidence, ten years after the fact."

Walker cleared his throat and offered a letter from one of his portfolios. "I believe this might offer some explanations. Not all, of course. We need to find Mr. Palmer first. But those burned scraps may be more important than the painting."

Halfway between the steward and the captain, Rafe took the letter. Frowning, he scanned the contents before handing it to Hunt, who produced his monocle to read it. It pretty much confirmed what Rafe had feared all along. He might not be a general, but he'd learned the enemy was wily.

Upset, Verity watched their every move. The instant Hunt set the letter down, she snatched it from the desk.

She gasped at the contents at the same time as Hunt explained to their audience. "Our solicitor located the Palmer family's solicitors and queried them. They are in the process of transferring the late Faith Palmer's trust funds to her uncle, her only surviving relation."

Verity's hands shook as she held the eye-opening letter. "They are calling my uncle my father's *executor*? Not his heir? He stood nothing to gain by my father's death?"

"The partial burned letters we found," Rafe reminded her. "One appeared to be an amendment to a will. The other mentions fraud and embezzlement. Had your father not died, your uncle may have been removed as executor as well, which would have ruined him completely."

Her big eyes widened, her long lashes nearly sweeping her eyebrows. "Uncle Warren worked for Father. He meant to change his will, cutting out my uncle? For fraud?"

"Reason to kill," Hunt said coldly. "He'd most likely been let go from the firm."

"As executor, your uncle had access to your funds, even if he wasn't heir," Walker said from the back of the room. "If your father could no longer trust his brother, he most likely intended to remove him as executor. One assumes the house was part of the trust, perhaps giving you and your mother a life estate, which is why you couldn't be removed."

Verity clutched the letter to her breasts, a part of her anatomy that Rafe greatly admired. She wasn't a slender woman. She wouldn't break in his hands. And he didn't know why he was thinking like that about a virgin—except he admired her stalwart, stubborn character as much as her pigeon-plump breasts.

"But I was told my father's business was failing, that there were no funds, and that was why my uncle set up his business to keep the house running."

"We'll have to verify circumstances," Walker said from his corner. "But my assumption would be that the burned letter mentioning embezzlement and fraud indicates what happened to some part of your father's fortune. What business was he in?"

"Shipping," she murmured with a puzzled frown. "He owned dozens of ships and handled the trade from his warehouse on the docks. It's why we lived in that area. He liked keeping an eye on his possessions. He'd started out quite poor."

"We can only speculate," Walker warned. "But if your uncle

worked for your father, he was probably entrusted with funds that he may have siphoned for his own purposes. The loss of a single ship would put your father into debt. If he discovered his savings were gone. . ."

Tears flowed down Verity's cheeks. Rafe crouched down beside her. "Perhaps you should rest. This has to be distressing. There is nothing that can be done until we find your uncle."

Her jaw set. "Oh, no, I am not resting until I find that monster. I want to push him under carriage wheels!" She glanced at the letter again as she seemed to recall more. "Clement! If he was my uncle's driver in the painting, he's also the one who deliberately ran over my foot! He knows more than he's telling! *He didn't think I'd live to complain!*"

The room rumbled with anger. Whoever had torn apart the cottage looking for the painting had done so with malice. And stupidity. Clement quite possibly fit the bill.

Rafe wished he could wrap Verity in wool and store her somewhere safe until the world was a happy place again, but that wasn't happening soon. "You think Clement knew your uncle meant to set fire to your home?"

She slumped. "He may not have known everything. We can't even prove the explosion wasn't an accident."

Rafe stood. "I fear that Mr. Palmer wished to claim what remained of your inheritance before the solicitors went looking for the real heir upon her twenty-fifth birthday. The coincidence is unlikely."

"He insured the house," Verity whispered in horror. "I remember him proudly placing the placard over the door so the fire pumps would find us. I thought he was *protecting* my home!"

That made much too much sense. Hunt whistled in shock. Rafe wanted to punch something, anything. But he had to use his head, not his hands, in his new position as bailiff.

Verity might not inherit her home, but she would come into insurance funds—if they could only keep her alive long enough to claim them.

Accustomed to taking orders, not giving them, Rafe had to cast his old role aside. No one else had any clear idea what to do. He knew how to organize a small troop. It was up to him to catch an embezzling killer.

"We have to assume we're dealing with a desperate man." Rafe returned to pacing. "Clement has admitted to driving the coach that killed Mr. Palmer, the elder. He has indicated that it is Mr. Palmer, the younger, who pushed Verity's father to his death. We have verified that Palmer has not told his niece that she is an heiress. Instead, someone attempts to kill her before she inherits. Unless he hired someone besides Clement, that could only be her executor—*her uncle*. It is very likely that Mr. Palmer is here to finish the task that the explosion failed to accomplish."

With all eyes on him, Rafe waited for someone with more experience or authority to argue with his conclusion, but no one did. They were respecting him, for reasons he did not entirely understand. He was an innkeeper, a mess sergeant. His instinct demanded that he find Warren Palmer, grab him by the neck, and shake him until his eyes bulged. But instinct didn't apply here.

He had to keep his anger harnessed to plot and plan instead of throttle. "We know, at the time Verity says a man pushed her, that Luther was with the carriage, and Clement was locked in the cellar. The person we chased wore a frockcoat, breeches, and boots. Unless all the culprits are into wearing costumes, I will assume her attacker was a man and not Mrs. Clement. The only person who wants her dead is her uncle. Only the servants have not mentioned traveling with him and no one has seen him."

"Palmer would have wanted to establish an alibi," Hunt noted. "He sent his servants to do the dirty work and probably spent these past weeks very visible in the city to establish that anything happening on the other side of the country had nothing to do with him."

"Threatening the gas company and the fire company and. . ." Verity murmured. "He was in the newssheets. He had to have sought them out."

Rafe nodded. "But his lackeys were incompetent, didn't acquire the evidence, and killed Miss Edgerton instead of robbing her. That all fits. Palmer held an ax over Clement's head, so his servant had no choice but to obey orders or risk gaol for running over Verity's father. Guiltfree, Luther did not care and moved on."

"I suppose Luther must have approached Miss Edgerton first," Verity said, following his every word. "He's a little more presentable than Clement. When she refused him, he gave up. He's lazy like that. Then he came here looking for a position. So Miss Edgerton was warned that my uncle was after the ax she held over his head."

Rafe grinned at her for using his words. She offered a faint smile back.

Minerva spoke before he could continue. "Can we assume that Miss Edgerton learned of Verity's presumed death and threatened Mr. Palmer with the law?"

"Most likely." Rafe paced in thought. "He may not have known precisely what was in the painting or how much evidence she had. He had to find out. Then the Clements must have warned him they'd seen someone who looked like his niece. . . He panicked and had to see for himself."

"Mrs. Clement—the woman who suggested marjoram for the stew—she ran when she saw me. She knew it was me! So she warned my uncle and he came here to kill me," Verity said in an even tone that didn't hide her fury. "He must be here in Gravesyde!"

Killing Verity would leave no one to question her uncle's access to her trust. Clement wasn't a reliable witness. Rafe worked through his thoughts aloud. "Palmer is a pampered gentleman, accustomed to his creature comforts. If he's just arrived, he won't know how to survive without servants to look after him. We cannot know which of them poisoned Miss Edgerton or if it was even intentional, but Palmer is on his own now. He either needs to hire a killer—unlikely when he's so far out of his element—or act quickly so he might scurry back to his rathole and pretend he was there all the time."

He turned to Verity. "Does he know how to shoot?"

She frowned in thought. "My father carried a sword and a rapier and had a knife collection. He only owned one pistol, and it was quite old, a relict of his sailing days. My uncle sold them all. As you say, he preferred lackeys. I believe the painting proves that."

Rafe nodded and swung on the sturdy curate who had been listening more than participating. "Mr. Upton, you know how to defend yourself?"

The clergyman blinked and straightened. "I do, sir. I grew up rough."

"You are the only one of us who matches Verity's height. How would you fare in skirts?"

FORTY-ONE: PAUL

"I feel like an utter imbecile because I am one, correct?" Paul muttered, taking Rafe's arm as if he were a weak female. Of course, with the long hem tangling around his boots, he could understand why women might need support to walk. And the insane, long-brimmed bonnet was worse than blinders on a horse. He couldn't see anyone coming at him from the side. How did women manage to walk?

"You are a soldier in the war on evil," Rafe muttered back, strolling slowly so he could pretend he was adjusting his stride to Verity's.

Daylight had fled by the time they descended the manor drive into the village. In the sliver of lamplight, if anyone watched, they'd only catch a glimpse of Rafe's bright curls and large form, and a figure in skirts wearing Verity's bonnet and carrying a cane.

"You need to buy Verity one of those walking sticks concealing a knife," Paul retorted. "I daresay she'd stab her uncle quick enough if she were adequately armed."

"But snatching the stick from her hand would be an attacker's first move. You have the strength to hang onto it. Verity isn't trained to throw a punch, pull a knife, or shoot."

When they reached the village street, Rafe slowed down to

greet the church's deacon, who merely nodded and wandered on, not recognizing Paul. "Although I fear she's furious enough to kick the man downstairs if offered the opportunity. And I'm surmising you won't."

"You're surmising correctly. I will defend myself and you, but I will not attack," Paul declared firmly.

"Which is how I want it. If the scoundrel is here, I want explanations, and then we can send him off to hang, as it should be. All you're to do is draw him out. He's a city man. He has to be tired of sleeping with fleas or whatever he's doing to hide himself. The soldiers are keeping an eye on the caravan, so he's probably not bunking there." Rafe opened his lantern wider as they approached the inn.

"You're assuming he's not only here but inside the inn, aren't you? Perhaps he's been hiding in the attic all along. The place is large enough to hide an army." Paul studied the dark façade of the sprawling old inn with its myriad of hiding places. "Where's Wolfie?"

"I had the blacksmith take him in. I didn't want Wolf scaring off our target." Rafe swung the lantern casually, illuminating different parts of the yard.

Paul memorized the layout. Henri had left his cart parked by the back door. Lumber, stones, and brick were stacked about, but none made for much concealment. He tried to surreptitiously study the inn windows, but he didn't dare allow light to fall on his face.

"You don't look much like Verity," Rafe said in amusement as they approached the front door. "Pull the shawl around you and hide what you don't have."

Paul felt for the hilt of his knife through the purse slit in his mother's skirt. Reassured it was where he could reach it, he pulled the shawl tighter with a black-gloved hand. He ought to resent that he was the only one slight enough to play a female role, but he wore robes every Sunday. Wardrobe didn't make the man.

278

"Do you think there has been time for everyone to be stationed?" Paul murmured as they stepped into the dark lobby.

"Time, yes, opportunity, unknown. It's not easy to slip unseen into a place most likely being watched. Henri may or may not be inside his cart. He may be lying in wait outside after pretending to head up the hill. We don't know where the enemy is. Our scouts aren't very useful." Wryness tinted Rafe's whisper as he set the lantern on the lobby desk.

"It's pretty hard to conceal Arnaud and Hunt," Paul admitted. He didn't want to consider where Jack and Fletcher were stationed. The ex-soldiers had carried rifles when they headed for the trees.

Rafe kept his voice low as he stomped around the lobby, shoving crates about. "They're about somewhere. Your mother will hack off heads if anything happens to you."

"The place smells vaguely of oil," Paul whispered. "Did you fill the lamps?"

"The women probably did while they were cleaning. I think I smell some sort of cleaning fluid. . . or they had a drunken party up there." Rafe spoke louder. "I'll go up and make sure it's safe. Heat some water, if you will."

Paul didn't reply. He concentrated on sounding like a woman walking. Instead of going to the kitchen, however, he hid behind the bar in the pub and stripped off the bonnet and damned skirt. If he had to fight, it would be in trousers. Let Palmer come looking for him.

With that thought, he set the straw bonnet on a large bottle, wrapped the shawl around a stool, and draped the skirt over a chair. Having created a tower of clothing, he carried it into the kitchen. In the dark, all that could be seen was a vague outline.

Now all they could do was wait—and pray.

FORTY-TWO: VERITY

VERITY HAD LISTENED TO THE MEN PLOT THROUGH DINNER. Unaccustomed to speaking up or arguing, she let them rattle on without her.

But this was her personal nightmare. If they were right. . . her own uncle had killed her father! And wanted her dead. It couldn't be more personal than that.

She supposed she ought to let Rafe do things legally. That's how he was, and she certainly appreciated that he wouldn't burn down anyone's home or push them under a carriage. But she had learned to defend herself by any means available, since there had never been anyone else to do so. She didn't have any qualms about using whatever means necessary to stop a scoundrel.

She simply didn't know how.

As the men went off to set a trap, the women gathered to worry in the withdrawing room after dinner. Verity refused to sit. She simply couldn't, not while Rafe and others were prepared to protect her worthless life.

Cuddling Marmie, she swallowed her fear of speaking to an audience of respectable ladies. "I think we should arm ourselves," she said uncertainly. When conversation stopped and all eyes turned to her, she trembled, but it didn't matter if she made a fool of herself. No one else should be harmed because of her. "We have no way of knowing that my uncle is at the inn. If he is in Gravesyde, it would be easy for him to learn that I am here, at the manor."

Minerva was instantly out of her seat. "Thank you. I agree. I am comfortable with a pistol and a knife. How about you?"

Not having thought that far, Verity gave her cane a wry glance. "A sword? A frying pan?"

Patience instantly popped up. "I have sharp hoes!"

Lavender removed a vicious pair of scissors from her sewing basket. Coming in late, Lady Elsa—not only a cook but an excellent horsewoman—suggested riding crops and whips and returned to the kitchen for suitable weaponry for the others.

"We need a signal," Mrs. Huntley—Clare—decided. "If we are to spread out, we need to sound an alarm if we see anything untoward."

The curate's mother, also the manor's housekeeper, arrived carrying a broom and a carpet beater. She nodded her head at this suggestion. "The place is too large for us to see each other. Perhaps if we shout something innocent, like *huzzah*?"

"Hallelujah," Patience said with a grin. "I could sing it."

Verity loved that these women had immediately leapt to her aid. She feared they would hurt themselves, however, and that had never been her intention. "I know you have a footman and butler at the main entrances. Do we need to guard all the doors?"

"I'll see that we have maids and footmen at every entrance to sound an alert, although guarding every window, or even room, is impossible," the housekeeper admitted.

"Quincy and his son can patrol the main corridor," Minerva suggested. "Does anyone know how to unlock Hunt's gun vault? They should probably be armed."

"I do." Clare rushed out to find the ex-boxer butler and his son.

"I suppose this is good practice," Thea said with a frown. "We are isolated and can't expect the men to always protect us. I might

PATRICIA RICE

manage a rapier if all I need to do is stab someone's toes. I hope
the boys are safely in bed and don't hear us or they'll be down
directly."

"I can't imagine the schoolroom is in any danger," Minerva
said, "but we should send a note up to Mr. Birdwhistle to warn
him of what we are doing. He might be a little alarmed by an
outbreak of *hallelujah*."

Verity tried to slip out with the others scattering to find
weapons, but Minerva caught up with her. "I'm not letting Paul
go into danger without me," she whispered resolutely. "So whatever you're planning, I'm with you."

"Perhaps, for the first time in my life, I am not planning
anything," Verity admitted. "I simply know I cannot let anyone be
harmed for my sake. I've lost too much. I have nothing. No one
will miss me if I'm gone. But the rest of you. . . have no reason to
sacrifice yourselves."

Minerva made an inelegant noise. "Rafe would burn down the
town if anything happened to you. You are one of us now. You are
not alone. We do not let criminals roam free. It may be akin to
eradicating rodents, hopeless, but crime has to be addressed."

"A female army of constables?" Verity suggested in amusement, only because she was very, very afraid.

They followed Clare into the captain's study. Verity claimed a
small sword. If she used her cane, she only had one spare hand.
She was far more comfortable with the cane. Minerva took a pistol
and expertly loaded it, then added a dirk to her arsenal. She was
petite and all the swords were large and heavy.

Verity tried to slip away again while the rest of the weapons
were distributed, but Minerva stayed with her. She supposed the
librarian had a reason to be concerned about her fiancé. Mr. Upton
was, after all, dressed as Verity.

"I don't want to ruin my new gown," Verity decided, trying to
balance her weapons. "I need to change."

"Boots," Minerva agreed. "Aprons for pockets. Cloaks for
concealment."

They hurried upstairs. Several of the others apparently had the same thought. Verity could hear them down the family side of the corridor as she entered her chamber in a front guestroom. Lavender had brilliantly designed her dinner gown for someone without a lady's maid, but it took a few minutes to remove it and pull on her old blacks. She tucked Marmie into a drawer of linen with a torn handkerchief the kitten liked to shred.

At the main stairs, she met Minerva wearing a concealing cloak. Together, they hurried through the manor and slipped into the dark night from the unused east wing by the drive, making certain a footman locked it behind them.

"The original medieval manor block was built like a fortress," Minerva said as they cautiously crossed to the stable without a lantern. "Whoever added the new wings added too many doors and windows for it to ever be used as a fortification again."

"Sharpshooters in all the towers?" Verity suggested, trying to keep her tone light. She had utterly no idea what she was doing but she welcomed the idea of a whip and riding crop.

Lady Elsa was there ahead of them. She had rounded up the stable lads—including Luther—and every weapon they could carry. Verity didn't think her uncle's former footman a wise idea.

"Unless you want to use him as a target, I suggest locking Luther in a stall," she said dryly as the new coach driver stumbled down the stairs from his room in stocking feet.

"A lure," Minerva cried happily. "Exactly what we need. If Mr. Palmer is anywhere about, he'll be certain to seek someone he knows for aid."

Luther protested volubly. One of the other stable men ran upstairs for Luther's boots.

"You'll be well guarded, sir," Lady Elsa said happily. "No one wants to harm you. Just stroll down the drive, make yourself visible."

Verity thought she might choke holding back laughter. This was deadly serious business, but the ladies. . . were fearless. And quite insane. She left Luther cowering in a corner, protesting.

283

Instead of guarding *inside* the manor as she'd proposed, the ladies were apparently slipping like shadows through the gardens and yard and around hedges, protecting the perimeter. Verity didn't think if they sang the entire Messiah, there would be enough hallelujahs to reach all ears, but she was glad she'd aroused awareness.

With a riding crop in her apron band, cane in one hand, sword in the other, she followed the row of trees lining the drive, keeping an eye on shadows.

She didn't know her uncle well, at all, she realized. She'd known he was a drunkard, a mean miser, and accustomed to city streets and servants to do his bidding. She supposed that might make him hideously uncomfortable in a country setting, more so than she had been. He couldn't ride about in a carriage and wouldn't appreciate taking dark lanes on foot.

Rafe was correct. If he was here, Uncle Warren had most likely hidden in the inn. But if he was the man who had pushed her, he'd escaped on a horse earlier. Would he return? He had to go back to London soon if he was to protect his alibi—but riding at night was treacherous.

Minerva drifted toward the orchard, on the east side of the hill. She probably knew footpaths that Verity didn't. She stayed with the drive that she could see rather than get lost.

There, further down the drive, the evergreens moved. There was no wind. Minerva couldn't see the movement from the path she'd taken. This could simply be one of the men keeping watch or going home for the evening. Well, she had no other plan. She might as well watch and follow too.

The overgrown grass muffled her feet as the distant shadow took a footpath away from the drive and down the hill. This concealed path seemed to lead in the direction of the chapel and inn, but that meant little, if Rafe had him guarding the inn.

Surrounded as it was by trees, the path couldn't be seen unless one was on it. She swallowed hard and hoped that wasn't her uncle, although the silhouette appeared the right height. A cloak prevented seeing more. Except for Mr. Upton, most of the gentlemen were taller than this, but she didn't know all the servants.

She heard a muffled curse and splashing. A brook ran along the manor property, she recalled, one that rushed down to the river on the other side of the hill. She'd been told the captain had recently built a new bridge on the carriage drive but apparently not for this path. Apparently the shadow wasn't as familiar with the path as she'd thought.

Her target squelched up the opposite bank. She carefully chose rocks to cross on. It hadn't rained recently, so the water was low.

As they crossed the field toward the chapel, the inn loomed large against the clear night sky. She knew Rafe and Mr. Upton had hoped to lure her uncle here, but if this were he. . . had he seen them going down the drive and simply took a different route?

As she watched, lamplight illuminated one of the inn's upper guestrooms. She held her breath, watching the window. The silhouette passing in front of it seemed large enough to be Rafe, and her heart pounded a little faster. He'd arrived safely. Clenching her weapons, she waited. A moment later, a light appeared in the kitchen window. She covered her mouth to smother a laugh at the silhouette of a stiff figure in a bonnet and what appeared to be a shawl. The curate? Did they really think that a shawl and bonnet resembled *her*?

The shadow she'd been following hesitated, then crouching down, scurried toward the crumbling wall around the inn. She caught her breath. That silly silhouette had caught his attention? Surely not. . .

He crossed at a broken place and slipped into the inn yard. Concealing himself like that could not mean anything good.

Where were the others? She didn't want to sound an alarm and have everyone rushing in and ruining the trap if this wasn't the killer.

She froze as the demons of uncertainty circled. Rafe was

risking his life for her! She had to decide and act *now*. Not ten long years later.

Setting her jaw, she approached the wall and shouted, "Uncle Warren!"

To her utter shock, the cloaked figure swung around and blackened the air with familiar curses. "You! You never did stay where you belonged!"

. . . as if she were the one at fault for making him come out here!

Instead of cowering like simple Faith, Verity drew on years of suppressed rage. There was only one reason for the reprehensible villain who had killed her father and destroyed her home to be in Gravesyde—to kill her too!

Without thinking twice, Verity sang *"Hallelujah, hallelujah,"* at the top of her lungs. Forgetting her broken foot and clumsiness, swinging her cane with the vigor of the song, she ran toward the man who wielded death and destruction.

He opened his lantern and a torch abruptly illuminated the dusty yard.

A torch. Recalling a fiery inferno emblazoned against a night sky. . . Sheer terror ripped through Verity.

FORTY-THREE: RAFE

FINDING THE SOURCE OF THE FISHY OIL AND ALCOHOL STENCH, RAFE took the stairs down, two at a time, shouting, "Upton, get out, stay low, behind the cart, but get the blazes *out*!"

Cursing until the air turned blue, he reached the kitchen, praying the curate had obeyed.

He had no way of knowing if the killer knew how to shoot, but he was almost certainly out there, waiting for his moment. Rafe had to spirit the curate away from the deadly inn and through the open yard without anyone seeing—a quandary.

Outside, a voice resembling Verity's rose in insane shrieks of *hallelujah.*

He must be hallucinating from oil fumes. Paul was already out the kitchen door by the time Rafe reached it. They ducked low behind Henri's cart, scanning the yard as more voices and shouts emerged from the night.

From this vantage point, he saw an open lantern and flames sputtering in the distance, just as he'd feared. The bastard had turned the inn into an incendiary bomb simply waiting to be lit, trusting a method that had worked before.

The wild screams escalated and. . . echoed? An entire chorus of *hallelujahs* carried up and down the hill.

"Run for the woods, if you can," Rafe warned the curate, wanting him well out of the way before the bomb ignited.

Even as Rafe broke from their hiding place, hoping to distract the killer from the curate, the singing dark silhouette of a vengeful angel manifested behind the cloaked madman holding a torch.

Verity! By all that was holy, she wielded a sword as well as her cane.

Gripping a blazing torch in one hand, lantern in the other, the cloaked scoundrel swung to meet his singing attacker. Before he could complete his clumsy turn, Verity walloped his head with her stick so hard that he staggered. As the villain tried to regain his balance, she swung again with the sword.

Fighting to dodge the blows and hang onto his torch, the cloaked form stumbled over a stone.

Before Rafe could even *think* about crossing the yard to save the insane angel from herself, the arsonous villain tumbled—onto his torch. Saturated by spilled fuel from the swinging lantern, the cloak ignited.

Verity's song escalated to screams, as did that of everyone converging on the inn.

Rafe watched in horror as the blaze rose into a bonfire. Turning, he rushed back to the kitchen, where he heaved the fifty-pound bag of flour over his shoulder. Trailing a path of white, he ran into the yard again to slice the burlap open over the burning cloak, smothering all but embers with flour.

Black fury roiled his soul as he grasped what the scoundrel intended, what he could still accomplish if the flames spread. Instead of running, the poor curate used his shabby coat to beat at the smoldering fire in the dead grass and debris.

Illuminated by flames, shadows raced down the hill to the pump.

Letting others dump water on the mix of flour and oil, Rafe caught Verity in his arms and carried her from the sight. Shivering and shaking, she wept against his chest while others doused the final sparks racing toward the inn.

Rocking her back and forth, he watched in unsympathetic rage as the fire died and people began to circle the villain. The gentlemen used their swords to remove the remaining fragments of smoldering cloak. What little that was left unscorched beneath revealed a stout man of middling height, with hanks of graying hair. The clergyman kneeled down and located an unscorched and unmoving wrist. Testing it, he shook his head.

"He's gone, sweetheart," Rafe whispered in her ear, offering her reassurances while waiting for his racing pulse to slow so he could think coherently. He was utterly amazed at what she had done. "You stopped him. He meant to torch the inn with us in it."

She buried her head in his shoulder, refusing to look.

Wielding an assortment of weapons, women spilled across the now dark yard. Rafe shook his head in disbelief but didn't disabuse them of their notion that they could have stopped a demented scoundrel with anything short of a shotgun. Or his own torch. Verity had risked her life to save the inn.

"You'll have to identify him, Miss Porter," Captain Huntley said, returning to his feet after taking a look at the half-baked corpse. "None of us recognize him."

"Clubfoot," she whispered. "Uncle Warren has a clubbed foot. I should have noticed his special boot and shouted sooner."

That explained the clumsiness of the man's actions. He'd fallen over his own feet. "He wore a cloak. Until he opened the lantern, you could not have seen his boot." Rafe stroked her hair. She'd lost her pins and he felt guilty enjoying the silken strands beneath his rough fingers. His heartbeat had barely slowed, but that could be because of the female bounty pressed against him.

"Flour." After examining a burned boot and confirming the misshapen foot, Henri dusted the detritus off his hands in disgust. "Who knew?"

"A cook who has to put out fires." Lady Elsa strode up like a Valkyrie carrying a whip instead of a sword.

"Oil and flour batter," Rafe said in disgust. "I'll never fry another chicken."

The lady glanced down at the victim with a visible shudder. "What a waste of good grain. I'll happily replace it for you, maybe with two sacks. I'm sure my trustees will agree that saving lives is a justifiable expense."

In his arms, Verity choked and coughed at the macabre promise. Experienced in war, Rafe understood black humor. An extremely wealthy heiress and an eccentric, Lady Elsa must have had brutal experiences in her past. Her husband emerged from the trees to hug her shoulders, kiss her streaming blond hair, and lead her away. There was a story for another day.

The captain studied the inn's thatch and the still smoldering torch. "You'd have lost the inn, but there might have been time to escape. It would have been useful to interrogate him."

Rafe shook his head vehemently. "The bastard emptied oil over the floors in the upper story, then for good measure, broke bottles of that alcoholic elixir. Heat from just a fireplace might ignite the fumes. That's how he blew up Verity's home."

"Barrels of whale oil," she murmured against his chest. "Uncle Warren claimed he was saving money by buying barrels of oil from a company going bankrupt. He stored them all over the house, for convenience, he said."

Rafe held her closer, wishing he could erase the horror of her memory by running his hands up and down her back, but he did not have the right to even hold her like this. For this brief moment out of time, he absorbed the pleasure of the rise and fall of her breasts and her racing heartbeat. She was alive, no thanks to her villainous uncle.

Captain Hunt practically growled as he studied the inn. "We'd better start scrubbing it down then. No lanterns or fires until we do."

The librarian took the curate's arm and the pair departed, whispering. Rafe assumed they'd take charge of the body. He needed to take charge of cleaning the inn, but he couldn't bear to let Verity go.

Hunt's wife decided for him, tapping Rafe's hands so he'd

release. . . the young lady, not a widow. "I'll take Verity up to the manor. A bit of brandy and sleep will help. Some."

He didn't have the right to kiss her hair as he'd seen the lieutenant do with his lady wife. Reluctantly, Rafe released her. Verity cast him a glance he couldn't interpret, then obediently followed Mrs. Huntley.

It would be a very long night.

"You may want to regain control of your arsenal." Rafe addressed Hunt, nodding toward the shadows slipping back up the drive. "I'm fairly certain your librarian was carrying a pistol and your housekeeper had a blunderbuss."

The captain snorted. "Clare had a rapier. I don't know what the devil she thought she could do with it."

"On the Continent, we used them for cooking vermin." Without another glance at the roasted corpse in the dirt, Rafe strode back to the inn to begin pumping water and restoring order. That, he knew how to do.

What he meant to do about Verity. . . required planning, a technique he had not mastered but hoped to learn.

Instinct might save his life, but it wouldn't win a woman's heart. He'd lived an aimless existence until now. With a worthy goal in sight, he'd learn to strategize.

TUESDAY

FORTY-FOUR: VERITY

The next morning, Verity sat on her manor guest bed, stroking Marmi, reluctant to go downstairs where people were indubitably discussing the prior evening's horrors. She didn't particularly understand her reluctance. She simply knew she never wished to think about last night, ever.

She was hiding again, yes.

She wondered if she might slip down to the inn and fix herself eggs. She knew how to do that. Would Rafe let her stay in one of the rooms until she knew what to do next?

She couldn't know what to do until she talked to solicitors, apparently. And the manor occupants were the ones who knew about solicitors and wills and estates and. . . so many things she hadn't learned about while she cowered from the world in her cellar. She'd sold all her father's legal tomes as too boring to comprehend.

A knock on her bedchamber door dragged her from her torpor.

"Verity? We need you downstairs, please. The heirs have written, and the Prescotts have left a letter, and Hunt wants to torture Mrs. Clement until she talks. It's becoming a little desperate." Minerva spoke through the closed panel.

She liked the librarian. She didn't want to cause her any trouble. Reluctantly, Verity tucked Marmie in her apron pocket and unlocked the door. "I didn't know whether to wear black again."

"Don't," Minerva said firmly. "You cannot possibly be related to a toad. The bronze is respectful. That's all that is necessary. Have you eaten? We can take a tray into the library where you won't be interrogated until you're ready."

A toad. Verity almost smiled at this description of her uncle. All her life, she'd tried to mind her mother's memory and be respectful, but the rude appellation appealed. Perhaps experience taught that not everyone deserved respect. She'd work out the dividing line some other time, preferably after breakfast.

Some while later, fortified by one of Lady Elsa's generous meals and Minerva's discussion of schoolbooks and students, Verity was better prepared when Captain Huntley entered the library. With him, he brought a dark-haired man in frockcoated attire carrying a portfolio of papers.

Hunt greeted her with a curt nod. "Miss Porter, I must send a report to assizes with the Clements. I need to clarify a number of issues before I'll be satisfied that I've covered all the angles. This is Garret Browning III, a solicitor from Stratford who handles our affairs. He has been helping us locate information on your father's death and estate, and he is also conferring with Mr. Culliver, Miss Edgerton's solicitor. Browning, this is Miss Palmer, who prefers not to use her family name."

The gentleman bowed to her as if she were a lady. Verity didn't know whether to stand or offer her hand or the proper etiquette at all. It had been so very long. . . Relying on memories of her mother, she smiled, nodded, and remained seated, stroking Marmie in her lap.

"Once we have established all proprieties, proof of your identity, verification of your uncle's death, and so forth, we will arrange to have your father's funds transferred to your name on the date of your birth, per his wishes." The solicitor set the portfolio in front of her, as if she had any notion what to do with it. "I fear any amendments to the original will were lost, which is why your uncle continued as your trustee."

"Not that it matters any longer," Minerva said carelessly, "but we have scraps of paper that show Verity's father meant to cut his brother out. What we would like to know is how Miss Edgerton came by them and if they had anything to do with her death."

That, Verity understood. Heart racing, she watched the solemn gentleman, hoping he had more magic wands.

Inheriting her home now that it was gone did not improve her circumstances. If her father had actually cut his brother off, and left his estate to her and her mother, she comprehended her uncle's angry greed and why her father had died. But she would like to know why Miss Edgerton had to die.

"We are hoping the Clements might offer insight," Hunt said. "I would like to bring Mrs. Clement in first, if Miss Porter would consent to join us to verify facts. Browning here can act as witness."

Nervously, Verity twisted her hands. "And Ra. . . Sgt. Russell? He knows far more than I do about the Clements' actions. As far as I'm aware, I've never met them."

"He spent the night scrubbing flammable liquids from the inn," Hunt said dryly. "We just woke him. This will be more about you than Miss Edgerton first. We'll see how to proceed after that."

Knotting her fingers to steady them, Verity nodded consent. While they waited for someone to bring up the prisoner, the solicitor sat next to her and showed her the portfolio. "The house was insured for a considerable sum, Miss Porter. If you wish to remain in Gravesyde, the proceeds will purchase almost any residence you desire and pay to repair and maintain it for years to come."

That brightened her day. "Miss Edgerton's cottage?"

"Mr. Culliver has received permission to sell the cottage since the heirs cannot afford to repair it. I'm certain they will happily sell it to the highest bidder," Hunt answered. "You should take time to be certain it's the wisest investment."

Verity's day measurably brightened. To have the cozy cottage for her home. . .

She had no means of keeping up the extensive gardens. The repairs and purchasing new furnishings would be a daunting task. Her hope fell, but she clung to the comforting notion of her own home—as she'd clung to her cellar.

"There is also a considerable investment fund in your name that has grown since your father's death," the solicitor continued. "One most likely intended to be your dowry. That is presumably what your uncle wished to acquire. It seems his counting house has sustained substantial financial losses, possibly due to embezzlement or incompetence. We can't say. We only know that the bank was preparing to transfer your funds to cover his debts until we stopped them." He pulled a statement from the bank from the stack of papers.

Verity gulped at the sum. She'd thought she might live on the few hundred pounds she'd stolen from her uncle. This was so very much more! But if her uncle had been deeply in debt. . . Surely one night's deposits hadn't plunged him into financial difficulties. His drunken carelessness was more likely.

"My uncle's family?" she asked, staring at the sum. "What happens to them?"

"That isn't your concern," Minerva admonished. "They never cared about how you fared, did they?"

They had not. Still. . . "I'm not them," Verity said softly, remembering how devastated she'd been when her father died. "Will they still have a home?"

"I believe the funds embezzled from your father most likely paid for it," the solicitor explained. "It was purchased shortly before his death."

She nodded, growing a little angry as she understood the pattern of greed. "My father's business, it wasn't bankrupt, was it? My uncle sold it."

"And used the funds to pay his debts, yes. It seems the younger Mr. Palmer had both a drinking and gambling habit, among other vices. It is not uncommon, I fear." The lawyer sounded gruff and unsympathetic. "Unless there are other funds, your aunt will most likely have to sell her home to pay his debts. Her daughters are grown and married. She won't be homeless."

She didn't know if that was fair, but she supposed she shouldn't worry about a woman who had never worried about her. Everyone had paid for Uncle Warren's vices. And her father had paid the ultimate price.

Verity had difficulty swallowing and greeted the arrival of Mrs. Clement with her jailer almost with relief. She couldn't fathom the loss, the tragedy, the evil that had her uncle had perpetrated. He'd even destroyed the lives of his servants. He could not have been a well man.

The soldier entering with the prisoner was very much a well man, proud, strong, a hard worker with a moral compass stronger than her own weak one. His gaze instantly fell on her, and she thrilled at the concern she saw there. She managed a smile for his benefit, and Rafe relaxed enough to shove the disheveled prisoner into a chair. The cobweb-infested, empty wine cellar prison wasn't an ideal chamber for maintaining appearances.

Mrs. Clement sat sullenly while introductions were made. She glared at Verity but glanced away when Rafe set a bottle of elixir on the table.

"Let me do this," Verity said, regaining her voice and interrupting the captain before he could speak. She needed to do this. She had to quit hiding and face facts in the broad light of day. "Mrs. Clement, how did you know Miss Edgerton?"

She could see the men tense, on the point of objecting. Inquiring about the governess wasn't their goal, but it was hers. The connection was there, if she could simply see it.

"You don't even remember, do you?" the woman sneered. "We was way below your notice."

"Might we have some tea?" Verity asked, not looking away, trying to recognize the flattened nose and hostile dark eyes lost in folds of flesh. "I was only fifteen when my father died. Children seldom notice anyone unless they want something. I don't remember you because you evidently did not regularly bring me books or tea or take me on outings, as Miss Edgerton did."

The older woman made a crude noise and rubbed at a smudge on her face. "That one thought she knew it all. I was the one what fetched the herbs she asked for. And she had the nerve to question my elixirs!"

The men sat back and shut up. Women talked to other women. Men intimidated. In her overlarge wing chair, Minerva quietly took notes, out of the prisoner's sight.

"So you worked in our kitchen?" Verity waited for the tea tray to be set down.

"I was the one what taught your cook to season," she said with a scoff. "Just because I can't read or write don't mean I don't know as much or more as that hatchet-faced baggage."

"Out of curiosity, how did Miss Edgewater know about your elixir?" Verity tried not to put words in the woman's mouth. She had a horrible notion of what happened now that she grasped how venal people could be. She wanted truth.

"Your mother appreciated my compound," Mrs. Clement said proudly. "She was a good woman."

And had spent the better part of her last years in bed with her medicines. Tensing, Verity merely nodded. "And Miss Edgewater objected?"

"Threw out my bottles, she did! I was glad to see the back of her."

"That was after my father died, wasn't it? My mother was bedridden with grief. You stayed but Miss Edgewater left." Verity struggled to put the words right. "Why did my uncle not let you go too?"

"Cause he needed me and Clem," The woman said proudly. "That baggage yelled and threatened him, said as how she meant to call the law if he turned everyone off. But me and Clem saw how we could finally get hitched, so we said we'd tell the Runners she was lying."

Standing behind Verity, Rafe squeezed her shoulder. Drawing strength from his touch, she filled the teacups, while she put together the next question. It wasn't easy skirting around the issue of her father's murder. "I'm surprised that my uncle didn't turn out me and my mother too. He didn't like us much."

Mrs. Clement shrugged. "The tart threatened him, said she had some sort of evidence, said if anything happened to you or your home, she'd lie, if she must, to see him hang. Stupid fool believed her."

It hadn't cost her uncle anything to leave Verity and her mother alone. As in everything, he'd simply taken the easiest route. Brave Miss Edgerton had kept them from being flung into the streets.

"And then I died," Verity said softly. Her uncle must have believed everyone, including Miss Edgerton, had forgotten invisible Faith Palmer after ten long years.

Mrs. Clement grimaced. "That was a nasty fire, I heard. Don't know how you escaped. Luther said as you was in there."

"Luther was in a pub and didn't see anything," Verity said in scorn. "So why did you visit Miss Edgerton all the way out here if I was dead?"

Caught by surprise, the prisoner replied without thinking.

"His Royal Pomposity wanted that painting, just like we told you. We was only following orders. You can't hold us for getting back what belonged to him." She sat back, satisfied she'd said all that needed to be said—while verifying everything Luther had told them.

"So my uncle sent you to retrieve a painting, Miss Edgerton refused to give it up, and then what happened?"

"The stupid boy didn't like being refused and wouldn't go back. So I had to do it." The old woman wrinkled her forehead. "It was like she was expecting me. Luther must have said something, 'cause she said she'd ordered more of my elixir. She meant to have it examined by an apothecary."

"Did that upset you?" Verity tried to sound sympathetic.

Mrs. Clement waved a careless hand. "Makes no matter to me and my customers what some rattle-pate says."

"But you still didn't have the painting, and you couldn't go home without it?"

The prisoner scowled. "It shoulda been simple. I mixed a sleeping powder, enough to keep her out while Clem and I searched. But a visitor started pounding on the door, and we had to leave. I didn't do nothing wrong, and we never found any painting, so you can't accuse us of stealing. You gotta let us go."

The old witch's "powder" and ignorance had put Miss Edgerton permanently to sleep.

Trying not to turn into a watering pot again, Verity glanced back at Rafe. He rubbed her shoulder comfortingly.

Captain Huntley nodded at the footman standing guard. "Take the prisoner back to the wine cellar. We'll let the judge decide whether it's murder."

They led her away, screaming vile curses.

FORTY-FIVE: RAFE

Terrified after learning of his employer's death, Clement admitted to no more than the accident of killing Verity's father and "accidentally" setting the cottage on fire. Neither man nor wife admitted to ransacking the cottage, but they were the only ones searching for the painting. The real villain was dead. Rafe left the gin-soaked lout in Hunt's hands for transportation to assizes and better minds than his.

With the crimes solved, a far more important task lay ahead. He didn't know if a rough military man could finesse his argument as nicely as Verity had done with her interrogation. He was a man of action, not charm. But he had an actual plan in place, which gave him some confidence.

He found Verity, as he'd feared, wistfully studying Miss Edgerton's cottage. Since she hadn't objected to his earlier reassurances, he tried the trick again, laying a hand on her shoulder and rubbing sympathetically. "Her heirs need the blunt. They authorized Mr. Culliver to sell everything, including the botanical plates. Mrs. Prescott had hoped the plates might help in finding her teacher's killer, but when they're printed, she'll sell the book to her fellow students who remember their teacher with fondness."

"Good to know her memory will go on." Sadly, she turned to stare down the empty village street. "It was lovely having a home, but I couldn't keep up the garden. I hope the new owners will allow Patience to take what she needs before they destroy it."

"Better," he said, hiding his immense relief that she was as practical as he thought. "Captain Huntley is offering for it. Now that the manor has funds, he wants it to properly house their steward."

She finally lifted her chin to study him, her thick velvet lashes sweeping upward in surprise. "He's buying it for Meera and Walker? Oh, that is perfect! Meera knows everything about herbs, and Patience can have her gardeners take care of the flowers. Lavender will have lavender for her scents!"

Arm draped daringly over her shoulders, Rafe steered her down the street. "Better, Hunt will turn the cottage's loft into a proper second floor, add servants' quarters, and a real stove. I believe Mrs. Walker intends to open an apothecary office in back."

"Where the women used to seeing Miss Edgerton will find her," she said in excitement. "I love this village. Do you think you could put me up for a little while at the inn until I find a room of my own—if I can talk Mrs. Underhill into joining me?"

This was where his plan became delicate. Rafe had had time to plan and to know what he wanted. But he had to think of her and not just himself. It wasn't quite the same as keeping his starving troop in provisions. She had choices. He had to acknowledge that.

"That's one possibility," he agreed, guiding her into the inn yard, where all signs of last night's horror had been swept away. The curate had arranged for a quiet burial. A load of lumber now rested where her uncle's conflagration had occurred. "Remember, you talked about creating a lending library?"

"We hardly have funds to. . ." She stopped herself as they entered the lobby. "I could, though, couldn't I? I'm not poor anymore."

"It's worth talking about." He'd had people in all morning, clearing up what he'd missed in the dark. Lighting lanterns while oil covered the floors had not been an option. The inn smelled of beeswax again. "Let me show you something, see what you think."

"What *I* think?" she asked in amusement.

He wanted to hear her happy again. Planning required determining goals, and her happiness was the first one.

He led her down the bedchamber corridor and opened a door. He'd left a lantern burning, since this closet had no windows for light. "It's only a small start, what I could do quickly, just to show you."

Peering in the doorway, she gasped and stepped inside, head swiveling as she took in the shelves of books. "My father's library! Where I can find a book without digging through crates. This is amazing! How did you. . ."

He pulled a book down and opened it on the battered table he'd dragged down from the attic. "Fletch helped me. We've discussed it. The curate and his intended want books available for the children, and adults, if possible. Fletch thinks we should have a gentleman's library, where guests can relax and read and enjoy drinks from the pub."

"No smoking," she said tartly. "Women and children allowed. Perhaps you could set hours for different groups."

"Excellent notion. I knew you'd be able to help. Upton thinks the church ladies might like a place to gather and sew and discuss fetes and such. Until he can raise funds for a chimney, the inn will be warmer than the chapel. If we use one of the larger rooms, added a few chairs—"

She actually clapped her hands in excitement. "I can see that. The room definitely needs to be larger. . ." She broke off and narrowed her eyes. "But you must earn money off every room to make improvements. One cannot earn money off a library."

He hid a smile. As he'd suspected, she had inherited her father's business sense. "I should rent it for meetings?"

She wrinkled her brow, thinking. "You could keep the adult library locked and offer a key to guests for an additional cost, perhaps. That won't be enough, but it's a start. Perhaps a small charge to reserve the room at certain hours? So you might earn off it all day. A lending library can charge subscription fees. I hate charging people, but until you're profitable. . ."

He loved watching her flush with excitement. This was the intelligent woman who had been abandoned in a cellar for too long, the one clever enough to accumulate a library, earn savings on nothing, and flee all alone.

She might be too smart for the likes of him, but if he struck while the iron was hot. . . He had his uses.

He tucked her hand into his elbow and led her to a much more spacious chamber, in the new addition, one with decent windows and level floors. He'd painted an old bedstead and a battered armoire in a pretty blue to match the print on the plain draperies Lavender had cut and hemmed for the mullioned panes. A braided carpet he'd bought from one of the cart women rested beside the bed. The washstand came from the manor attic. Ornately carved cherry, it had seen better days, but the chipped china washbasin with blue flowers fit on it. A matching chamber pot was visible beneath the still unadorned bed.

"I thought. . . Since you're to teach. . ." What he wanted and what he ought to say differed and tied his tongue in knots.

"For me?" At his nod, she leaned into him, resting her head trustingly against his shoulder and gazing about in awe. "It's beautiful. Will you do the cooking? I can keep the ledgers and learn to order the maids and maybe even help with the garden, but I don't think I'll ever cook as well as you do."

He swelled with pride, then reminded himself that she was an heiress. He was an impoverished ex-soldier. She could do better.

No, she couldn't. No one would cherish her more than he.

She glanced up at him, and this time, she had a wicked glint in her eyes. "I do not mind offering Mrs. Underhill a place as my companion. But you would soon fill the inn with family and servants and leave no room for guests. Did you want me to share your best chamber with Mrs. Underhill? And where would you sleep?"

And there it was, the opening he needed. And she'd deliberately offered it. They were practical people. She read books on geography, not romance. He issued orders, not pretty phrases. From the way she leaned into him, he hoped they had more than a meeting of minds.

"Clever puss," he murmured, lowering his head to brush his mouth against plush lips. "I'd like to sleep with you, if you will allow. Do you think you might consider a rufus-haired old soldier as husband if he promises to cook for you forever?"

In reply, she reached up to wrap her arms around his neck and bring his head closer.

Her kiss was everything he'd imagined and more.

COUPLES

GRAVESYDE MANOR MYSTERIES

Book #1 *The Secrets of Wycliffe Manor*: Captain Alistair Reid
Huntley and Clarissa (Clare) Knightley
Book #2 *The Mystery of the Missing Heiress:* Lt. Honorable John
(Jack) Cecil de Sackville and Lady Elspeth (Elsa) Laurel Villiers
Book #3 *The Bones in the Orchard:* Patience Upton and Henri
Lavigne
Book #4 *The Question of the Wedding Pearls*: weddings
Book #5 *The Case of the Purloined Pages:* Minerva (Penn) Peniston
and Paul Upton
Book #6 *The Dilemma of a Dead Scholar*: Arnaud Lavigne and
Dorothea (Thea) Reid Talbot

GRAVESYDE VILLAGE MYSTERIES

Book #1 *The Villain's Fatal Plot*: Verity Porter and Sgt. Rufus
Russell (Rafe)

GRAVESYDE PRIORY MYSTERY

The Secrets of Wycliffe Manor
Book #1

Be wary of what you wish for. . .

In Regency England:

The descendant of adventuring—dead—aristocrats, Clarissa Knightley supplements a modest inheritance by penning gothic novels that cost more than they earn. Upon learning that she has mysteriously inherited a share of an earl's estate, she rashly packs up her household. In remote Gravesyde Priory, she hopes to find a safe haven and family who will welcome her and her young nephew.

Instead, she discovers a drunken American army captain, his African servant, and ancient, surly caretakers. Terrified, prepared to flee, Clare is lured to linger by the prospect of secret diaries, hidden jewels, and an increasingly intriguing man. Then a killer strikes.

The crumbling manor's ominous and baffling history offers

fascinating fodder for Clare's horror novels—if only she can survive real-life madmen and a spectral murderer who may seek the jewels at any price.

Buy The Secrets of Wycliffe Manor

The Mystery of the Missing Heiress
Book #2

Wycliffe Manor, a magnet for murder...

On a long-delayed errand to remote Wycliffe Manor, ex-Lieutenant Jack de Sackville stumbles across the murdered body of London dandy, Basil Culpepper, in the hedgerow, a long way from his usual haunts. To Jack's dismay, he discovers the earl's daughter Culpepper ruined hiding in Wycliffe's kitchen.

Disguised as a lowly cook, Lady Elspeth Villiers may have liked to shoot Culpepper for ruining her life, but she dropped out of sight for more immediate reasons than an old scandal —her wealth has become the focus of greedy men. The arrival of Jack, the man she's adored since childhood, along with Culpepper's corpse, mean her hiding place is no longer safe.

But once Lady Elsa reveals herself to the unconventional inhabitants of Wycliffe Manor, they become the protective family she has never known. Outraged to learn the beautiful woman he once loved and lost has become a target of greed, Jack joins the investigation into Culpepper's death.

With a murderer on the loose, the amateur sleuths must unravel a deadly tangle of kidnappers and counterfeiters or the

Manor's eccentric inhabitants will be in as much danger as their cook.

Buy *The Mystery of the Missing Heiress*

The Bones in the Orchard
Book #3

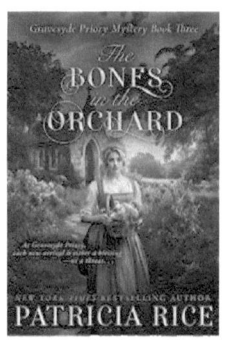

At Gravesyde Priory, each new arrival is either a blessing—or a threat. . .

Wycliffe Manor has been neglected for decades. Its new heirs are determined to create a welcoming home. Yet soon after the latest family moves into the nearby parsonage, bones are uncovered in the orchard. . . and odd strangers arrive.

When her curate father returns his family to Gravesyde for the marriages of the manor's heirs, gawky spinster Patience Upton has high expectations—until her father is murdered. Shock at learning her father had a mysterious past, leads to alarm that the killer may have been after his notebook, which she now possesses.

After the chapel is ransacked and a witness killed, it's clear the murderer isn't done. Desperate to find the truth, Patience accepts the aid of Henri Lavigne, Wycliffe Manor's smooth-talking rake. Intent on saving his new home and family from danger, Henri is drawn to the clergyman's guileless daughter but wonders if she hasn't reason to conceal the killer's identity.

Before there will be any courting, much less marrying, the inhabitants of the manor realize if they want a chance at a future, they must hunt the killer themselves. But are they hunting one murderer. . . or more?

Buy The Bones in the Orchard

The Question of the Wedding Pearls
Book #4

Will death ruin the perfect wedding?

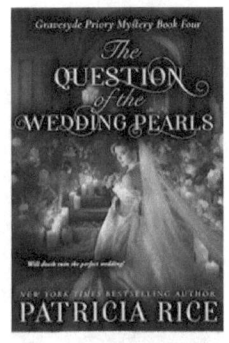

Bestselling author Patricia Rice brings you another haunting country house mystery in Regency England. . .

Spinster and secret novelist Clarissa Knightley and her gruff American engineer, Captain Huntley, along with their friend and cousin, the Honorable Jack de Sackville and Lady Elspeth, are to wed at last! In anticipation of the double wedding, friends and family are gathering at moldering Wycliffe Manor—until a dying stranger is discovered on the neglected grounds.

Despite the tragedy, aristocratic wedding guests, and their retinues, foreign and domestic, continue to arrive, not all by invitation. Compounding the bedlam, tales of missing pearls and ghostly encounters precede a second alarming death. Fearing that a killer lurks inside the manor walls, Clare and Hunt are swept up in a whirlwind of secret bigotries, deceit, and increasing peril. Before their family's joyful plans veer into heartbreak, can they put an end to mayhem and catch a killer?

Buy The Question of the Wedding Pearls

The Case of the Purloined Pages
Book #5

Death stalks the library. . .Bestselling author Patricia Rice brings you another haunting country house mystery in Regency England...

Minerva Peniston, intrepid spinster and booklover, is determined to capture the villain who tried to shoot a duke at a book auction— imperiling her father's position and the only home she's ever known. And now the same wealthy biblio-philes are gathering at Wycliffe Manor...

Paul Upton, over-educated and impoverished curate, has volunteered to assist the residents of Wycliffe Manor in preparing for a book auction to save the village and the manor's future. When an intriguing wallflower drags him into aiding her quest to find a potential killer, he agrees for her safety, and to keep trouble from upending the long-awaited nuptials of the manor's owner.

Despite their efforts, Minerva's chatty book-collecting friend is strangled before the auction begins. A killer on the loose threatens to upend both sale and wedding. Paul and Minerva must deter-mine what secrets the garrulous victim revealed. . . and to whom. . . before the murderer strikes again.

With valuable manuscripts at risk and a half dozen more potential victims on hand, only an unlikely white-knight and mousy spinster can save the auction and the wedding. As much as Minerva adores books, even she knows they aren't worth dying for.

Buy The Case of the Purloined Pages

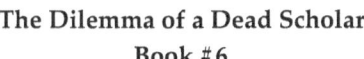

The Dilemma of a Dead Scholar
Book #6

*At Wycliffe Manor, a legendary pirate treasure draws danger... .***Bestselling author Patricia Rice brings you another haunting country house mystery in Regency England. . .**

An heiress haunted by ghosts, Dotty Dorothea knows her family believes her mad. Fearing fortune hunters who would lock her and her awkward little brother in an asylum, she flees behind the ancient walls of Wycliffe Manor.

A French artist and émigré, his soul bearing scars from a French prison, Comte Arnaud Lavigne has lost everything to war. His only foreseeable future is restoring bad artwork in his cousin's decrepit manor. Mad heiresses aren't his concern, until the day a mathematical scholar is murdered. The deceased leaves a coded journal that might lead to Wycliffe Manor's lost treasure—inside the sealed tower the terrified heiress swears is haunted.

Ghosts don't exist as far as Arnaud is concerned, but killers and thieves are real, especially when stolen treasure is involved. How is he to work with the dotty heiress when neither of them trusts the other—or themselves? But the inhabitants of Wycliffe Manor, young and old, are in peril unless a heartless killer and thief is caught. . .

Buy *The Dilemma of a Dead Scholar*

Book View Café
304 S. Jones Blvd. Suite #2906
Las Vegas NV 89107

ABOUT THE AUTHOR

With several million books in print and *New York Times* and *USA Today's* bestseller lists under her belt, former CPA Patricia Rice is one of romance's hottest authors. Her emotionally-charged contemporary and historical romances have won numerous awards, including the *RT Book Reviews* Reviewers Choice and Career Achievement Awards. Her books have been honored as Romance Writers of America RITA® finalists in the historical, regency and contemporary categories.

A firm believer in happily-ever-after, Patricia Rice is married to her high school sweetheart and has two children. A native of Kentucky and New York, a past resident of North Carolina and Missouri, she currently resides in Southern California, and now does accounting only for herself.

ALSO BY PATRICIA RICE

The World of Magic:

The Unexpected Magic Series

MAGIC IN THE STARS

WHISPER OF MAGIC

THEORY OF MAGIC

AURA OF MAGIC

CHEMISTRY OF MAGIC

NO PERFECT MAGIC

The Magical Malcolms Series

MERELY MAGIC

MUST BE MAGIC

THE TROUBLE WITH MAGIC

THIS MAGIC MOMENT

MUCH ADO ABOUT MAGIC

MAGIC MAN

The California Malcolms Series

THE LURE OF SONG AND MAGIC

TROUBLE WITH AIR AND MAGIC

THE RISK OF LOVE AND MAGIC

Crystal Magic

SAPPHIRE NIGHTS

TOPAZ DREAMS

CRYSTAL VISION

WEDDING GEMS

The Regency Nobles Series

THE GENUINE ARTICLE

THE MARQUESS

ENGLISH HEIRESS

IRISH DUCHESS

Regency Love and Laughter Series

CROSSED IN LOVE

MAD MARIA'S DAUGHTER

ARTFUL DECEPTIONS

ALL A WOMAN WANTS

Rogues & Desperadoes Series

LORD ROGUE

MOONLIGHT AND MEMORIES

SHELTER FROM THE STORM

WAYWARD ANGEL

DENIM AND LACE

CHEYENNES LADY

Dark Lords and Dangerous Ladies Series

LOVE FOREVER AFTER

SILVER ENCHANTRESS

DEVIL'S LADY

DASH OF ENCHANTMENT

INDIGO MOON

Too Hard to Handle

TEXAS LILY

TEXAS ROSE

TEXAS TIGER

TEXAS MOON

Mystic Isle Series

MYSTIC ISLE

MYSTIC GUARDIAN

MYSTIC RIDER

MYSTIC WARRIOR

Mysteries:

Family Genius Series

EVIL GENIUS

UNDERCOVER GENIUS

CYBER GENIUS

TWIN GENIUS

TWISTED GENIUS

Tales of Love and Mystery

BLUE CLOUDS

GARDEN OF DREAMS

NOBODY'S ANGEL

VOLCANO

CALIFORNIA GIRL

Historical Mysteries

Graneside Priory Series

THE SECRETS OF WYCLIFFE MANOR

THE MYSTERY OF THE MISSING HEIRESS

THE BONES IN THE ORCHARD

THE QUESTION OF THE WEDDING PEARLS

THE CASE OF THE PURLOINED PAGES

THE DILEMMA OF A DEAD SCHOLAR

Graneside Village Mysteries

THE VILLAIN'S FATAL PLOT

Urban Fantasies

Writing as Jamie Quaid

.

ABOUT BOOK VIEW CAFÉ

 *Book View Café* LLC (BVC) is an author-owned cooperative of professional writers, publishing in a variety of genres including fantasy, romance, mystery, and science fiction — with 90% of the proceeds going to the authors. Since its debut in 2008, BVC has gained a reputation for producing high-quality ebooks. BVC's ebooks are DRM-free and are distributed around the world. The cooperative is now bringing that same quality to its print editions.

BVC authors include New York Times and USA Today best-sellers as well as winners and nominees of many prestigious awards.

www.ingramcontent.com/pod-product-compliance
Lightning Source LLC
Chambersburg PA
CBHW021457110726
47899CB00001BA/197